S0-BNG-728

The Giving Earth

The Giving Earth

A John G. Neihardt Reader

Edited and with an
introduction by
Hilda Neihardt Petri

University of Nebraska Press
Lincoln and London

Copyright © 1991 by the
University of Nebraska Press
All rights reserved
Manufactured in the
United States of America
The paper in this book meets
the minimum requirements
of American National
Standard for Information
Sciences—Permanence
of Paper for
Printed Library Materials,
ANSI Z39.48 – 1984.
Library of Congress Cataloging-
in-Publication Data
Neihardt, John Gneisenau,
1881-1973.
The giving earth :
a John G. Neihardt reader /
edited and with
an introduction by
Hilda Neihardt Petri.
p. cm.
ISBN 0-8032-3325-6 (cloth)
I. Petri, Hilda Neihardt.
II. Title.
PS3727.E35A6 1992
811'.52—dc20   90-28609 CIP
Frontispiece:
John G. Neihardt on his farm,
Skyrim, near Columbia,
Missouri, 1955

The title of this reader, taken from the poem "Easter," was chosen because it represents a theme that runs through all of Neihardt's works, from his early lyrics and short stories to his mature writings—that of love and veneration for the Earth, "the only mother, she who has shown mercy to her children." This love for Mother Earth, or Planet Earth, has of recent years increasingly been felt by many persons in many lands, and it may well be a vital force in preserving for ourselves and all living things the wonder and the security of "the Giving Earth."

Contents

INTRODUCTION xi

LYRIC POEMS 1

Let Me Live Out My Years 3

The Sound My Spirit Calls You 3

Invitations 5

If This Be Sin 6

The Temple of the Great Outdoors 7

Prayer for Pain 10

Gæa, Mother Gæa! 11

The Red Wind Comes! 15

Cry of the People 17

The Child's Heritage 18

The Lyric Deed 20

April Theology 21

Easter 23

When I Have Gone Weird Ways 24

L'Envoi 25

SHORT STORIES   27

Dreams Are Wiser Than Men   29

The Alien   42

THE RIVER AND I   61

Through the Region of Weir   63

A CYCLE OF THE WEST   85

The Song of Three Friends   87

The Up-Stream Men   89

The Song of Hugh Glass   111

Graybeard and Goldhair   113

The Song of Jed Smith   135

The Rendezvous   137

The Song of the Indian Wars   169

The Sowing of the Dragon   171

The Death of Crazy Horse   176

The Song of the Messiah   189

The Spirit World   191

The Dance   193

BLACK ELK SPEAKS   205

The Offering of the Pipe   209

The Butchering at Wounded Knee   214

WHEN THE TREE FLOWERED   221

Why the Island Hill Was Sacred   221

Going on Vision Quest   232

Hold Fast; There Is More!   244

ALL IS BUT A BEGINNING   255

The Battle of Wisner   257

Four Things Are Good   268

PATTERNS AND COINCIDENCES   275

The Passing of the Gods   275

Back Home in Bancroft   277

LITERARY CRITICISM:

THE ESSAYS   285

The White Radiance   287

Literature and Environment   292

The Decline of Swearing   296

For What Purpose Did God Create Man?   299

Introduction

By Hilda Neihardt Petri

The purpose in bringing together representative selections from the work of John Neihardt in *The Giving Earth* is to entertain and enlighten—and to point the way to further enrichment. It is hoped that the reader will seek out and savor, in their entirety, not only the classics—*Black Elk Speaks, A Cycle of the West,* and *When the Tree Flowered*—but also the lyrics, essays, and short stories that brought my father his first fame. To be introduced to them is to understand more about life in the early American West—and still more about the eternal human spirit. *The Giving Earth* proceeds more or less chronologically, revealing along the way the spiritual and artistic growth of John Neihardt.

He was born John Greenleaf Neihardt in the small Illinois town of Sharpsburg on January 8, 1881. That middle name testified to his father's love of poetry. Nicholas Neihardt and Alice May Culler—my grandparents—both came from Indiana, near Coal City. After their marriage they moved with baby John from Illinois to western Kansas, where they lived in a sod house with relatives. John's earliest experiences there would be reflected in his literary work. The Kansas prairie fire that he witnessed at age five is realistically described in *The Song of Three Friends*. The old homestead is remembered in *Patterns and Coincidences*.

Success eluded Nicholas Neihardt, and he moved his family to Kansas City, where he found work as a streetcar conductor. It was seed time for young John's imagination. One day, holding on to his father as they stood on the bluffs above the flooding Missouri, he viewed with terror and awe the mighty river that would figure importantly in his writings. When John was ten years old, Nicholas Neihardt left the family. He was too weak to complete his many schemes for material success, and Alice Neihardt was too strong to be a victim. The sadness of a young boy who loses his father is recalled in *All Is But a Beginning*. Alice Neihardt took John and his two sisters, Lulu and Grace, to the farm of her brother, George Culler, near Wayne, Nebraska. That period, too, is described in my father's autobiography. By the time Alice moved her children into Wayne, she was supporting them as a seamstress.

Young John was already an eager student who read widely. One of his earliest treasures was a paperbound edition of Tennyson's *Idylls of the King* (obtained by hoarding soap wrappers), which he carried in a hip pocket while working in the beet fields. The writing of poetry became his life's ambition after his completed plans for a turbine engine did not materialize because there was no money to build it. In Wayne, his mother contacted Professor Pyle of the new Nebraska Normal School. The upshot was that John was allowed to attend the college and earn his tuition by ringing the bell for classes. He progressed so well that his teachers had to study at night to keep up with him, as they later admitted. After graduating in 1896 (at age fifteen) from the regular course, and in 1897 from the scientific course, he taught in a country school for one year—just long enough to confirm that writing, not teaching or anything else, was to be his life work. About that time his mother and sisters moved to Bancroft, Nebraska, where he joined them.

For a poet, John Neihardt was unusually physical. A trained wrestler and boxer, he could lift his own weight—125 pounds—over his head with one arm. His chest was expansive and the power behind his fist was surprising. A fight promoter, seeing the young poet cause the bell to ring loudly on a carnival punching machine, offered to make him a featherweight boxing champion. When he declined, the promoter remarked, "What's the matter? Do you hate money?" No, he did not hate money; it was just not then, nor would it ever be, the motivating force for any decision he might make. Although he chose the intellectual and spiritual over the physical, it seems clear that his physical as well as mental and spiritual power lent his writing its masculine verve. John Neihardt was never, to use his phrase, a "lily-fingered" poet.

Short fiction first brought him financial success. Beginning in 1901, he published short stories in the *Overland Monthly* and other magazines with regularity. Two of his most popular, "The Alien" and "Dreams Are Wiser

Than Men," are included in this volume. At this time he dropped "Greenleaf" from his name and substituted "Gneisenau," after Neidhardt von Gneisenau, a German forebear. It will be noted that he omitted the first "d"; from that time on he was John Gneisenau Neihardt.

After 1908 he turned away from short stories to concentrate on poetry. *A Bundle of Myrrh* was published the year before to modest acclaim. Poems like "If This Be Sin," which is included in this volume, were considered quite daring and "frank" back then. Perhaps *A Bundle* achieved greatest effect in circulating among a group of young artists in Paris. One of them, a New Yorker studying with Auguste Rodin, was captivated by Neihardt's poetry and wrote to him in Nebraska, breathing these words as she posted the letter: "Oh, God, let him not be married!" He answered, they corresponded for about six months, exchanged photographs—and then in November 1908 Mona Martinsen, daughter of the international financier Rudolph Vincent Martinsen, stepped off the train to find a very nervous John Neihardt waiting for her. Fashionably dressed and modeling a broad-brimmed velvet hat, this young woman from another world almost frightened him. He jokingly remarked later that for a moment he wanted desperately to turn and run! But, recognizing him, she called "John!" so eagerly that all panic fled. They were married the next day at a friend's home in Omaha and returned to Bancroft to set up housekeeping.

In spite of such different backgrounds, my mother and father made a very successful marriage. They both believed in and based their lives on the same "higher" values. Mona Martinsen had given up a promising career as a sculptress because, in her words, "I believed his art was greater than mine." (She did not, however, entirely give up sculpture; her busts of my father and other subjects were in demand.) Fifty years later our family was planning their Golden Wedding anniversary, which sadly did not take place because of Mother's untimely death following an automobile accident. The loss of her left Father with the appearance of one who had been hit with a sledgehammer; she had, he said, "built herself into the walls of my world." Their union was truly a partnership of ideals and goals, and it must be considered as part of any proper discussion of his later works. It was impossible to speak of John without also speaking of Mona Neihardt.

The summer preceding his marriage, John Neihardt descended the Missouri River from the head of navigation at Ft. Benton, Montana, to Sioux City, Iowa, and wrote about the adventure in a series of articles for *Outing Magazine*. Those articles were later collected as chapters in *The River and I* (1910). The opening one, "The River of an Unwritten Epic," anticipates my father's later work, *A Cycle of the West*. But the one included in this volume carries the striking title of "The Region of Weir."

The short stories, the lyrics, the articles—all were preparing my father for some great work. Casting about for a subject, he considered writing about the French Revolution and began researching it. But my mother, believing not only in him but also in the peculiarly American adventure, urged him to write about it. "Oh, John," she said, "write about what you *know*!" Years later he told a reporter: "I did, and it just came up through the soles of my feet." And so *A Cycle of the West* was conceived. Writing when the white old-timers and the Indians who had made history still lived, he was able to incorporate their first-hand reports with his own scholarly research, and this happy blending of sources gives a certain lifelike authenticity to his work. My father devoted twenty-nine of his most productive years to writing *A Cycle of the West*.

The five "Songs" of the *Cycle* were not written in chronological order, but were so arranged when collected in 1949 in one volume. *The Song of Three Friends* (1919) plays out earliest in time. It deals with the exploits of the Ashley-Henry fur traders who ascended the Missouri River in the 1820s. The three dissimilar comrades of the title—Mike Fink, Will Carpenter, and Frank Talbeau—are described in the chapter included in this anthology. Composed first, but placed second in the *Cycle, The Song of Hugh Glass* (1915) tells the dramatic story of a hunter and trapper who literally crawled many miles to cheat death and even a score. The narrative, part of which is excerpted here, gives a "feel" for the wildness and vastness of the Great Plains before it was settled by whites. The great migration west and its perils are related in *The Song of the Indian Wars* (1925). Although sincerely sympathetic with the Native Americans whose land was being invaded, Neihardt also presents the side of the whites and places events in historical perspective. The first chapter and the last—describing the death of Chief Crazy Horse and the close of the wars—have been selected for this volume. Finally, the reader is led to parts of *The Song of the Messiah* (1935), poignant in its portrayal of the Ghost Dance and the death of Sitting Bull.

In preparing to write *The Song of the Messiah,* Neihardt went to the Pine Ridge Reservation in South Dakota to see a Sioux holy man named Black Elk, who was known to have had some connection with the Ghost Dance movement. To Black Elk, my father appeared as the one who was meant to record his teachings. The result of their collaboration was *Black Elk Speaks* in 1932 and *When the Tree Flowered,* published nearly twenty years later. When the latter book appeared, the former was out of print, having been remaindered by William Morrow and Company. *Black Elk Speaks* came to roaring life after it was reprinted in 1961 by the University of Nebraska Press.

During his long career, John Neihardt made his living not only by creative writing but also by reviewing books and by lecturing widely at colleges and universities. Most of the lectures were not written and therefore are unavailable. An exception was the one that was later collected in *Poetic Values: Their Reality and Our Need for Them* (1925). That book provides a lucid discussion of the importance of the arts in our lives and points out that "poetic" values are actually compatible with scientific ideas as expressed in the new physics. Although not excerpted for this anthology, *Poetic Values* has recently been reprinted by the University of Nebraska Press.

My father's essays and autobiographical writings have not been omitted from *The Giving Earth*. In reviewing a book, he often used the subject of it as a springboard for an essay on a related philosophical concern—such as "Literature and the Environment" and "The White Radiance." During the last years of his life, he began to write his memoirs, and what he completed before his death is printed in two volumes, *All Is But a Beginning* (1972) and *Patterns and Coincidences* (1978). Chapters from each have been included here.

Detailed biography is outside the scope of this introduction, but it must be said that John G. Neihardt lives on in his works and in the memory of those of us who loved him. He died at my home near Columbia, Missouri, on November 3, 1973, surrounded by family and friends. After a lifetime of adventures, literary and actual, he had embarked on what he had anticipated would be the final "great adventure."

Lyric Poems

My father's lyric poetry was written when he was quite young and, with few exceptions, was discontinued when he began A Cycle of the West *in 1912. I have selected poems that provide variety, that express important aspects of John Neihardt's beliefs, and that have been most popular.*

The first, "Let Me Live Out My Years," has been quoted often. It so caught the fancy of a number of readers that they came to think of it as their own creation. "Battle Cry" was also greatly admired; the famous trial attorney Clarence Darrow once recited it during a passionate argument in court.

John Neihardt was early a strong advocate of free verse, two examples of which are included here: "The Sound My Spirit Calls You" and "Temple of the Great Outdoors." Although he had been a proponent of free verse at a time when it was not generally accepted, he later abandoned it, deciding that the stricter form and rhyme scheme demanded increased concentration of thought and resulted in greater power.

Among the other lyrics included here, "Cry of the People" and "The Red Wind Comes" will be found more than slightly prophetic in view of political events, some recent. About "April Theology," the poet remarked at age ninety-two, "Although I

*wrote it when I was very young, it expresses today my attitude
toward the world and all living things."*

All but two of the following poems were published in *The Collected
Poems of John G. Neihardt* (New York: Macmillan, 1926). "April Theol-
ogy" appeared in *The Quest* (New York: Macmillan, 1916). "The
Lyric Deed" appeared in the *St. Louis Post-Dispatch,* June 19, 1927, and
was reprinted in *Current American Literature,* 1 (January–March 1928):
4. All except "The Lyric Deed" were reprinted in *Lyric and Dramatic
Poems* (University of Nebraska Press, 1973, 1991).

Let Me Live Out My Years

Let me live out my years in heat of blood!
Let me die drunken with the dreamer's wine!
Let me not see this soul-house built of mud
Go toppling to the dust—a vacant shrine!

Let me go quickly like a candle light
Snuffed out just at the heyday of its glow!
Give me high noon—and let it then be night!
Thus would I go.

And grant me, when I face the grisly Thing,
One haughty cry to pierce the gray Perhaps!
O let me be a tune-swept fiddlestring
That feels the Master Melody—*and snaps!*

The Sound My Spirit Calls You

I would I knew some slow soft sound to call you:
Some slow soft syllable that would linger on the lip
As loath to pass, because of its own sweetness.

I cannot shape the sound—tho' I have heard it;
Heard it in the night-wind and the rush of the rain;
Heard it in the dull monotony of the dozing noon;

Heard it among the leaves when Winds were fagged at
    nightfall!

Kind as the shade, this sound:
Kind as the dull blue shade that blade-like cuts
A kingdom of coolness from the cruel Noon:
Soft as the kiss of the Stream to the drooping Leaf;
Sad as the pale Sun's smile over the Blizzard's bier;
Deep and resonant as distant thunder after a day of heat;
Mystic as the dream of the illimitable Prairie under the
    August glare;
Mysterious as the blue haze in which the turbid River
    dwindles to a creek!

I cannot speak the language of the Hills.
I am unskilled to sing the notes of the June Southwind.
The Noon croons not with such a tongue as mine.
Yet—even tho' I be dead, this sound shall call you for
    me!
In the still blue nights—listen, and you shall hear it!
In the burst of the storm it shall be as a whisper to you!
The Morning shall sing it for you and the Sunset paint its
    meaning,
Even upon a background of burning gold, and from the
    palette of the Rainbow!

I would that my tongue could shape this sound my spirit
    calls you.
It would be as a rose-leaf becoming vocal;
As a honeycomb talking of sweetness!

And it would pass slowly and gloriously as a sunset
    passes;
Gloriously and lingeringly it would die away,
To be like fragrance remembered.

Invitations

I

O come with me and through my gardens run,
And we shall pluck strange flowers that love the sun,
Of which the sap is blood, the petals flame,
The sweet, forbidden blossoms of no name!
O splendid are my gardens walled with night,
Dim-torched with stars and secret for delight;
And winds breathe there the lure of smitten strings,
Vocal of the immensity of things!
Come, Wailer out of Nothing, nowhere hurled,
Frustrate the bitter purpose of the World!
Thou shalt drink deep of all delights that be—
So come with me!

II

I have a secret garden where sacred lilies lift
White faces kind with pardon, to hear my shrift.
And all blood-riot falters before those faces there;
Bowed down at quiet altars, my hours are monks at
    prayer.

There through my spirit kneeling the silence thrills and
    sings
The cosmic brother feeling of growing, hopeful things:
Old soothing Earth a mother; a sire the shielding Blue;
The Sun a mighty brother—and God is in the dew.
O Garden hushed and splendid with lily, star and tree!
There all vain dreams are ended—so come with me!

If This Be Sin

Can this be sin?
This ecstasy of arms and eyes and lips,
This thrilling of caressing finger-tips,
This toying with incomparable hair?
(I close my dazzled eyes, you are so fair!)
This answer of caress to fond caress,
This exquisite maternal tenderness?
How could so much of beauty enter in,
If this be sin?

Can it be wrong?
This cry of flesh to flesh, so like a song?
This fusing of two atoms with a kiss,
Hurled to the black and pitiless abyss?

Can it be crime
That we should snatch one happy hour from Time—

Time that has naught but death for you and me?
(How soon, O Dearest, shall we cease to be!)
And could one frenzied hour of love or lust
Augment the final tragedy of dust?

Although we be two sinners burned with bliss,
Kiss me again, that warm round woman's kiss!
Close up the gates of gold! I go not in—
If this be sin.

The Temple of the Great Outdoors

Lo! I am the builder of a temple!
Even I, who groped so long for God
And laughed the broken laugh to find the darkness
    empty,
I am the builder of a temple!

The toiling shoulders of my dream heaved up the arch
And set the pillars of the Dawn,
The burning pillars of the Evening and the Dawn,
Under the star-sprent, sun-shot, moon-enchanted dome
    of blue!

And I, who knew no God,
Stood straight, unhumbled in my temple:
I did not fear the Mystery of Darkness,

And I was only glad to feel the rush of sunlight in my
blood!

I did not bend the knee.
I was unafraid, unashamed, careless and defiant.
I stood as in the centre of the universe and laughed!

And in my temple there were songs and organ tones,
And there was a silent Something holier than prayer.
I heard the winds and the streams and the sounds of
many birds:
I heard the shouting of storms and the moaning of snows;
I heard my heart, and it was lifted up in song.
The Wind passing in a gust was as though an organ had
been stricken by the hands of a capricious Master!
There was a movement in the air, motion in the leaves, a
stirring in the grass,
Even as of the reverent moving about of a congregation.
Yet I stood alone in my temple; I stood alone and was not
afraid.

But once a Something glided into my temple
And I became afraid!
As the Moon-Woman of the Greeks the Something
seemed,
Lithe and swift and pale,
A fitting human sheath for the keen chaste spirit of a
sword!
And then it seemed my temple was too small.

The Presence filled it to the furthest nook!
There was no lonesomeness in any cranny!

I knelt—and was afraid!

I felt the Presence in the winds;
I heard it in the streams;
I saw it in the restless changing of the clouds!
I tried to be as I had been, unbending, not afraid—
   godless.

Subtle as the scent of the unseen swinging censer of the
   wild flowers
That Presence crept upon me!
I fled from the terrible sunlight that burned the dome of
   my temple!
Childlike I hid my head in the darkness!
But I am not alone.

Where I have laughed defiantly into the blind emptiness,
Something moves!
I have placed my irreverent hand upon a Something in
   the shadow!
I tremble lest the Thing shall illumine itself as the dawn;
I tremble lest at last I must see God—
See God and laugh no more.

Prayer for Pain

I do not pray for peace nor ease,
Nor truce from sorrow:
No suppliant on servile knees
Begs here against to-morrow!

Lean flame against lean flame we flash,
O Fates that meet me fair;
Blue steel against blue steel we clash—
Lay on, and I shall dare!

But Thou of deeps the awful Deep,
Thou breather in the clay,
Grant this my only prayer—O keep
My soul from turning gray!

For until now, whatever wrought
Against my sweet desires,
My days were smitten harps strung taut,
My nights were slumbrous lyres.

And howsoe'er the hard blow rang
Upon my battered shield,
Some lark-like, soaring spirit sang
Above my battle-field;

And through my soul of stormy night
The zigzag blue flame ran.

I asked no odds—I fought my fight—
Events against a man.

But now—at last—the gray mist chokes
And numbs me. *Leave me pain!*
O let me feel the biting strokes
That I may fight again!

Gæa, Mother Gæa!

Gæa, Mother Gæa, now at last,
Wearied with too much seeking, here I cast
My soul, my heart, my body down on thee!
Dust of thy dust, canst thou not mother me?

Not as an infant weeping do I come;
These tears are tears of battle; like a drum
Struck by wild fighting hands my temples throb;
Sob of the breathless swordsman is my sob,
Cry of the charging spearman is my cry!

O Mother, not as one who craves to die
I fall upon thee panting. Fierce as hate,
Strong as a tiger fighting for his mate,
Soul-thewed and eager for yet one more fray—
O Gæa, Mother Gæa, thus I pray!

Have I not battled well?
My sword has ripped the gloom from many a hell
To let the sweet day kiss my anguished brow!
O, I have begged no favors until now;
Have asked no pity, though I bit the dust;

For always in my blood the battle-lust
Flung awful sword-songs down my days and nights.
But now at last of all my golden fights
The greatest fight is on me—and I pray.
O let my prayer enfold thee as the day,
Crush down upon thee as the murky night,
Rush over thee a thunder-gust, alight
With swift electric blades! Nay, let it be
As rain flung down upon the breast of thee!
With something of the old Uranian fire
I kiss upon thee all my deep desire.

If ever in the silence round about,
Thy scarlet blossoms smote me as a shout;
If ever I have loved thee, pressed my face
Close to thy bosom in a lonesome place
And breathed thy breath with more than lover's
    breathing;
If ever in the spring, thy great trees, seething
With hopeful juices, felt my worship-kiss—
Grant thou the prayer that struggles out of this,
My first blood-cry for succor in a fight!

Alone I shouldered up the crushing night,
Alone I flung about me halls of day,
Unmated went I fighting on my way,
Lured on by some far-distant final good,
Unwarmed by grudging fires of bitter wood,
Feeding my hunger with my tiger heart.
Mother of things that yearn and grow, thou art!
The Titan brood sucked battle from thy paps!
O Mother mine, sweet-breasted with warm saps,
Once more Antæus touches thee for strength!
My victories assail me! Now at length
My lawless isolation dies away!
For Mother, giving Mother, like the day
Flung down from midnight, she who was to be
Floods all the brooding thunder-glooms of me!
And in the noon-glow that her face hath wrought,
Stands forth the one great foe I have not fought—
The close-ranked cohorts of my selfish heart.

Suckler of virile fighting things thou art!
Breathe in me something of the tireless sea;
The urge of mighty rivers breathe in me!
Cloak me with purple like thy haughty peaks;
O arm me as a wind-flung cloud that wreaks
Hell-furies down the midnight battle-murk!
Fit me to do this utmost warrior's work—
To face myself and conquer!

Mother dear,
Thou seemest a woman in this silence here;

And 'tis thy daughter who hath come to me
With all the wise, sad mother-heart of thee,
Thy luring wonder and immensity!
For in her face strong sweet earth passions brood:
I feel them as in some wild solitude
The love-sweet panting summer's yearning pain.

Teach me the passion of the wooing rain!
Teach me to fold her like a summer day
To kiss her in the great good giant way,
As Uranus amid the cosmic dawn!

Now all the mad spring revelling is gone,
And comes the fruiting summer! Let me be
Deep-rooted in thy goodness as a tree,
Strong in the storms with skyward blossomings!
Teach me the virile trust of growing things,
The wisdom of slow fruiting in the sun!

I would be joyous as the winds that run
Light footed on the wheatfields. O for her,
I would be gentle as the winds that stir
The forest in the noon hush. Lift me up!
Fill all my soul with kindness as a cup
With cool and bubbling waters! Mother dear,
Gæa, great Gæa, 'tis thy son—O hear!

The Red Wind Comes!

Too long mere words have thralled us. Let us think!
O ponder, are we "free and equal" yet?
That July bombast, writ with blood for ink,
Is blurred with floods of unavailing sweat!

An empty sound we won from Royal George!
Yea, till a greater fight be fought and won,
A sentimental show was Valley Forge,
A mawkish, tawdry farce was Lexington!

No longer blindfold Justice reigns; but leers
A barefaced, venal strumpet in her stead!
The stolen harvests of a hundred years
Are lighter than a stolen loaf of bread!

O pious Nation, holding God in awe,
Where sacred human rights are duly priced!
Where men are beggared in the name of Law,
Where alms are given in the name of Christ!

The Country of the Free?—O wretched lie!
The Country of the Brave?—Yea, let it be!
One more good fight, O Brothers, ere we die,
And this shall be the Country of the Free!

What! Are we cowards? Are we doting fools?
Who built the cities, fructified the lands?

We make and use, but do we own the tools?
Who robbed us of the product of our hands?

A tiger-hearted Tyrant crowned with Law,
Whose flesh is custom and whose soul is greed!
Ubiquitous, a nothing clothed in awe,
We sweat for him and bleed!

Daft Freedom sings the glory of his reign;
Religion is a pander of his lust:
Surviving tyrants, he eludes the vain,
Tyrannicidal thrust.

Yea, and *we* serve this Insult to our God!
Gnawing our crusts, we render Cæsar toll!
We labor with the back beneath his rod,
His shackles on the soul!

He is a System—wrought for human hogs!
So long as we shall hug a hoary Lie,
And gulp the vocal swill of demagogues,
The Fat shall rule the sty!

Behold potential plenty for us all!
Behold the pauper and the plutocrat!
Behold the signs prophetic of thy fall,
O Dynast of the Fat!

Lo, even now the haunting, spectral scrawl!
Lo, even now the beat of hidden wings!

The ghosts of millions throng thy banquet hall,
O guiltiest and last of all the kings!

Beware the Furies stirring in the gloom!
They mutter from the mines, the mills, the slums!
No lie shall stay or mitigate thy doom—
The Red Wind comes!

Cry of the People

Tremble before thy chattels,
Lords of the scheme of things!
Fighters of all earth's battles,
Ours is the might of kings!
Guided by seers and sages,
The world's heart-beat for a drum,
Snapping the chains of ages,
Out of the night we come!

Lend us no ear that pities!
Offer no almoner's hand!
Alms for the builders of cities!
When will you understand?
Down with your pride of birth
And your golden gods of trade!
A man is worth to his mother, Earth,
All that a man has made!

We are the workers and makers!
We are no longer dumb!
Tremble, O Shirkers and Takers!
Sweeping the earth—we come!
Ranked in the world-wide dawn,
Marching into the day!
The night is gone and the sword is drawn
And the scabbard is thrown away!

The Child's Heritage

O, there are those, a sordid clan,
With pride in gaud and faith in gold,
Who prize the sacred soul of man
For what his hands have sold.

And these shall deem thee humbly bred:
They shall not hear, they shall not see
The kings among the lordly dead
Who walk and talk with thee!

A tattered cloak may be thy dole
And thine the roof that Jesus had:
The broidered garment of the soul
Shall keep thee purple-clad!

The blood of men hath dyed its brede,
And it was wrought by holy seers
With sombre dream and golden deed
And pearled with women's tears.

With Eld thy chain of days is one:
The seas are still Homeric seas;
Thy sky shall glow with Pindar's sun,
The stars of Socrates!

Unaged the ancient tide shall surge,
The old Spring burn along the bough:
The new and old for thee converge
In one eternal Now!

I give thy feet the hopeful sod,
Thy mouth, the priceless boon of breath;
The glory of the search for God
Be thine in life and death!

Unto thy flesh, the soothing dust;
Thy soul, the gift of being free:
The torch my fathers gave in trust,
Thy father gives to thee!

The Lyric Deed

We sighed and said, the world's high purpose falters;
    Here in the West, the human hope is sold;
Behold, our cities are but monstrous altars
    That reek in worship to the Beast of Gold!

Now no rapt silence hears the bard intoning;
    Our lurid stacks paint out the ancient awe,
And lock-step millions to the motor's moaning
    Are herded into Moloch's yawning maw.

With men we stoke our diabolic fires;
    Of smithied hearts the soaring steel is made
To dwarf and darken all our godward spires
    With drunken towers of Trade.

We said it, blinded with the sweat of duty,
    And now, behold! emerging from the dark,
Winged with the old divinity of beauty,
    Our living dream mounts morning like a lark!

Of common earth men wrought it, and of wonder;
    With lightning have men bitted it and shod;
The throat of it is clothed with singing thunder—
    And Lindbergh rides with God!

We have not known, but surely now we know it;
    Not thus achieve venality and greed:

The dreaming doer is the master poet—
 And lo! the perfect lyric in a deed!

The sunset and the world's new morning hear it;
 Ecstatic in the rhythmic motor's roar,
Not seas shall sunder now the human spirit,
 For space shall be no more!

April Theology

O to be breathing and hearing and feeling and seeing!
O the ineffably glorious privilege of being!
All of the World's lovely girlhood, unfleshed and made
 spirit,
Broods out in the sunlight this morning—I see it, I hear
 it!

So read me no text, O my Brothers, and preach me no
 creeds;
I am busy beholding the glory of God in His deeds!
See! Everywhere buds coming out, blossoms flaming,
 bees humming!
Glad athletic growers up-reaching, things striving, be-
 coming!

O, I know in my heart, in the sun-quickened, blossom-
 ing soul of me,

This something called self is a part, but the world is the
    whole of me!
I am one with these growers, these singers, these earnest
    becomers—
Co-heirs of the summer to be and past æons of summers!

I kneel not nor grovel; no prayer with my lips shall I
    fashion.
Close-knit in the fabric of things, fused with one com-
    mon passion—
To go on and become something greater—we growers
    are one;
None more in the world than a bird and none less than
    the sun;
But all woven into the glad indivisible Scheme,
God fashioning out in the Finite a part of His dream!

Out here where the world-love is flowing, unfettered,
    unpriced,
I feel all the depth of the man-soul and girl-heart of
    Christ!
'Mid this riot of pink and white flame in this miracle
    weather,
Soul to soul, merged in one, God and I dream the vast
    dream together.
We are one in the doing of things that are done and to be;
I am part of my God as a raindrop is part of the sea!

What! House me my God? Take me in where no blos-
    soms are blowing?

Roof me in from the blue, wall me in from the green and
    the wonder of growing?
Parcel out what is already mine, like a vender of staples?
See! Yonder my God burns revealed in the sap-drunken maples!

Easter

Once more the northbound Wonder
Brings back the goose and crane,
Prophetic Sons of Thunder,
Apostles of the Rain.

In many a battling river
The broken gorges boom;
Behold, the Mighty Giver
Emerges from the tomb!

Now robins chant the story
Of how the wintry sward
Is litten with the glory
Of the Angel of the Lord.

His countenance is lightning
And still His robe is snow,
As when the dawn was brightening
Two thousand years ago.

O who can be a stranger
To what has come to pass?
The Pity of the Manger
Is mighty in the grass!

Undaunted by Decembers,
The sap is faithful yet.
The giving Earth remembers,
And only men forget.

When I Have Gone Weird Ways

When I have finished with this episode,
Left the hard up-hill road,
And gone weird ways to seek another load,
O Friend, regret me not, nor weep for me—
Child of Infinity!

Nor dig a grave, nor rear for me a tomb,
To say with lying writ: "Here in the gloom
He who loved bigness takes a narrow room,
Content to pillow here his weary head—
For he is dead."

But give my body to the funeral pyre,
And bid the laughing fire,
Eager and strong and swift as my desire,

Scatter my subtle essence into Space—
Free me of Time and Place.

Sweep up the bitter ashes from the hearth!
Fling back the dust I borrowed from the Earth
Unto the chemic broil of Death and Birth—
The vast Alembic of the cryptic Scheme,
Warm with the Master-Dream!

And thus, O little House that sheltered me,
Dissolve again in wind and rain, to be
Part of the cosmic weird Economy:
And O, how oft with new life shalt thou lift
Out of the atom-drift!

L'Envoi

Seek not for me within a tomb;
You shall not find me in the clay!
I pierce a little wall of gloom
To mingle with the Day!

I brothered with the things that pass,
Poor giddy Joy and puckered Grief;
I go to brother with the Grass
And with the sunning Leaf.

Not Death can sheathe me in a shroud;
A joy-sword whetted keen with pain,
I join the armies of the Cloud,
The Lightning and the Rain.

O subtle in the sap athrill,
Athletic in the glad uplift,
A portion of the Cosmic Will,
I pierce the planet-drift.

My God and I shall interknit
As rain and Ocean, breath and Air;
And O, the luring thought of it
Is prayer!

Short Stories

The two stories that follow are taken from the collection Indian Tales and Others *(1926). Both were written early in the twentieth century while John Neihardt lived in Bancroft, Nebraska, on the edge of the Omaha Indian Reservation. Through his close association with the Omaha people, my father gained the knowledge that enabled him to write stories such as "Dreams Are Wiser Than Men," published in* Tom Watson's Magazine *in 1905. Reading them, Dr. Susan LaFlesche Picotte, the daughter of the last chief of the Omahas, Iron Eyes, commented: "His sympathetic insight into the mysticism and spiritual nature of the race gives him a true understanding of Indian character."*

Included here is perhaps the most popular of all his stories, "The Alien." After it appeared in Munsey's *magazine in 1906, editors bombarded him with requests for "another* Alien." *But his career was about to take another turn, and after 1908 he wrote no more short stories.*

The following stories were collected in *The Lonesome Trail* (New York: John Lane, 1907) and *Indian Tales and Others* (New York: Macmillan, 1926; reprinted Lincoln: University of Nebraska Press, 1988).

Dreams Are Wiser Than Men

Rain Walker lay upon the brown grass without the circle of the village; and it was the time when the maize is gathered—the brown, drear time. He lay with ear pressed to the earth.

"What are you doing?" asked one who walked there.

"I?" said Rain Walker; and his eyes and face were not good to see as he raised his head. The dying time seemed also in his face. "The growers are coming up, and I am listening to their breathing," he said.

And the questioner walked on with a strange smile; for it was not the time of the coming of the growers.

Rain Walker stood in the center of the village and held his face to the sky.

"What are you doing?" said one who walked there.

"I?" and there was twilight in Rain Walker's eyes as he looked upon the questioner. "I shot an arrow into the air. It did not come back, so I am always looking for it."

And the questioner smiled and went on walking; for no arrow rises that does not fall. A child knows that.

And the people said: "It is all because Mad Buffalo, the Ponca, took his squaw. He took her, and she went. It was after the summer's feasting and talking together that she went. Rain Walker is not forgetting."

And Rain Walker sat much alone; he sat much alone making strange songs not pleasant to hear. And as he made songs he made weapons. He fashioned him a *man-de-hi,* which is a long spear, tipped with sharp flint; and he sang. He wrought a *za-zi-man-di,* which is a great bow; and sang all the time. They were hate songs that he sang; they snarled.

He shaped many arrows; he headed them with sharp flints and tipped them with the feathers of the hawk; and all the time he sang. He made a *we-ak-ga-di,* which is an ugly club. He sang to himself and to the weapons that he made. To the harsh, snarling airs he wrought the weapons. The songs went into them, and they looked like things that might hate much.

And one drew near who was walking. "Why do you make war things?" said he.

"I?" and Rain Walker threw himself upon his stomach, writhing toward the questioner like a big snake. "I am a rattlesnake," he said, "*hiss-ss-ss-s!* go away! I sting!"

And the man went, for it is not good to see a man act like a snake.

And one night the weapons were finished. All that night the people heard the voice of Rain Walker singing. They said: "Those are the songs of one who wishes to go on the warpath!"

And in the morning Rain Walker came out of his lodge. The squaws trembled to see him; and the men wondered. For he had wept and his eyes were wild.

And Rain Walker raised a hoarse voice into the morning stillness before all the people: "Where is my woman—she who cooked for me and made my lodge pleasant? Tell me; for I walk there that the crows may eat me!"

The people shivered as though his voice were the breath of the first frost.

"You need not make words, my kinsmen; I know. I walk there and the crows shall eat me."

He went forth from the door of his lodge and came to the place where the head chief lived among the Hungas. He raised the door flap. "A-ho!" said he, for the chief was within eating. "I, Rain Walker, stand before you. I have words to say."

"Speak," said the chief.

"I am wronged. I wish war! I wish to see the Poncas destroyed!"

The head chief gazed long into the tear-washed eyes of Rain Walker, and he said: "It is a big thing to take that trail. It makes the wailing of women; it makes hunger; it makes the crying of *zhinga zhingas* for fathers that lie in lonesome places and never ride back. It is a hard path to take. I will think."

And it happened after the thinking of the big chief that a council was called—a coming-together of the leaders of the bands.

And the leaders came together, and sat with big thoughts. It was evening, and among the assembled leaders sat Rain Walker. His face was thin and cruel as a stone axe stained with blood.

Then the big chief raised his voice, and words to be heard grew there in the big lodge. "This man who sits with us has been wronged. When our brothers, the Poncas, were among us for the feasting and the talking together, Mad Buffalo was among them.

"A woman is a thing not to be understood. Now she dies on long winter trails for a man, or grows old and wrinkled suckling his *zhinga zhingas*; and now she leaves him for another; yet it is the same woman. I knew a wise man once; but he shook his head about these things; and so do I.

"You know of whom I speak. It was Sun Eyes; and she was this man's woman. Mad Buffalo smiled, and she went with him.

"And this man has come to me crying for war," continued the head chief. "Think hard, and let us talk together."

And he of the Big Elk band said: "Let the Poncas come down in the night and drive away our ponies, and I will gather my band about me. But it has not been so."

And he of the Hawk band said: "Let the Poncas destroy our gardens, and I will think of my weapons."

And he of the No-Teeth band said: "Let the Poncas speak ill of us, and my band will put on war paint."

Then a silence grew and the head chief filled it with few words. "Let us pass the pipe; and all who smoke it smoke for war."

And there were ten chiefs in the council, sitting in a circle. The first touched the pipe lightly and passed it on as though it burned his fingers; and so the second and third, even to the tenth. And next to him sat Rain Walker. His breath came dryly through his teeth, like a hot wind in a parched gulch. With hands that trembled he grasped his pipe from the tenth, who had not placed it to his lips. Rain Walker placed it to his lips nervously, eagerly, as one who touches a cool water bowl after a long thirst. He struck a flint and lit it. Then he arose to his feet, tall, straight, trembling—a rage grown into a man!

"*I smoke!*" he cried; "I smoke, and through all the sunlights that come I will walk alone and kill! The lonesome walker—I am he!

"I shall speak to the snake, and he shall teach me his creeping and his stinging. I shall speak to the elk, and he shall teach me his fleetness, his strength that lasts, his fury when he turns to fight. And I shall speak to the hawk and learn the keenness of his eyes!"

Rain Walker puffed blue streamers of smoke into the still twilight of the lodge, seeming something more than man in the fog he made.

"I smoke!" he cried; and his cry had changed into a song of snarling sounds and sounds that wailed. "I smoke, and I smoke alone; my brothers will not take the pipe with me. In lonesome places shall I walk with my hate, and not even the lone hawk in the farthest hills shall hear me make aught but a hate cry. I have no longer any people! I am a tribe—the tribe that walks alone! The *zhinga zhingas* of the women that are not yet born shall hear my name, and it shall be like a nightwind wailing when the spirits walk and the fires are blue! I will forget that I am the son of a woman; I will think myself the son of a snake, that bore me on a hot rock in a lonesome place. I will think that I never tasted woman's milk, but only venom stewed by the hot sun. And now I walk alone."

His cry had fallen to a low wail that made the flesh of the hearers creep, although they were leaders and brave.

And with eyes that peered far ahead as into impenetrable distances Rain Walker strode out of the lodge. The night was coming; he went forth to meet it, walking.

As he walked toward the night his thoughts were of *choobay* (holy) things. He thought much of the spirits, and he reached a high hill as he walked. It was high; therefore it was a *choobay* place. And he climbed to the summit, bare of grass and white with flaked rocks against the sky, that darkened fast as the Night walked.

Then he lit his pipe and made *choobay* smoke. He wished to have the good *wakundas* with him, even though he walked alone. For well he knew that no man can walk quite alone. So he extended the pipe stem to the west, the south, the east, the north, and he cried, "O you who cause the four winds to reach a place, help me! I stand needy!" Then he extended the pipe stem toward the earth, and he said, "O Venerable Man who lives at the bottom, here I stand needy!" And to the heavens he held the stem and cried, "O Grandfather who lives above, I stand needy; I, Rain Walker! Though my brothers treat me badly, yet I think you will help me!"

And he felt much stronger.

Then, with his weapons about him, he set his face to the south, for there in the flat lands of Nebraska lay the village of the Poncas.

And he walked in lonesome places all night. A coyote trotted past him and sat at some distance. "O brother Coyote," said Rain Walker, "I am on the warpath; teach me your long running and your snapping!" The coyote whined and went into a gulch.

"I walk alone, and none relieves my sorrow!"

So sang Rain Walker; and singing thus he walked into the morning. And the prairie was gray with frost and very big, and the skies were filled with a quiet, so that a far crow cawing faintly made a shout. Having nothing to eat he sang, and hunger went away. His song filled the world, for he walked alone where it was very silent.

To the hawk he cried for keenness of eyes; but the hawk circled on and was only a speck. Nothing heard the man who walked alone.

He killed a rabbit and ate; he found a stream and drank. Then he met the Night walking again, and they walked together until they met the Day; and the man saw below him in the flat lands of Nebraska the jumbled mud village of the Poncas.

And it happened that the people in the village were moving very early. There was a neighing of ponies and a shouting of men and a scolding and laughing of women. It was the time of the bison hunt, and they were going forth that day.

Rain Walker lay in the brown grass at the hilltop and watched with wistful eyes the merry ones as the long, thin file left the village, the riders and the walkers and the drags. It is pleasant to go on the hunt. Rain Walker felt that he would never go again.

His face softened; then suddenly it changed and became again as a barbed war arrow. Mad Buffalo rode, and after him went Sun Eyes walking! Her head hung low like a thing wilted by the frost. She laughed not; she, too, seemed as one who walked alone.

When the long, thin line, like a huge snake writhing westward into the hills, had disappeared, Rain Walker got up and walked fast. He walked fast, for he wished to be near the place of camping when the night came. And it was so.

He lay at a distance, watching the fires flare into the night and feeling very hungry, for he caught the scent of the boiling kettles. They smelled like home. And when the people had eaten and the fires had fallen, Rain Walker said, "Now I will begin my war. I need a pony, the Poncas have them."

He crawled upon his hands and knees to where the herd grazed. There had been no watch set, for all the tribes were at peace, except the tribe that walked alone.

And Rain Walker rode away into the night. He had big thoughts as he rode.

The hunting was poor that year; it happened so, they say. Still toward the place where the evening goes went the tribe, peering into far places for the bison; and ever there was one who crept near the tepees at night and heard the words of the Poncas, which are the same as the Omahas speak.

And they wandered, hunting, in the places where the sandhills are—the dreary places.

And one day it happened, they say, that a coyote and a hawk and some crows saw two men in a very lonesome place among the sand hills. They alone saw. And the two met, riding. One was a Ponca gone forth to seek the unappearing herd. He was tall and well made, and his pony was spotted. The other was also even as the first, although not a Ponca; but his pony was not spotted.

And when they met a great cry went up from the one whose pony was not spotted. The coyote and the hawk and the crows heard and saw. It seemed a strange cry in the silence that lived there. Then he who rode the spotted pony turned and fled; but an arrow is swifter than a pony, though it be wind-footed; and he who fled fell upon the sand and the pony ran at some distance and stopped. He looked on also.

And the two men met. He with the arrow in his back arose with a groan from the sand and growled as the other approached and dismounted. They seemed as two who had met and parted enemies.

They seized each other and rolled upon the sand. The coyote whined, the crows cawed, but the hawk only watched. But all the while the ponies neighed.

And the sting of the arrow weakened one, but he fought like a bear. He made a good fight. But the other fixed his hands upon his enemy's throat until the silent places were filled with a gurgling and a rasping of breath that came hard. Then there was only silence. The coyote ran away, the crows and the hawk flew. The ponies alone watched now.

And the man whose pony was not spotted arose and laughed very loud—only it was not the laugh of a glad man. Then the man who laughed stripped off the garments of the other and put them upon himself. Then he built a fire and lit his pipe and made *choobay* smoke. Then he spoke to the various *wakundas* that were somewhere there in the silence.

"I have killed my enemy. I will burn his heart and give you the ashes, O Grandfathers!"

The crows heard this, for they had come back looking for their feast.

And the man burned the heart of his enemy and scattered the ashes, singing a brave song all the while. He had learned to do this from the Kansas; it is their custom.

Then the man got on the spotted pony and rode away, bearing with him the weapons of the man who stayed. And when he was gone the crows and the coyote came and made harsh noises at each other, for each was hungry, and there was a feast spread there upon the sand.

And it happened that evening, they say, that one rode into the Ponca camp and went to the tepee where Sun Eyes, the Omaha woman, waited for someone.

The man who came had his whole face hidden with a piece of buckskin, having eye and mouth holes in it. And Sun Eyes was cooking over a fire before her tepee.

"Ho, Mad Buffalo!" she said; "you have not found the bison. Why have you hidden your face?"

"I found no bison," said the man, "but I saw something in the hills which caused me to hide my face."

And Sun Eyes looked keenly at the man, for she thought it was some *wakunda* he had seen.

"Why do you speak in a strange voice?" said she; and she trembled as she said it.

"He who has seen something is never the same again!" said he.

And while the woman wondered the two ate together. And as the man ate he laughed very pleasantly at times like a man who is very glad.

"Why do you laugh, Mad Buffalo?" said the woman.

"Because I was very hungry for something, and I have it now," said the man.

And when he had ceased eating he sang glad songs, and again the woman questioned.

"I sing because of what I saw in the hills," said he.

And this seemed very strange to the woman. But it is not allowed that one should question a man who has seen a *wakunda.*

And it happened that the man was pleased to speak evil words of Rain Walker, and Sun Eyes hung her head; her eyes were wet.

Then said the man, having seen: "Why do you act so? Do you want him? Behold! Am I not as good to see as Rain Walker?"

And he acted as one who is almost angry and a little sad. But the woman only sobbed a very little sob, for as the chief said in the council, a very wise man does not know the ways of a woman.

And it happened that night, they say, that, as the two slept, Sun Eyes dreamed a strange dream that made her cry out. And the two sat up startled.

"What is it?" said the man.

"A dream!" sobbed Sun Eyes.

"What dream?" said the man, and his voice seemed kind.

"I cannot tell; I do not wish to be beaten."

"Tell it, Sun Eyes. Was it about Rain Walker?"

She did not answer.

"Do not be afraid," he said. And she spoke.

"I dreamed that I saw my *zhinga zhinga* that I am carrying. And it was Rain Walker's. It had his face, and it looked upon me with hate. It pushed me away when I offered my breast. It would take no milk from me. And it seemed that its look pierced me like a barbed arrow. Thus I awoke, and cried out."

The woman was weeping, and a tremor ran through the man. She felt it as he leaned against her, and she thought it anger.

"Take me there where I came from—to the village of my people!" she cried. "You are big and good to see, and many women will follow you! Take me to my people; Dreams are wiser than men; the *wakundas* send them. I wish to go back, that my child may smile and take my breast."

And the man rose and began dressing for the trail.

"I will take you back," said he. "Dreams are wiser than men."

And before the day walked the two went forth on the long trail, back to the village of the woman's people.

The man went before and the woman followed, bearing the burdens of the trail. But when the dawn came the man did a strange thing. He took the burdens upon his own shoulders, saying nothing. It seemed his heart had been softened; but his face being hidden, the woman could not see what was there.

And the trail was long; but the man was kind. He seemed no longer the Mad Buffalo. He made fires and pitched the tepee like a squaw. He spoke soft words.

And after many days of traveling the two came, as the Night was beginning to walk, to the brown brow of the hill beneath which lay the village of the Omahas.

And the man said: "There are your people. Go!"

And the woman moaned, saying: "He will not take me, and the dream will be true. Never on the long trail did my heart fail; but now I am weak."

But the man said: "Sun Eyes, had not Rain Walker ever a soft heart? He will take you back. Look!"

And the woman, who had been gazing through tears upon the village of her people, turned and saw that the man had torn the buckskin from his face. She gave a cry and shrank from what she saw.

But the man took her gently by the hand.

"He will take you back," he said; "dreams are wiser than men!"

The Alien

Through the quiet night, crystalline with the pervading spirit of the frost, under prairie skies of mystic purple pierced with the glass-like glinting of the stars, fled Antoine.

Huge and hollow-sounding with the clatter of the pinto's hoofs hung the night above and about—lonesome, empty, bitter as the soul of him who fled.

A weary age of flight since sunset; and now the midnight saw the thin-limbed, long-haired pony slowly losing his nerve, tottering, rasping in the throat. With spike-spurred heels the rider hurled the beast into the empty night.

"Gwan! you blasted cayuse! you overgrown wolfdog! Keep up that tune; I'm goin' somewheres. What'd I steal you fer? Pleasure? I reckon; pleasure for the half-breed! Gwan!"

Suddenly rounding a bank of sand, the pinto sighted the broad, ice-bound river, a stream of glinting silver under the stars. Sniffing and crouching upon its haunches at the sudden glow that dwindled a gleaming thread into the further dusk, the jaded beast received a series of vicious jabs from the spike-spurred heels. It groaned and lunged forward again, taking with uncertain feet the glaring path ahead, and awakening dull, snarling thunder in the under regions of the ice. Slipping, struggling, doing its brute best to overcome fatigue and the uncertainty of its path, the pinto covered the ice.

"Doin' a war dance, eh?" growled the man with bitter mirth, gouging the foaming bloody flanks of the animal. "Gwan! Set up that tune; I want fast music, 'cause I'm goin' somewheres—don't know where—somewheres out there in the shadders! Come here, will you? Take that and that and *that*! By the——!"

The brutal cries of the man were cut short as he shot far over the pommel, lunging headlong over the pinto's head, and striking with head and shoulders upon the glare ice. When he stopped sliding he lay very still for a few moments. Then he groaned, sat up, and found that the bluffs and the river and the stars and the universe in general were whirling giddily, with himself for the dizzy center.

With uncertain arms he reached out, endeavoring to check the sickening motion of things with the sheer force of his powerful hands. He was thrown down like a weakling wrestling with a giant. He lay still, cursing in a whisper, trying to steady the universe, until the motion passed, leaving in his nerves the sickening sensation incident to the sudden ending of a rapid flight.

With great care Antoine raised himself upon his elbows and gazed about him with an imbecile leer. Then he began to remember; remembered that he was hunted; that he was an outcast, a man of no race; remembered dimly, and with a malignant grin, a portion of a long series of crimes; remembered that the last was horse-stealing and that some of the others concerned blood. And as he remembered, he felt with horrible distinctness the lariat tightening about his neck—the lariat that the men of Cabanne's trading post were bringing on fleet horses, nearer, nearer through the silent night.

Antoine shuddered and got to his feet, looming huge against the star-spent surface of the ice, as he turned a face of bestial malevolence down trail and listened for the beat of hoofs. There was only the dim, hollow murmur that dwells at the heart of silence.

"Got a long start," he observed, with the chuckle of a man whom desperation has made careless. "Hel-*lo!*"

A pale, semicircular glow, like the flare of a burning straw stack a half day's journey over the hills, had grown up at the horizon of the east; and as the man stared, still in a maze from his recent fall, the moon heaved a tarnished silver arc above the rim of sky, flooding with new light the river and the bluffs. The man stood illumined—a big brute of a man, heavy-limbed, massive-shouldered, with the slouching stoop and the alert air of an habitual skulker. He moved uneasily, as though he had suddenly become visible to some lurking foe. He glanced nervously about him, fumbled at the butt of a six-shooter at his belt, then catching sight of the blotch of huddled dusk that was the fallen pinto, the meaning of the situation flashed upon him.

"That cussed cayuse! Gone and done hisself like as not! Damn me! the whole creation's agin me!"

He made for the pony, snarling viciously as though its exhausted, lacerated self were the visible body of the inimical universe. He grasped the reins and jerked them violently. The brute only groaned and let its weary head fall heavily upon the ice.

44

"Get up!"

Antoine began kicking the pony in the ribs, bringing forth great hollow bellowings of pain.

"O, you won't get up, eh? Agin me too, eh? Take that, and that and *that*! I wished you was everybody in the whole world and hell to oncet! I'd make you beller now I got you down! Take *that*!"

The man with a roar of anger fell upon the pony, snarling, striking, kicking, but the pony only groaned. Its limbs could no longer support its body. When Antoine had exhausted his rage, he got up, gave the pony a parting kick on the nose, and started off at a dogtrot across the glinting ice toward the bluffs beyond.

Ever and anon he stopped and whirled about with hand at ear. He heard only the murmur of the silence, broken occasionally by the whine and pop of the ice and the plaintive wail of the coyotes somewhere in the hills, like the heartbroken cry of the prairie, yearning for the summer.

"O, I wouldn't howl if I was you," muttered the man to the coyotes; "I wished I was a coyote or a gray wolf, knowin' what I do. I'd be a man-killer and a cattle-killer, I would. And then I'd have people of my own. Wouldn't be no cur of a half-breed runnin' from his kind. O, I wouldn't howl if I was you!"

He proceeded at a swinging trot across the half mile of ice and halted under the bluffs. He listened intently. A far sound had grown up in the hollow night—vague, but unmistakable. It was the clatter of hoofs far away, but clear in faintness, for the cold snap had made the prairie one vast soundingboard. A light snow had fallen the night before, and the trail of the refugee was traced in the moonlight, distinct as a wagon track.

Antoine felt the pitiless pinch of the approaching lariat as he listened. Then his accustomed bitter weariness of life came upon the pariah.

"What's the use of me runnin'? What am I runnin' to? Nothin'—only more of the same thing I'm runnin' from; lonesomeness and hunger and the like of that. Gettin' awake stiff and cold and half starved and cussin' the daylight 'cause it's agin me like everything else, and gives me away. Sneakin' around in the brush till dark, eatin' when I can like a damned wolf, then goin' to sleep hopin' it'll never get day. But it always does. It's all night somewheres, I guess, spite of what the missionaries says. That's fer me—night always! No comin' day, no gettin' up, somewhere to hide snug in always!"

He walked on with head dropped forward upon his breast, skirting the base of the bluffs, now seemingly oblivious of the sound of hoofs that grew momentarily more distinct.

As he walked, he was dimly conscious of passing the dark mouth of a hole running back into the clay of a bluff. He proceeded until he found himself again at the edge of the river, staring down into a broad, black fissure in the ice, caused, doubtless, by the dash of the current crossing from the other side.

A terrible, dark, but alluring thought seized him. Here was the place—the doorway to that place where it was always night! Why not go in? There would be no more running away, no more hiding, no more hatred of men, no more lonesomeness! Here was the place at last.

He stepped forward and stooped to gaze down into the door of night. The rushing waters made a dismal, moaning sound.

He stared transfixed. Yes, he would go!

Suddenly a shudder ran through his limbs. He gave a quick exclamation of terror! He leaped back and raised his face to the skies.

How kind and soft and gentle and good to look upon was the sky! He gazed about—it was so fair a world! How good it was to breathe! He longed to throw his great, brute arms about creation and clutch it to him, and hold it! He wished to live.

The hoofs!

The distant muffled confusion of sound had grown into distinct, staccato notes. The pursuers were now less than a mile away. Soon they would reach the river.

With the quick instinct of the hunted beast, Antoine knew his means of safety. His footprints led to the ice-fissure. He decided that none should lead away. He could not be pursued under ice. Stooping so that he could look between his legs, he began retracing his steps, walking backward, placing his feet with great care where they had fallen before. Thus he came again to the hole in the clay bluff, and disappeared. His trail had passed within a foot of the hole, which was overhung by a jutting point of sandstone. No snow had fallen at the entrance; he left no trail as he entered.

Stopping upon his hands and knees, he listened and

could hear distinctly the sharp crack of hoofs upon the ice and the pop and thunder of the frozen surface.

"Here's *some* luck," muttered Antoine. He crawled on into the nether darkness of the hole that grew more spacious as he proceeded. As he crawled, the sound of pursuing hoofs grew dimmer. Antoine half forgot them. His keen sense had caught the peculiar musty odor of animal life. He felt a stuffy warmth in his nostrils as he breathed.

Suddenly out of the dark ahead grew up two points of phosphorescent light. Antoine fell back upon his haunches with a little growl of surprise. Years of wild lonesome life had made him more beast than man.

The lights slowly came closer, growing more brilliant. Then there was a harsh, rasping growl and a sound of sniffing. Antoine waited until the expanding pupils of his eyes could grasp the situation with more distinctness. "Can't run," he mused. "Lariat behind, somethin' growlin' in front. It's one more fight. Here goes fer my damnedest. Rather die mad and fightin' than jump into cold water or stick my head through a rawhide necktie!"

He crawled on carefully. The lights approached with a strange swaying motion. Then of a sudden came a whine, a sharp, savage yelp, and Antoine felt his cheek ripped open with a stroke of gnashing teeth!

He felt for an instant the hot breath of the beast, the trickle of hot blood on his cheek; and then all that was human in him passed. He growled and hurled the sinewy body of his unseen foe from him with a blow of his bear-like paw.

The dark hole echoed a muffled howl of anger, and in an instant man and beast rolled together in the darkness.

At last the man knew that it was a gray wolf he fought. He reached for its throat, but felt his hand caught in a hot, wet, powerful trap of teeth. He grasped the under jaw with a grip that made his antagonist howl with pain. Then with his other hand he felt about in the darkness, groping for the throat.

He found it, seized it with a vise-like clutch, shut his teeth together, and threw all of the power of his massive frame into the struggle.

Slowly the struggles of the wolf became weaker. The lean, hairy form fell limp, and the man laughed with a sobbing, guttural mirth—for he was master.

Then again he felt the trickle of blood upon his cheek, the ache of his bitten hand. His anger returned with double fury. He kicked the limp body as he lay beside it, never releasing his grip.

Suddenly he forgot to kick. There were sounds! He heard the *thump thump* of hoofs passing his place of refuge. Then they ceased. There were sounds of voices coming dimly; then after a while the hoofs passed again, and there was a voice that said "saved hangin' anyway."

The hoof beats grew dimmer, and Antoine knew by their hollow sound that his pursuers had begun to cross the ice on the back trail. He again gave his attention to the wolf. It lay still. A feeling of supreme comfort came over Antoine. It was sweet to be a master. He laid his head upon the wolf's motionless body. He was very weary, he had conquered, and he would sleep upon his prey.

He awoke feeling a warm, rasping something upon his wounded cheek. A faint light came in at the entrance of the place. It was morning. In his sleep Antoine had moved his head close to the muzzle of the wolf. Now, utterly conquered, bruised, unable to arise, the brute was feebly licking the blood from the man's wound.

Antoine's sense of mastery after his sound sleep made him kind for once. He was safe and something had caressed him, although it was only a soundly beaten wolf.

"You pore devil!" said Antoine with a sudden softness in his voice; "I done you up, didn't I? You hain't so bad, I guess; but if I hadn't done you, I'd got done myself. Hurt much, you pore devil, eh?"

He stroked the side of the animal, whereupon it cried out with pain.

"Pretty sore, eh? Well, as long as I'm bigger'n you, I'll be good to you. I ain't so bad, am I? You treat me square and you won't never get no bad deals from the half-breed; mind that. Hel-*lo*! you're a *Miss* Wolf, ain't you? Well, for the present, I'm a Mister Wolf, and I'm a good un! Let me hunt you up a name; somethin' soft like a woman, 'cause you did touch me kind of tender like. *Susette*!—that's it—*Susette*. You're Susette now. I hain't got no people, so I'm a wolf from now on, and my name's Antoine. Susette and Antoine—sounds pretty good, don't it? Say, I know as much about bein' a wolf as you do. Can't teach me nothin' about sneakin' and hidin' and fightin'! Say, old girl, *hain't* I a tol'able good fighter now? O, I know I am, and when you need it again, you're goin' to get it good and hard, Susette; mind that.

Hain't got nothin' to eat about the house, have you, old girl? Then, bein' head of the family with a sick woman about, I'm goin' huntin'. Don't you let no other wolf come skulkin' around! You know me! I'll wear his skin when I come back, if you don't mind!"

And he went out.

Before noon he returned bringing three jack rabbits, having shot them with his six-shooter. "Well, Susette," said he, "got any appetite?"

He passed his hand over the wolf's snout caressingly. The wolf flinched in fear, but the man continued his caresses until she licked his hand.

"Now, we're friends and we can live together peaceable, can't we? Took a big family row, though. Families needs stirrin' up now and then, I reckon."

He skinned a rabbit and cut off morsels of meat.

"Here, Susette, I'm goin' to fill your hide first, 'cause you've been so good since the row that I'm half beginnin' to love you a little. There, that's it—eat. Does me good to see you eat, pore, sick Susette!"

The wolf took the morsels from his hand and a look almost tame came into her eyes. When she had eaten a rabbit, Antoine had a meal of raw flesh. Then he sat down beside her and stroked her nose and neck and flanks. There was an air of home about the place. He was safe and sheltered, had a full stomach, and there was a fellow creature near him that showed kindness, although it had been won with a beating. But this man had long been accustomed to possessing by violence, and he was satisfied.

"Susette," he said in a soft voice; "don't get mean again when you get well. I want to live quiet and like somethin' that likes me oncet. If you'll be good, I'll get you rabbits and antelope and birds, and you won't need to hunt no more nor go about with your belly flappin' together. And I know how to make fire—somethin' you don't know, wise as you be; and I'll keep you warm and pet you.

"Is it a bargain? All you need to do is just be good, keepin' your teeth out'n my cheek. I've been lonesome always. I hain't got no people. Do you know who your dad was, Susette? Neither do I. Some French trader was mine, I guess. We're in the same boat there. My mother was an Omaha. O Susette, I know what it means to set a stranger in my mother's lodge. 'Wagah peazzha!' [no good white man], that's what the Omahas called me ever since I was a little feller. And the white men said 'damn Injun.' And where am I? O, hangin' onto the edge of things, gettin' ornry and nasty and bad! I've stole horses and killed people and cussed fer days, Susette. And I want to rest; I want to love somethin'. Cabanne's men down at the post would laugh to hear me sayin' that. But I do. I want to love somethin'. Tried to oncet; her name was Susette, jest like your'n. She was a trader's daughter—a pretty French girl. That was before I got bad. I talked sweet to her like I'm a talkin' to you, and she kind of liked it. But the old man Lecroix—that was her dad— he showed me the trail and he says: 'Go that way and go fast, you damn Injun!"

"I went, Susette, but I made him pay, I did. I seen him

on his back a-grinnin' straight up at the stars; and since then I hain't cared much. I killed several after that, and I called 'em all Lecroix!

"Be a good girl, Susette, and I'll stick to you. I'm a good fighter, you know, and I'm a good grub-hunter, too. I learned all that easy."

He continued caressing the wolf, and she licked his hand when he stroked her muzzle.

Days passed; the heavy snows came. Antoine nursed his bruised companion back to health. Through the bitter nights he kept a fire burning at the entrance of the hole. The depth of the snow made it improbable that any should learn his whereabouts; and by that time the news must have spread from post to post that Antoine, the outlaw half-breed, had drowned himself in the ice-fissure.

The man had used all his ammunition, and his six-shooter had thus become useless. With the skill of an Indian he wrought a bow and arrows. He made snow-shoes and continued to hunt, keeping the wolf in meat until she grew strong and fat with the unaccustomed luxurious life.

Also she became very tame. During her weakness the man had subdued her, and through the long nights she lay nestled within the man's great arms and slept.

When the snow became crusted, Antoine and Susette went hunting together, she trotting at his heels like a dog. To her he had come to be only an unusually large wolf—a good fighter.

One evening in late December, when the low moon threw a shaft of cold silver into the mouth of the lair,

Antoine lay huddled in his furs, listening to the long, dirge-like calls of the wolves wandering inward from the vast pitiless night. Susette also listened, sitting upon her haunches beside the man with her ears pricked forward. When the far away cries of her kinspeople arose into a compelling major sound, dying away into the merest shadow of a pitiful minor, she switched her tail uneasily, shuffled about nervously, sniffing and whining.

Then she began pacing with an eager swing up and down the place to the opening and back to the man, sending forth the cry of kinship whenever she reached the moonlit entrance.

"Night's cold, Susette," said Antoine; " 'tain't no time fer huntin'. Hain't I give you enough to eat? Come here and snuggle up and let's sleep."

He caught the wolf and with main force held her down beside him. She snarled savagely and snapped her jaws together, struggling out of his arms and going to the opening where she cried out into the frozen stillness. The answer of her kind floated back in doleful chorus.

"Don't go!" begged the man. "Susette, my pretty Susette! I'll be so lonesome."

As the chorus died, the wolf gave a loud yelp and rushed out into the night. A terrible rage seized Antoine. He leaped from his furs and ran out after the wolf. She fled with a rapid, swinging trot over the scintillating snow toward the concourse of her people. The man fled after, slipping, falling, getting up, running, and ever the wolf widened the glittering stretch of snow between them. To Antoine, the ever-widening space of glinting coldness vaguely symbolized the barrier that seemed growing between him and his last companion.

"Susette, O, Susette!" he cried at last, breathless and exhausted. His cry was dirgelike, even as the wolves'.

She had disappeared in the dusk of a ravine. Antoine, huddled in the snows with his face upon his knees, sobbed in the winter stillness. At last, with slow and faltering step, he returned to his lair; and for the first time in months he felt the throat-pang of the alien.

He threw himself down upon the floor of the cave and cursed the world. Then he cursed Susette.

"It's some other wolf!" he hissed. "Some other gray dog that she's gone to see. O, damn him! damn his gray hide! I'll kill her when she comes back!"

He took out his knife and began whetting it viciously upon his boot.

"I'll cut her into strips and eat 'em! Wasn't I good to her? O, I'll cut her into strips!"

He whetted his knife for an hour, cursing the while through his set teeth. At last anger grew into a foolish madness. He hurled himself upon the bunch of furs beside him and imagined that they were Susette. He set his teeth into the furs, he crushed them with his hands, he tore at them with his nails. Then in the impotence of his anger, he fell upon his face and sobbed himself to sleep.

Strange visions passed before him. Again he killed Lecroix, and saw the dead face grinning at the stars. Again he sat in his mother's lodge and wept because he was a stranger. Again he was fleeing from a leather noose that hung above him like a black cloud, and circled and lowered and raised and lowered until it swooped down upon him and closed about his neck.

With a yell of fright he awoke from his nightmare. His head throbbed, his mouth was parched. At last day came in sneakingly through the opening—a dull, melancholy light; and with it came Susette, sniffling, with the bristles of her neck erect.

"Susette! Susette!" cried the man joyfully.

He no longer thought of killing her. He seized her in his arms; he kissed her frost-whitened muzzle; he caressed her; he called her a woman. She received his kisses with disdain. Whereat the man redoubled his acts of fondness. He fed her and petted her as she ate; whereas the bristles on her neck fell. She nosed him half fondly.

And Antoine, man-like, was glad again.

He ate none that day. He said to himself, "I won't hunt till it's all gone; she can have it all." He was afraid to leave Susette. He was afraid to take her with him again into the land of her own people.

All day he was kind to her with the pitiful kindness of a doting lover for his unfaithful mistress.

That night she consented to lie within his arms, and Antoine cried softly as he whispered into her ear: "Susette, I hain't a goin' to be jealous no more. You've been a bad girl, Susette. Don't do it again. I won't be mean less'n you let *him* come skulkin' round here, damn his gray hide! But O, Susette"—his voice was like a spoken pang—"I wisht—I wisht I was that other wolf!"

The next morning Antoine did not get up. He felt sore and exhausted. By evening his heart was beating like a hammer. His head ached and swam; his burning eyes saw strange, uncertain visions.

"Susette," he called, "I hain't quite right; come here and let me touch you again."

Night was falling and Susette sat sullenly apart, listening for the call of her people. She did not go to him. All night the man tossed and raved. After a lingering age of delirious wanderings, dizzy flights from huge pitiless pursuers, he became conscious of the daylight. He raised his head feebly and looked about the den. Susette was gone. A fury of jealousy again seized Antoine. She had gone to that other wolf—he felt certain of that. He tried to arise, but the fever had weakened him so that he lay impotent, torn alternately with anger and longing.

Suddenly a frost-whitened snout was thrust in at the opening. It was Susette. The man was too weak to cry out his joy, but his eyes filled with a soft light.

Susette entered sniffing strangely, whining and switching her tail as she came. At her heels followed another gray wolf—a male, larger-boned, lanker, with a more powerful snout. He whined and moved his tail nervously at sight of the man.

Antoine lay staring upon the intruder. "So that's him," thought the man; "I wisht I could get up."

A delirious anger shook him; he struggled to arise, but could not. "O God," he moaned; it was an unusual thing for this man to say the word so; "O God, please le' me get up and fight!"

A harsh growl stopped him. The gray intruder approached him with a rapid, sinuous movement of the tail. His jaws grinned with long sharp teeth displayed. The rage of hunger was in his eyes fixed steadily upon the sick man.

Antoine stared steadily into the glaring eyes of his wolfish rival, already crouching for the spring.

On a sudden, a strange exhilaration came over the man. He seemed drinking in the essence of life from the pitiless stare of his adversary. His great limbs, seeming devitalised but a moment before, now tingled to their extremities with a sudden surging of the wine of life. His eyes, which the fever had burned into the dullness of ashes, flamed suddenly again with the eager lust of fight.

He raised himself upon his haunches, beast-like, and with the lifting of a sneering lip that disclosed his grinding teeth, he gave a cry that was both a snarl and a sob.

Antoine met the impetuous spring of the wolf with the downward blow of a fist, and sprang whining upon his momentarily worsted foe. Never before had he fought in all his bitter pariah life as now he fought for the possession of his last companion.

His antagonist was larger than Susette, the survivor of many moonlit battles in the frozen wilderness of hills.

Lacerated with the snapping of powerful jaws, bleeding from his face and hands, the man felt that he was winning. With a whining cry, less than half human, he succeeded in fixing his left hand upon the hairy throat, crushed the wolf down upon its back, and with prodigious strength, began pressing the fingers of his right hand in between the protruding lower ribs. He would tear them out! He would thrust his hand in among the vitals of his foe!

All the while Susette, whining and switching her tail, watched with glowing eyes the struggle of the males.

At this juncture she arose with a nervous, threatening swaying of the head, approached the two cautiously, then hurled herself into the encounter. She leaped with a savage yelp upon him who had long been her master.

The man's grip relaxed. He fell back and threw out his arms in which once more the weakness of the fever came.

"Susette!" he gasped; "I was good to you; I—"

His voice was choked into a wheeze. Susette had gripped him by the throat, and the two were upon him.

The River and I

In the summer of 1908, Neihardt and a companion descended the Missouri River in a small boat. Sailing from the head of navigation at Fort Benton, Montana, to Sioux City, Iowa, a distance of some two thousand miles, they saw the river in its original state before the great dams were built. In the chapter excerpted here, their boat is said to have a motor. As it happened, the unavailability of parts for the motor made it necessary to turn to manpower, and most of the voyage was completed in a rowboat.

Neihardt described the adventure in a series of articles commissioned by the editor of Outing Magazine, *which paid an advance to make the trip possible. In 1910 the articles were collected in a book entitled* The River and I. *It has become something of a classic. Choosing the chapter to be included here was not easy, but "The Region of Weir" is a favorite and is typical of the book.*

The following selection was first published in *Putnam's Magazine*, 1909, then in the book *The River and I* (1910, 1927; reprinted Lincoln: University of Nebraska Press, 1968).

Through the Region of Weir

We awoke with light hearts on the second morning of the voyage. All about us was the sacred silence of the wilderness dawn. The coming sun had smitten the chill night air into a ghostly fog that lay upon the valley like a fairy lake.

We were at the rim of the Bad Lands and there were no birds to sing; but crows, wheeling about a sandstone summit, flung doleful voices downward into the morning hush—the spirit of the place grown vocal.

Cloaked with fog, our breakfast fire of driftwood glowed ruddily. What is there about the tang of wood-smoke in a lonesome place that fills one with glories that seem half memory and half dream? Crouched on my haunches, shivering just enough to feel the beauty there is in fire, I needed only to close my eyes, smarting with the smoke, to feel myself the first man huddled close to the first flame, blooming like a mystic flower in the chill dawn of the world!

Perhaps that is what an outing is for—to strip one down to the lean essentials, press in upon one the glorious privilege of being one's self, unique in all the universe of innumerable unique things. Crouched close to your wilderness campfire, the great Vision comes easily out of the smoke. Once again you feel the bigness of your world, the tremendous significance of everything in it—including yourself—and a far-seeing sadness grips you. Living in the flesh seems so transient, almost a pitiful thing in the last analysis. But somehow you feel that there is something bigger—not beyond it, but all about it continually. And you wonder that you ever hated anyone. You know, somehow, there in the smoky silence, why men are noble or ignoble; why they lie or die for a principle; why they kill, or suffer martyrdom; why they love and hate and fight; why women smile under burdens, sin splendidly or sordidly—and why hearts sometimes break.

And expanded by the bigness of the empty silent spaces about you, like a spirit independent of it and outside of it all, you love the great red straining Heart of Man more than you could ever love it at your desk in town. And you want to get up and move—push on through purple distances—whither? Oh, anywhere will do! What you seek is at the end of the rainbow; it is in the azure of distance; it is just behind the glow of the sunset, and close under the dawn. And the glorious thing about it is that you know you'll never find it until you reach that lone, ghostly land where the North Star sets, perhaps. You're merely glad to know that you're not a vegetable—and that the trail never really ends anywhere.

Just now, however, the longing for the abstract had the semblance of a longing for the concrete. It always has that semblance, for that matter. You never really want what you think you are seeking. Touch the substance—and away you go after the shadow!

Around the bend lay Sioux City. Around what bend? What matter? Somewhere down stream the last bend lay, and in between lay the playing of the game. Any bend will do to sail around! There's a lot of fun in merely being able to move about and do things. For this reason I am overwhelmed with gratitude whenever I think that, through some slight error in the cosmic process, the life forces that glow in me might have been flung into a turnip—*but weren't!* The thought is truly appalling— isn't it? The avoidance of that one awful possibility is enough to make any man feel lucky all his life. It's such fun to awaken in the morning with all your legs and arms and eyes and ears about you, waiting to be used again! So strong was this thought in me when we cast off, that even the memory of Bill's amateurish pancakes couldn't keep back the whistle.

The current of the Black Bluffs Rapids whisked us from the bank with a giddy speed, spun us about a right-angled bend, and landed us in a long quiet lake. Contrary to the average opinion, the Upper Missouri is merely a succession of lakes and rapids. In the low-water season, this statement should be italicised. When you are pushing down with the power of your arms alone the rapids show you how fast you want to go, and the lakes show you that you can't go that fast. For the teaching of patience, the arrangement is admirable. But when head winds blow, a three-mile reach means about a two-hour fight.

This being a very invigorating morning, however, the engine decided to take a constitutional. It ran. Below the mouth of the Marias River, twenty minutes later, we grounded on Archer's Bar and shut down. After dragging her off the gravel, we discovered that the engine wished to sleep. No amount of cranking could arouse it. Now and then it would say "*squash*," feebly rolling its wheel a revolution or two—like a sleepy-head brushing off a fly with a languid hand.

A light breeze had sprung up out of the west. The stream ran east and northeast. We hastily rigged a tarp on a pair of oars spliced for a mast, and proceeded at a carefree pace. The light breeze ruffled the surface of the slow stream;

"——yet still the sail made on
A pleasant noise till noon."

In the lazy heat of the mounting sun, tempered by the cool river draught, the yellow sandstone bluffs, whimsically decorated with sparse patches of greenery, seemed to waver as though seen through shimmering silken gauze. And over it all was the hush of a dream, except when, in a spasmodic freshening of the breeze, the rude mast creaked and a sleepy watery murmur grew up for a moment at the wake.

Now and then at a break in the bluffs, where a little coulee entered the stream, the gray masses of the bullberry bushes lifted like smoke, and from them, flamelike, flashed the vivid scarlet of the berry-clusters, smiting the general dreaminess like a haughty cry in a silence.

A wilderness indeed! It seemed that waste land of which Tennyson sang, "where no man comes nor hath come since the making of the world." I thought of the steamboats and the mackinaws and the keel-boats and the thousands of men who had pushed through this dream-world and the thought was unconvincing. Fairies may have lived here, indeed; and in the youth of the world, a glad young race of gods might have dreamed gloriously among the yellow crags. But surely we were the first men who had ever passed that way—and should be the last.

Suddenly the light breeze boomed up into a gale. The *Atom,* with bellying sail, leaped forward down the roughening water, swung about a bend, raced with a quartering wind down the next reach, shot across another bend—and lay drifting in a golden calm. Still above us the great wind buzzed in the crags like a swarm of giant bees, and the waters about us lay like a sheet of flawless glass.

With paddles we pushed on lazily for an hour. At the next bend, where the river turned into the west, the great gale that had been roaring above us, suddenly struck us full in front. Sucking up river between the wall rocks on either side, its force was terrific. You tried to talk while facing it, and it took your breath away. In a few minutes, in spite of our efforts with the paddles, we lay pounding on the shallows of the opposite shore.

We got out. Two went forward with the line and the third pushed at the stern. Progress was slow—no more than a mile an hour. The clear water of the upper river is always cold, and the great wind chilled the air. Even under the August noon it took brisk work to keep one's teeth from chattering. The bank we were following became a precipice rising sheer from the river's edge, and the water deepened until we could no longer wade. We got in and poled on to the next shallows, often for many minutes at a time barely holding our own against the stiff gusts. For two hours we dragged the heavily laden boat, sometimes walking the bank, sometimes wading in mid-stream, sometimes poling, often swimming with the line from one shallow to another. And the struggle ended as suddenly as it began. Upon rounding the second bend the head wind became a stern wind, driving us on at a jolly clip until nightfall.

During the late afternoon, we came upon a place where the Great Northern Railroad touches the river for the last time in five hundred miles. Here we saw two Italian section hands whiling away their Sunday with fishing rods. I went ashore, hoping to buy some fish. Neither of the two could speak English, and Italian sounds to me merely like an unintelligible singing. However, they gave me to understand that the fish were not for sale, and my proffered coin had no persuasive powers.

Still wanting those fish, I rolled a smoke, carelessly whistling the while a strain from an opera I had once heard. For some reason or other that strain had been in my head all day. I had gotten up in the morning with it; I had whistled it during the fight with the head wind. The Kid called it "that Dago tune." I think it was something from *Il Trovatore*.

Suddenly one of the little Italians dropped his rod, stood up to his full height, lifted his arms very much after the manner of an orchestra leader and joined in with me. I stopped—because I saw that he *could* whistle. He carried it on with much expression to the last thin note with all the ache of the world in it. And then he grinned at me.

"Verdi!" he said sweetly.

I applauded. Whereat the little Italian produced a bag of tobacco. We sat down on the rocks and smoked together, holding a wordless but perfectly intelligible conversation of pleasant grins.

That night we had fish for supper! I got them for a song—or, rather, for a whistle. I was fed with more than fish. And I went to sleep that night with a glorious thought for a pillow: Truth expressed as Art is the universal language. One immortal strain from Verdi, poorly whistled in a wilderness, had made a Dago and a Dutchman brothers!

Scarcely had the crackling of the ruddy log lulled us to sleep, when the night had flitted over like a shadow, and we were cooking breakfast. A lone, gray wolf, sitting on his haunches a hundred paces away, regarded us curiously. Doubtless we were new to his generation; for in the evening dusk we had drifted well into the Bad Lands.

Bad Lands? Rather the Land of Awe!

A light stern wind came up with the sun. During the previous evening we had rigged a cat-sail, and noiselessly we glided down the glinting trail of crystal into the "Region of Weir."

On either hand the sandstone cliffs reared their yellow masses against the cloudless sky. Worn by the ebbing floods of a prehistoric sea, carved by the winds and rains of ages, they presented a panorama of wonders.

Rows of huge colonial mansions with pillared por-

ticoes looked from their dizzy terraces across the stream
to where soaring mosques and mystic domes of worship
caught the sun. It was all like the visible dream of a
master architect gone mad. Gaunt, sinister ruins of me-
dieval castles sprawled down the slopes of unassailable
summits. Grim brown towers, haughtily crenellated,
scowled defiance on the unappearing foe. Titanic stools
of stone dotted barren garden slopes, where surely gods
had once strolled in that far time when the stars sang and
the moon was young. Dark red walls of regularly laid
stone—huge as that the Chinese flung before the advance
of the Northern hordes—held imaginary empires asun-
der. Poised on a dizzy peak, Jove's eagle stared into the
eye of the sun, and raised his wings for the flight deferred
these many centuries. Kneeling face to face upon a lone-
some summit, their hands clasped before them, their
backs bent as with the burdens of the race, two women
prayed the old, old woman prayer. The snow-white
ruins of a vast cathedral lay along the water's edge, and
all about it was a hush of worship. And near it, arose the
pointed pipes of a colossal organ—with the summer
silence for music.

With a lazy sail we drifted through this place of awe;
and for once I had no regrets about that engine. The
popping of the exhaust would have seemed sacrilegious
in this holy quiet.

Seldom do men pass that way. It is out of the path of
the tourist. No excursion steamers ply those awesome
river reaches. Across the sacred whiteness of that cathe-
dral's imposing mass, no sign has ever been painted

telling you the merits of the best five-cent cigar in the world! Few besides the hawks and the crows would see it, if it were there.

And yet, for all the quiet in this land of wonder, somehow you cannot feel that the place is unpeopled. Surely, you think, invisible knights clash in tourney under those frowning towers. Surely a lovelorn maiden spins at that castle window, weaving her heartache into the magic figures of her loom. Stately dames must move behind the shut doors of those pillared mansions; devotees mutter Oriental prayers beneath those sun-smitten domes. And amid the awful inner silence of that cathedral, white-robed priests lift wan faces to their God.

Under the beat of the high sun the light stern wind fell. The slack sail drooped like a sick-hearted thing. Idly drifting on the slow glassy flood, we seemed only an incidental portion of this dream in which the deepest passions of man were bodied forth in eternal fixity. Towers of battle, domes of prayer, fanes of worship, and then— the kneeling women! Somehow one couldn't whistle there. Bill and the Kid, little given to sentiment, sat quietly and stared.

Late in the afternoon we found ourselves out of this "Region of Weir." Great wall rocks soared above us. Consulting our map, we found that we were nearing Eagle Rapids, the first of a turbulent series. I had fondly anticipated shooting them all under power. So once more I decided to go over that engine. We landed at the wooded mouth of a little ravine, having made a trifle over twenty miles that day.

With those tools of the engine doctor—an air of mystery and a monkey-wrench—I unscrewed everything that appeared to have a thread on it, and pulled out the other things. The odds, I figured, were in my favor. A sick engine is useless, and I felt assured of either killing or curing. I did something—I don't know what; but having achieved the complete screwing up and driving in of things—*it went!*

So on the morning of the fourth day, we were up early, eager for the shooting of the rapids. We had understood from the conversation of the seemingly wise, that Eagle Rapids was the first of a series that made the other rapids we had passed through look like mere ripples on the surface. In some of those we had gone at a very good clip, and several times we had lost our rudder.

I remembered how the steamboats used to be obliged to throw out cables and slowly wind themselves up with the power of the "steam nigger." I also remembered the words of Father de Smet: "There are many rapids, ten of which are very difficult to ascend and very dangerous to go down."

We had intended from the very first to get wrecked in one or all of these rapids. For this reason we had distributed forward, aft, and amidships, eight five-gallon cans, soldered airtight. The frail craft would, we figured, be punctured. The cans would displace nearly three hundred and fifty pounds of water, and the boat and engine, submerged, would lose a certain weight. I had made the gruesome calculation with fond attention to detail. I decided that she should be wrecked quite arithmetically. We should be able, the figures said, to recover the engine and patch the boat. We had provided three life-preservers, but one had been stolen; so I had fancied what a bully fight one might have if he should be thrown out into the mad waters without a life-preserver.

I have never been able to explain it satisfactorily; it is one of the paradoxes; but human nature seems to take a weird delight in placing in jeopardy that which is dearest. Even a coward with his fingers clenched desperately on the ragged edge of hazard, feels an inexplicable thrill of glory. Having several times been decently scared, I know.

One likes to take a sly peep behind the curtain of the big play, hoping perhaps to get a slight hint as to what machinery hoists the moon, and what sort of contrivance flings the thunder and lightning, and many other things that are none of his business. Only, to be sure, he intends to get away safely with his information. When you think you see your finish bowing to receive you, something happens in your head. It's like a sultry sheet of rapid fire lapping up for a moment the thunder-shaken night—and discovering a strange land to you. And it's really good for you.

Under half speed we cruised through the windless golden morning; and the lonesome canyon echoed and re-echoed with the joyful chortle of the resurrected engine. We had covered about ten miles, when a strange sighing sound grew up about us. It seemed to emanate from the soaring walls of rock. It seemed faint, yet it arose above the din of the explosions, drowned out the droning of the screw.

Steadily the sound increased. Like the ghost of a great wind it moaned and sighed about us. Little by little a new note crept in—a sibilant, metallic note as of a tense sheet of silk drawn rapidly over a thin steel edge.

We knew it to be the mourning voice of the Eagle Rapids; but far as we could see, the river was quiet as a lake. We jogged on for a mile, with the invisible moaning presence about us. It was somewhat like the intangible something you feel about a powerful but sinister personality. The golden morning was saturated with it.

Suddenly, turning a sharp bend about the wall of rock that flanked the channel, a wind of noise struck us. It was like the hissing of innumerable snakes against a tonal background of muffled continuous thunder. A hundred yards before us was Eagle Rapids—a forbidding patch of writhing, whitening water, pricked with the upward thrust of toothlike rocks.

The first sight of it turned the inside of me mist-gray. Temporarily, wrecks and the arithmetic of them had little charm for me. I seized the spark-lever, intending to shut down. Instead, I threw it wide open. With the resulting leap of the craft, all the gray went out of me.

I grasped the rudder ropes and aimed at a point where the sinuous current sucked through a passage in the rocks like a lean flame through a windy flue. Did you ever hear music that made you see purple? It was that sort of purple I saw (or did I hear it like music?) when we plunged under full speed into the first suck of the rapids. We seemed a conscious arrow hurled through a gray, writhing world, the light of which was noise. And then, suddenly, the quiet, golden morning flashed back; and we were ripping the placid waters of a lake.

The Kid broke out into boisterous laughter that irritated me strangely: "Where the devil do you suppose our life-preservers are?" he bawled. "They're clear down under all the cargo!"

A world of wonderful beauty was forging past us. In the golden calm, the scintillant sheet of water seemed to be rushing backward, splitting itself over the prow, like a fabric woven of gold and silver drawn rapidly against a keen stationary blade.

The sheer cliffs had fallen away into pine-clad slopes, and vari-colored rocks flung notes of scarlet and gold through the sombre green of the pines—like the riotous treble cries of an organ pricking the sullen murmur of the bass. So still were the clean waters that we seemed midway between two skies.

We skirted the base of a conical rock that towered three hundred feet above us—a Titan sentinel. It was the famous Sentinel Rock of the old steamboat days. I shut the engine down to quarter speed, for somehow from the dizzy summit a sad dream fell upon me and bade me linger.

I stared down into the cold crystal waters at the base of the rock. Many-colored mosses, sickly green, pale, feverish red, yellow like fear, black like despair, purple like the lips of a strangled man, clung there. I remembered an old spring I used to haunt when I was just old enough to be awed by the fact of life and frightened at the possibility of death. Just such mosses grew in the depths of that spring. I used to stare into it for hours.

It fascinated me in a terrible way. I thought Death looked like that. Even now I am afraid I could not swim long in clear waters with those fearful colors under me. I am sure they found Ophelia floating like a ghastly lily in such a place.

Filled with a shadow of the old childish dread, I looked up to the austere summit of the Sentinel. Scarred and haggard with time it caught the sun. I thought of how long it had stood there just so, under the intermittent flashing of moon and sun and star, since first its flinty peak had pricked through the hot spume of prehistoric seas.

Fantastic reptiles, winged and finned and fanged, had basked upon it—grotesque, tentative vehicles of the Flame of Life! And then these flashed out, and the wild sea fell, and the land arose—hideous and naked, a steaming ooze fetid with gasping life. And all the while this scarred Sentinel stared unmoved. And then a riot of giant vegetation all about it—divinely extravagant, many-colored as fire. And this too flashed out—like the impossible dream of a god too young. And the Great Change came, and the paradox of frost was in the world, stripping life down to the lean essentials till only the sane, capable things might live. And still the Titan stared as in the beginning. And then, men were in the land—gaunt, terrible, wolf-like men, loving and hating. And La Verendrye forged past it; and Lewis and Clark toiled under it through these waters of awful quiet. And then the bull boats and the mackinaws and the packets. And all these flashed out; and still it stood unmoved. And I came—and I too would flash out, and all men after me and all life.

I viewed the colossal watcher with something like terror—the aspect of death about its base and that cynical glimmer of sunlight at its top. I flung the throttle open, and we leaped forward through the river hush. I wanted to get away from this thing that had seen so much of life and cared so little. It depressed me strangely; it thrust bitter questions within the charmed circle of my ego. It gave me an almost morbid desire for speed, as though there were some place I should reach before the terrible question should be answered against me.

We fled down five or six miles of depressingly quiet waters. Once again the wall rocks closed about us. We seemed to be going at a tediously slow pace, yet the two thin streams of water rushed hissing from prow to stern. A strange mood was upon me. Once when I was a boy and far from home, I awoke in the night with a bed of railroad ties under me, and the chill black blanket of the darkness about me. I wanted to get up and run through that damned night—anywhere, just so I went fast enough—stopping only when exhaustion should drag me down. And yet I was afraid of nothing tangible; hunger and the stranger had sharpened whatever blue steel there was in my nature. I was afraid of being still! Were you ever a homesick boy, too proud to tell the truth about it?

I felt something of that boy's ache as we shot in among the wall rocks again. It was a psychic hunger for something that does not exist. Oh, to attain the terrible speed one experiences in a fever-dream, to get somewhere before it is too late, before the black curtain drops!

To some this may sound merely like the grating of overwrought nerves. But it is more than that. All religions grew out of that most human mood. And whenever one is deeply moved, he feels it. For even the most matter-of-fact person of us all has now and then a suspicion that this life is merely episodic—that curtain after curtain of darkness is to be pierced, world after world of consciousness and light to be passed through.

Once more the rocks took on grotesque shapes— utterly ultra-human in their suggestiveness. Those who have marveled at the Hudson's beauty should drop down this lonesome stretch.

We shot through the Elbow Rapids at the base of the great Hole-in-the-wall Rock. It was deep and safe— much like an exaggerated millrace. It ran in heavy swells, yet the day was windless.

In the late afternoon we shot the Dead Man's Rapids, a very turbulent and rocky stretch of water. We went through at freight-train speed, and began to develop a slight contempt for fast waters. That night we camped at the mouth of the Judith River on the site of the now forgotten Fort Chardon. We had made only ninety-eight miles in four days. It began to appear that we might be obliged to finish on skates!

We were up and off with the first gray of the morning.

We knew Dauphin Rapids to be about seventeen miles below, and since this particular patch of water had by far the greatest reputation of all the rapids, we were eager to make its acquaintance.

The engine began to show unmistakable signs of getting tired of its job. Now and then it barked spitefully, had half a notion to stop, changed its mind, ran faster than it should, wheezed and slowed down—acting in an altogether unreasonable way. But it kept the screw humming nevertheless.

Fortunately it was going at a mad clip when we sighted the Dauphin. There was not that sibilance and thunder that had turned me a bit gray inside at first sight of the Eagle. The channel was narrow, and no rocks appeared above the surface. But speed *was* there; and the almost noiseless rolling of the swift flood ahead had a more formidable appearance than that of the Eagle. Rocks above the surface are not much to be feared when you have power and a good rudder. But we drew about twenty-two inches of water, and I thought of the rocks under the surface.

I had, however, only a moment to think, for we were already traveling a good eighteen miles, and when the main swirl of the rapids seized us, we no doubt reached twenty-five. I was grasping the rudder ropes and we were all grinning a sort of idiotic satisfaction at the amazing spurt of speed, when——

Something was about to happen!

The Kid and I were sitting behind the engine in order to hold her screw down to solid water. Bill, decorated with a grin, sat amidships facing us. I caught a pink flash in the swirl just under our bow, and then *it happened!*

The boat reared like a steeple-chaser taking a fence! The Kid shot forward over the engine and knocked the grin off Bill's face! Clinging desperately to the rudder ropes, I saw, for a brief moment, a good three-fourths of the frail craft thrust skyward at an angle of about forty-five degrees. Then she stuck her nose in the water and her screw came up, howling like seven devils in the air behind me! Instinctively, I struck the spark-lever; the howling stopped,—and we were floating in the slow waters below Dauphin Rapids.

All the cargo had forged forward, and the persons of Bill and the Kid were considerably tangled. We laughed loud and long. Then we gathered ourselves up and wondered if she might be taking water under the cargo. It developed that she wasn't. But one of our grub boxes, containing all the bacon, was missing. So were the short oars that we used for paddles. While we laughed, these had found some convenient hiding-place.

We had struck a smooth bowlder and leaped over it. A boat with the ordinary launch construction would have opened at every seam. The light springy tough construction of the *Atom* had saved her. Whereat I thought of the Information Bureau and was well pleased.

Altogether we looked upon the incident as a purple spot. But we were many miles from available bacon, and when, upon trial, the engine refused to make a revolution, we began to get exceedingly hungry for meat.

Having a dead engine and no paddles, we drifted. We

drifted very slowly. The Kid asked if he might not go ashore and drive a stake in the bank. For what purpose? Why, to ascertain whether we were going up or down stream! While we drifted in the now blistering sun, we talked about *meat*. With a devilish persistence we quite exhausted the subject. We discussed the best methods for making a beefsteak delicious. It made us very hungry for meat. The Kid announced that he could feel his backbone sawing at the front of his shirt. But perhaps that was only the hyperbole of youth. Bill confessed that he had once grumbled at his good wife for serving the steak too rare. He now stated that at the first telegraph station he would wire for forgiveness. I advised him to wire for money instead and buy meat with it. Personally I felt a sort of wistful tenderness for packing-houses.

That day passed somehow, and the next morning we were still hungry for meat. We spent most of the morning talking about it. In the blistering windless afternoon, we drifted lazily. Now and then we took turns cranking the engine.

We were going stern foremost and I was cranking. We rounded a bend where the wall rocks sloped back, leaving a narrow arid sagebrush strip along both sides of the stream. I had straightened up to get the kink out of my back and mop the sweat out of my eyes, when I saw something that made my stomach turn a double somersault.

A good eight hundred yards down stream at the point of a gravel-bar, something that looked like and yet unlike a small cluster of drifting, leafless brush moved slowly into the water. Now it appeared quite distinct, and now it seemed that a film of oil all but blotted it out. I blinked my eyes and peered hard through the baffling yellow glare. Then I reached for the rifle and climbed over the gunwale. I smelled raw meat.

Fortunately, we were drifting across a bar, and the slow water came only to my shoulders. The thing eight hundred yards away was forging across stream by this time—heading for the mouth of a coulee. I saw plainly now that the brush grew out of a head. It was a buck with antlers.

Just below the coulee's mouth, the wall rocks began again. The buck would be obliged to land above the wall rocks, and the drifting boat would keep him going. I reached shore and headed for that coulee. The sagebrush concealed me. At the critical moment, I intended to show myself and start him up the steep slope. Thus he would be forced to approach me while fleeing me. When I felt that enough time had passed, I stood up. The buck, shaking himself like a dog, stood against the yellow sandstone at the mouth of the gulch. He saw me, looked back at the drifting boat, and appeared to be undecided.

I wondered what the range might be. Back home in the plowed field where I frequently plug tin cans at various long ranges, I would have called it six hundred yards—at first. Then suddenly it seemed three or four hundred. Like a thing in a dream the buck seemed to waver back and forth in the oily sunlight.

"Call it four hundred and fifty," I said to myself, and let drive. A spurt of yellow stonedust leaped from the cliff a foot or so above the deer's back. Only four hundred? But the deer had made up his mind. He had urgent business on the other side of that slope—he appeared to be over-due.

I pumped up another shell and drew fine at four hundred. That time his rump quivered for a second as though a great weight had been dropped on it. But he went on with increased speed. Once more I let him have it. That time he lost an antler. He had now reached the summit, two hundred feet up at the least.

He hesitated—seemed to be shivering. I have hunted with a full stomach and brought down game. But there's a difference when you are empty. In that moment before you kill, you became the sort of fellow your mother wouldn't like. Perhaps the average man would feel a little ashamed to tell the truth about that savage moment. I got down on my knee and put a final soft-nosed ball where it would do the most good. The buck reared, stiffened, and came down, tumbling over and over.

That night we pitched camp under a lone scrubby tree at the mouth of an arid gulch that led back into the utterly God-forsaken Bad Lands. It was the wilderness indeed. Coyotes howled far away in the night, and div-ing beaver boomed out in the black stream.

We built half a dozen fires and swung above them the choice portions of our kill. And how we ate—with what glorious appetites!

It is good to sit with a glad-hearted company flinging words of joyful banter across very tall steins. It is good to draw up to a country table at Christmas time with turkey and pumpkin-pies and old-fashioned puddings before you, and the ones you love about you. I have been deeply happy with apples and cider before an open fire-place. I have been present when the brilliant sword-play of wit flashed across a banquet table—and it thrilled me. *But* ——

There is no feast like the feast in the open—the feast in the flaring light of a night fire—the feast of your own kill, with the tang of the wild and the tang of the smoke in it!

A Cycle of the West

In 1912, at the age of thirty-one, John Neihardt turned from lyric poetry and prose and began the work that would demand his major effort for the next twenty-nine years. Composed of five "songs," A Cycle of the West *begins in 1822, when the first Ashley-Henry band of trappers departed from St. Louis, and closes with the massacre of Big Foot's people at Wounded Knee in 1890, an event that signaled the end of Indian resistance on the plains.*

My father viewed this time of discovery, exploration, and settlement as "a genuine epic period, differing in no essential from the other great epic perods that marked the advance of the Indo-European peoples out of Asia and across Europe." It was a time, he said, "of intense individualism, a time when society was cut loose from its roots, a time when an old culture was being overcome by that of a powerful people driven by ancient needs and greeds."

This is not the place for a detailed discussion of the poetic form of The Song of Three Friends, The Song of Hugh Glass, The Song of Jed Smith, The Song of the Indian Wars, *and* The Song of the Messiah. *But a word is in order. At first blush, the reader might assume that the rhyme scheme is that of the familiar couplet. However, closer examination re-veals that both the sense and the breathing time carry over from the end of one line to the middle of the next, thus avoiding the monotonous singsong effect so often associated with the rhyming couplet.*

A Cycle of the West *is widely recognized as a masterwork. As one reviewer wrote, it is "told with Homeric directness, with the same joy in life and the same regret in death."*

The Song of Three Friends

A notice appeared in the March 20, 1822, issue of the Missouri Republican, *printed in St. Louis:*

TO ENTERPRISING YOUNG MEN

The subscriber wishes to engage one hundred young men to ascend the Missouri River to its source, there to be employed for one, two or three years. For particulars, enquire of Major Andrew Henry, near the lead mines in the County of Washington, who will ascend with, and command, the party; or of the subscriber near St. Louis.

(signed) William H. Ashley.

The unattached and adventurous read the advertisement and responded. Their story, told in The Song of Three Friends, *begins:*

One hundred strong they flocked to Ashley's call
That spring of eighteen hundred twenty-two;
For tales of wealth, out-legending Peru,
Came wind-blown from Missouri's distant springs,
And that old sireny of unknown things
Bewitched them, and they could not linger more.

The Song of Three Friends *was published in 1919. For this anthology I have selected the chapter entitled "The Up-Stream Men," which introduces the central characters and offers a preview of the action. The line "tales of wealth out-legending*

Peru" refers to rumors of the seemingly unlimited supply of fine furs to be gathered by trappers in the upriver country. As John Neihardt points out in his introduction to A Cycle of the West: *"Out of those trapper bands came all of the great continental explorers after Lewis and Clark."*

"The Up-Stream Men" is from *The Song of Three Friends* (New York: Macmillan, 1919, 1941); reprinted in *A Cycle of the West* (1949; Lincoln: University of Nebraska Press, 1963, 1991) and *The Mountain Men* (Lincoln: University of Nebraska Press, 1971).

The Up-Stream Men

               When Major Henry went
Up river at the head of Ashley's band,
Already there were robins in the land.
Home-keeping men were following the plows
And through the smoke-thin greenery of boughs
The scattering wild-fire of the fruit bloom ran.

Behold them starting northward, if you can.
Dawn flares across the Mississippi's tide;
A tumult runs along the waterside
Where, scenting an event, St. Louis throngs.
Above the buzzling voices soar the songs
Of waiting boatmen—lilting *chansonettes*
Whereof the meaning laughs, the music frets,
Nigh weeping that such gladness can not stay.
In turn, the herded horses snort and neigh
Like panic bugles. Up the gangplanks poured,
Go streams of trappers, rushing goods aboard
The snub-built keelboats, squat with seeming sloth—
Baled three-point blankets, blue and scarlet cloth,
Rum, powder, flour, guns, gauderies and lead.
And all about, goodbyes are being said.
Gauche girls with rainy April in their gaze
Cling to their beardless heroes, count the days
Between this parting and the wedding morn,
Unwitting how unhuman Fate may scorn
The youngling dream. For O how many a lad

Would see the face of Danger, and go mad
With her weird vixen beauty; aye, forget
This girl's face, yearning upward now and wet,
Half woman's with the first vague guess at woe!

And now commands are bellowed, boat horns blow
Haughtily in the dawn; the tumult swells.
The tow-crews, shouldering the long cordelles
Slack from the mastheads, lean upon the sag.
The keelboats answer lazily and drag
Their blunt prows slowly in the gilded tide.
A steersman sings, and up the riverside
The gay contagious ditty spreads and runs
Above the shouts, the uproar of the guns,
The nickering of horses.

                So, they say,
Went forth a hundred singing men that day;
And girlish April went ahead of them.
The music of her trailing garment's hem
Seemed scarce a league ahead. A little speed
Might yet almost surprise her in the deed
Of sorcery; for, ever as they strove,
A gray-green smudge in every poplar grove
Proclaimed the recent kindling. Aye, it seemed
That bird and bush and tree had only dreamed
Of song and leaf and blossom, till they heard
The young men's feet; when tree and bush and bird
Unleashed the whole conspiracy of awe!
Pale green was every slough about the Kaw;

About the Platte, pale green was every slough;
And still the pale green lingered at the Sioux,
So close they trailed the marching of the South.
But when they reached the Niobrara's mouth
The witchery of spring had taken flight
And, like a girl grown woman over night,
Young summer glowed.

              And now the river rose,
Gigantic from a feast of northern snows,
And mightily the snub prows felt the tide;
But with the loud, sail-filling South allied,
The tow-crews battled gaily day by day;
And seldom lulled the struggle on the way
But some light jest availed to fling along
The panting lines the laughter of the strong,
For joy sleeps lightly in the hero's mood.
And when the sky-wide prairie solitude
Was darkened round them, and the camp was set
Secure for well-earned sleep that came not yet,
What stories shaped for marvel or for mirth!—
Tales fit to strain the supper-tightened girth,
Looped yarns, wherein the veteran spinners vied
To color with a lie more glorified
Some thread that had veracity enough,
Spun straightway out of life's own precious stuff
That each had scutched and heckled in the raw.
Then thinner grew each subsequent guffaw
While drowsily the story went the rounds
And o'er the velvet dark the summer sounds

Prevailed in weird crescendo more and more,
Until the story-teller with a snore
Gave over to a dream a tale half told.

And now the horse-guards, while the night grows old,
With intermittent singing buffet sleep
That surges subtly down the starry deep
On waves of odor from the manless miles
Of summer-haunted prairie. Now, at whiles,
The kiote's mordant clamor cleaves the drowse.
The horses stamp and blow; about the prows
Dark waters chug and gurgle; as with looms
Bugs weave a drone; a beaver's diving booms,
Whereat bluffs grumble in their sable cowls.
The devil laughter of the prairie owls
Mocks mirth anon, like unrepentant sin.
Perceptibly at last slow hours wear thin
The east, until the prairie stares with morn,
And horses nicker to the boatman's horn
That blares the music of a day begun.

So through the days of thunder and of sun
They pressed to northward. Now the river shrank,
The grass turned yellow and the men were lank
And gnarled with labor. Smooth-lipped lads matured
'Twixt moon and moon with all that they endured,
Their faces leathered by the wind and glare,
Their eyes grown ageless with the calm far stare
Of men who know the prairies or the seas.
And when they reached the village of the Rees,

One scarce might say, This man is young, this old,
Save for the beard.

                Here loitered days of gold
And days of leisure, welcome to the crews;
For recently had come the wondrous news
Of beaver-haunts beyond the Great Divide—
So rich a tale 'twould seem the tellers lied,
Had they not much fine peltry to attest.
So now the far off River of the West
Became the goal of venture for the band;
And since the farther trail lay overland
From where the Great Falls thundered to no ear,
They paused awhile to buy more ponies here
With powder, liquor, gauds and wily words.
A horse-fond people, opulent in herds,
The Rees were; and the trade was very good.

Now camped along the river-fringing wood,
Three sullen, thunder-brewing, rainless days,
Those weathered men made merry in their ways
With tipple, euchre, story, jest and song.
The marksmen matched their cleverness; the strong
Wrestled the strong; and brawling pugilists
Displayed the boasted power of their fists
In stubborn yet half amicable fights.
And whisky went hell-roaring through the nights
Among the lodges of the fuddled Rees.
Thus merrily the trappers took their ease,
Rejoicing in the thread that Clotho spun;

For it was good to feel the bright thread run,
However eager for the snipping shears.

O joy long stifled in the ruck of years!
How many came to strange and bitter ends!
And who was merrier than those three friends
Whom here a song remembers for their woe?

Will Carpenter, Mike Fink and Frank Talbeau
Were they—each gotten of a doughty breed;
For in the blood of them the ancient seed
Of Saxon, Celt and Norman grew again.
The Mississippi reared no finer men,
And rarely the Ohio knew their peers
For pluck and prowess—even in those years
When stern life yielded suck but to the strong.
Nor in the hundred Henry took along
Was found their match—and each man knew it well.
For instance, when it suited Mike to tell
A tale that called for laughter, as he thought,
The hearer laughed right heartily, or fought
And took a drubbing. Then, if more complained,
Those three lacked not for logic that explained
The situation in no doubtful way.
"Me jokes are always funny" Mike would say;
And most men freely granted that they were.

A lanky, rangy man was Carpenter,
Quite six feet two from naked heel to crown;
And, though crow-lean, he brought the steelyard down

With twice a hundred notched upon the bar.
Nor was he stooped, as tall men often are;
A cedar of a man, he towered straight.
One might have judged him lumbering of gait,
When he was still; but when he walked or ran,
He stepped it lightly like a little man—
And such a one is very good to see.
Not his the tongue for quip or repartee;
His wit seemed slow; and something of the child
Came o'er his rough-hewn features, when he smiled,
To mock the porching brow and eagle nose.
'Twas when he fought the true import of those
Grew clear, though even then his mien deceived;
For less in wrath, he seemed, than mildly grieved—
Which made his blows no whit less true or hard.
His hair was flax fresh gleaming from the card;
His eyes, the flax in bloom.

     A match in might,
Fink lacked five inches of his comrade's height,
And of his weight scarce twenty pounds, they say.
His hair was black, his small eyes greenish gray
And restless as though feeling out of place
In such a jocund plenilunar face
That seemed made just for laughter. Then one saw
The pert pugnacious nose, the forward jaw,
The breadth of stubborn cheekbones, and one knew
That jest and fight to him were scarcely two,
But rather shifting phases of the joy
He felt in living. Careless as a boy,

Free handed with a gift or with a blow,
And giving either unto friend or foe
With frank good will, no man disliked him long.
They say his voice could glorify a song,
However loutish might the burden be;
And all the way from Pittsburg to the sea
The Rabelaisian stories of the rogue
Ran wedded to the richness of his brogue.
And wheresoever boatmen came to drink,
There someone broached some escapade of Fink
That well might fill the goat-hoofed with delight;
For Mike, the pantagruelizing wight,
Was happy in the health of bone and brawn
And had the code and conscience of the faun
To guide him blithely down the easy way.
A questionable hero, one might say:
And so indeed, by any civil law.
Moreover, at first glimpse of him one saw
A bull-necked fellow, seeming over stout;
Tremendous at a heavy lift, no doubt,
But wanting action. By the very span
Of chest and shoulders, one misjudged the man
When he was clothed. But when he stripped to swim,
Men flocked about to have a look at him,
Moved vaguely by that body's wonder-scheme
Wherein the shape of God's Adamic dream
Was victor over stubborn dust again!

O very lovely is a maiden, when
The old creative thrill is set astir

Along her blood, and all the flesh of her
Is shapen as to music! Fair indeed
A tall horse, lean of flank, clean-limbed for speed,
Deep-chested for endurance! Very fair
A soaring tree, aloof in violet air
Upon a hill! And 'tis a glorious thing
To see a bankfull river in the spring
Fight homeward! Children wonderful to see—
The Girl, the Horse, the River and the Tree—
As any suckled at the breast of sod;
Dissolving symbols leading back to God
Through vista after vista of the Plan!
But surely none is fairer than a man
In whom the lines of might and grace are one.

Bronzed with exposure to the wind and sun,
Behold the splendid creature that was Fink!
You see him strolling to the river's brink,
All ease, and yet tremendously alive.
He pauses, poised on tiptoe for the dive,
And momently it seems the mother mud,
Quick with a mystic seed whose sap is blood,
Mysteriously rears a human flower.
Clean as a windless flame the lines of power
Run rhythmic up the stout limbs, muscle-laced,
Athwart the ropy gauntness of the waist,
The huge round girth of chest, whereover spread
Enormous shoulders. Now above his head
He lifts his arms where big thews merge and flow
As in some dream of Michelangelo;

And up along the dimpling back there run,
Like lazy serpents stirring in the sun,
Slow waves that break and pile upon the slope
Of that great neck in swelling rolls, a-grope
Beneath the velvet softness of the skin.
Now suddenly the lean waist grows more thin,
The deep chest on a sudden grows more deep;
And with the swiftness of a tiger's leap,
The easy grace of hawks in swooping flight,
That terrible economy of might
And beauty plunges outward from the brink.

Thus God had made experiment with Fink,
As proving how 'twere best that men might grow.

One turned from Mike to look upon Talbeau—
A little man, scarce five feet six and slim—
And wondered what his comrades saw in him
To justify their being thus allied.
Was it a sort of planetary pride
In lunar adoration? Hark to Mike:
"Shure I declare I niver saw his like—
A skinny whiffet of a man! And yit—
Well, do ye moind the plisint way we mit
And how he interjooced hisself that day?
'Twas up at Pittsburg, liquor flowin' fray
And ivrybody happy as a fool.
I cracked me joke and thin, as is me rule,
Looked round to view the havoc of me wit;
And ivrywan was doubled up wid it,

Save only wan, and him a scrubby mite.
Says I, and shure me language was polite,
'And did ye hear me little joke?' says I.
'I did' says he. 'And can't ye laugh, me b'y?'
'I can't' says he, the sassy little chap.
Nor did I git me hand back from the slap
I give him till he landed on me glim,
And I was countin' siventeen of him
And ivry dancin' wan of him was air!
Faith, whin I hit him he was niver there;
And shure it seemed that ivry wind that blew
Was peltin' knuckles in me face. Hurroo!
That toime, fer wance, I got me fill of fun!
God bless the little whiffet! It begun
Along about the shank of afthernoon;
And whin I washed me face, I saw the moon
A-shakin' wid its laughther in the shtrame.
And whin, betoimes, he wakened from his drame,
I says to him, 'Ye needn't laugh, me b'y:
A cliver little man ye are,' says I.
And Och, the face of me! I'm tellin' fac's—
Ye'd wonder did he do it wid an ax!
'Twas foine! 'Twas art!"
                              Thus, eloquent with pride,
Mike Fink, an expert witness, testified
To Talbeau's fistic prowess.

                              Now they say
There lived no better boatmen in their day
Than those three comrades; and the larger twain

In that wide land three mighty rivers drain
Found not their peers for skill in marksmanship.
Writes one, who made the long Ohio trip
With those boon cronies in their palmy days,
How once Mike Fink beheld a sow at graze
Upon the bank amid her squealing brood;
And how Mike, being in a merry mood,
Shot off each wiggling piglet's corkscrew tail
At twenty yards, while under easy sail
The boat moved on. And Carpenter could bore
A squirrel's eye clean at thirty steps and more—
So many say. But 'twas their dual test
Of mutual love and skill they liked the best
Of all their shooting tricks—when one stood up
At sixty paces with a whisky cup
Set brimming for a target on his head,
And felt the gusty passing of the lead,
Hot from the other's rifle, lift his hair.
And ever was the tin cup smitten fair
By each, to prove the faith of each anew:
For 'twas a rite of love between the two,
And not a mere capricious feat of skill.
"Och, shure, and can ye shoot the whisky, Bill?"
So Mike wound end a wrangle. "Damn it, Fink!
Let's bore a pair of cups and have a drink!"
So Carpenter would stop a row grown stale.
And neither feared that either love might fail
Or either skill might falter.

Thus appear
The doughty three who held each other dear
For qualities they best could comprehend.

Now came the days of leisure to an end—
The days so gaily squandered, that would seem
To men at length made laughterless, a dream
Unthinkably remote; for Ilion held
Beneath her sixfold winding sheet of Eld
Seems not so hoar as bygone joy we prize
In evil days. Now vaguely pale the skies,
The glimmer neither starlight's nor the morn's.
A rude ironic merriment of horns
Startles the men yet heavy with carouse,
And sets a Ree dog mourning in the drowse,
Snout skyward from a lodge top. Sleepy birds
Chirp in the brush. A drone of sullen words
Awakes and runs increasing through the camp.
Thin smoke plumes, rising in the valley damp,
Flatten among the leathern tents and make
The whole encampment like a ghostly lake
Where bobbing heads of swimmers come and go,
As with the whimsy of an undertow
That sucks and spews them. Raising dust and din,
The horse-guards drive their shaggy rabble in
From nightlong grazing. *Voyageurs,* with packs
Of folded tents and camp gear on their backs,
Slouch boatward through the reek. But when prevails
The smell of frying pans and coffee pails,

They cease to sulk and, greatly heartened, sing
Till ponies swell the chorus, nickering,
And race-old comrades jubilate as one.

Out of a roseless dawn the heat-pale sun
Beheld them toiling northward once again—
A hundred horses and a hundred men
Hushed in a windless swelter. Day on day
The same white dawn o'ertook them on their way;
And daylong in the white glare sang no bird,
But only shrill grasshoppers clicked and whirred,
As though the heat were vocal. All the while
The dwindling current lengthened, mile on mile,
Meandrous in a labyrinth of sand.

Now e'er they left the Ree town by the Grand
The revellers had seen the spent moon roam
The morning, like a tipsy hag bound home.
A bubble-laden boat, they saw it sail
The sunset river of a fairy tale
When they were camped beside the Cannonball.
A spectral sun, it held the dusk in thrall
Nightlong about the Heart. The stars alone
Upon the cluttered Mandan lodges shone
The night they slept below the Knife. And when
Their course, long westward, shifted once again
To lead them north, the August moon was new.

The rainless Southwest wakened now and blew
A wilting, worrying, breath-sucking gale

That roared one moment in the bellied sail,
Next moment slackened to a lazy croon.
Now came the first misfortune. All forenoon
With line and pole the sweating boatmen strove
Along the east bank, while the horseguards drove
The drooping herd a little to the fore.
And then the current took the other shore.
Straight on, a maze of bar and shallow lay,
The main stream running half a mile away
To westward of a long low willow isle.
An hour they fought that stubborn half a mile
Of tumbled water. Down the running planks
The polesmen toiled in endless slanting ranks.
Now swimming, now a-flounder in the ooze
Of some blind bar, the naked cordelle crews
Sought any kind of footing for a pull;
While gust-bedevilled sails, now booming full,
Now flapping slack, gave questionable aid.

The west bank gained, along a ragged shade
Of straggling cottonwoods the boatmen sprawled
And panted. Out across the heat-enthralled,
Wind-fretted waste of shoal and bar they saw
The string of ponies ravelled up a draw
That mounted steeply eastward from the vale
Where, like a rampart flung across the trail,
A bluff rose sheer. Heads low, yet loath to graze,
They waxed and withered in the oily haze,
Now ponies, now a crawling flock of sheep.

Behind them three slack horseguards, half asleep,
Swayed limply, leaning on their saddle-bows.

The boat crews, lolling in a semi-doze,
Still watch the herd; nor do the gazers dream
What drama nears a climax over stream,
What others yonder may be watching too.
Now looming large upon the lucent blue,
The foremost ponies top the rim, and stare
High-headed down the vacancies of air
Beneath them; while the herders dawdle still
And gather wool scarce halfway up the hill—
A slumbrous sight beheld by heavy eyes.

But hark! What murmuring of far-flung cries
From yonder pocket in the folded rise
That flanks the draw? The herders also hear
And with a start glance upward to the rear.
Their spurred mounts plunge! What do they see but dust
Whipped skyward yonder in a freakish gust?
What panic overtakes them? Look again!
The rolling dust cloud vomits mounted men,
A ruck of tossing heads and gaudy gears
Beneath a bristling thicket of lean spears
Slant in a gust of onset!

Over stream
The boatmen stare dumbfounded. Like a dream
In some vague region out of space and time
Evolves the swiftly moving pantomime

Before those loungers with ungirded loins;
Till one among them shouts "*Assiniboines!*"
And swelling to a roar, the wild word runs
Above a pellmell scramble for the guns,
Perceived as futile soon. Yet here and there
A few young hotheads fusillade the air,
And rage the more to know the deed absurd.
Some only grind their teeth without a word;
Some stand aghast, some grinningly inane,
While some, like watch-dogs rabid at the chain,
Growl curses, pacing at the river's rim.

So might unhappy spirits haunt the dim
Far shore of Styx, beholding outrage done
To loved ones in the region of the sun—
Rage goaded by its own futility!

For one vast moment strayed from time, they see
The war band flung obliquely down the slope,
The flying herdsmen, seemingly a-grope
In sudden darkness for their saddle guns.
A murmuring shock! And now the whole scene runs
Into a dusty blur of horse and man;
And now the herd's rear surges on the van
That takes the cue of panic fear and flies
Stampeding to the margin of the skies,
Till all have vanished in the deeps of air.
Now outlined sharply on the sky-rim there
The victors pause and taunt their helpless foes
With buttocks patted and with thumbs at nose

And jeers scarce hearkened for the wind's guffaw.
They also vanish. In the sunwashed draw
Remains no sign of what has come to pass,
Save three dark splotches on the yellow grass,
Where now the drowsy horseguards have their will.

At sundown on the summit of the hill
The huddled boatmen saw the burial squad
Tuck close their comrades' coverlet of sod—
Weird silhouettes on melancholy gray.
And very few found anything to say
That night; though some spoke gently of the dead,
Remembering what that one did or said
At such and such a time. And some, more stirred
With lust of vengeance for the stolen herd,
Swore vaguely now and then beneath their breath.
Some, brooding on the imminence of death,
Grew wistful of their unreturning years;
And some who found their praying in arrears
Made shift to liquidate the debt that night.

But when once more the cheerful morning light
Came on them toiling, also came the mood
Of young adventure, and the solitude
Sang with them. For 'tis glorious to spend
One's golden days large-handed to the end—
The good broadpieces that can buy so much!
And what may hoarders purchase but a crutch
Wherewith to hobble graveward?

On they pressed
To where once more the river led them west;
And every day the hot wind, puff on puff,
Assailed them; every night they heard it sough
In thickets prematurely turning sere.

Then came the sudden breaking of the year.

Abruptly in a waning afternoon
The hot wind ceased, as fallen in a swoon
With its own heat. For hours the swinking crews
Had bandied scarcely credible good news
Of clouds across the dim northwestward plain;
And they who offered wagers on the rain
Found ready takers, though the gloomy rack,
With intermittent rumbling at its back,
Had mounted slowly. Now it towered high,
A blue-black wall of night across the sky
Shot through with glacial green.

A mystic change!
The sun was hooded and the world went strange—
A picture world! The hollow hush that fell
Made loud the creaking of the taut cordelle,
The bent spar's groan, the plunk of steering poles.
A bodeful calm lay glassy on the shoals;
The current had the look of flowing oil.
They saw the cloud's lip billow now and boil—
Black breakers gnawing at a coast of light;

They saw the stealthy wraith-arms of the night
Grope for the day to strangle it; they saw
The up-stream reaches vanish in a flaw
Of driving sand: and scarcely were the craft
Made fast to clumps of willow fore and aft,
When with a roar the blinding fury rolled
Upon them; and the breath of it was cold.
There fell no rain.

          That night was calm and clear:
Just such a night as when the waning year
Has set aflare the old Missouri wood;
When Greenings are beginning to be good;
And when, so hollow is the frosty hush,
One hears the ripe persimmons falling—*plush!*—
Upon the littered leaves. The kindly time!
With cider in the vigor of its prime,
Just strong enough to edge the dullest wit
Should neighbor folk drop in awhile to sit
And gossip. O the dear flame-painted gloam,
The backlog's sputter on the hearth at home—
How far away that night! Thus many a lad,
Grown strangely old, remembered and was sad.
Wolves mourned among the bluffs. Like hanks of wool
Fog flecked the river. And the moon was full.

A week sufficed to end the trail. They came
To where the lesser river gives its name
And meed of waters to the greater stream.
Here, lacking horses, they must nurse the dream

Of beaver haunts beyond the Great Divide,
Build quarters for the winter trade, and bide
The coming up of Ashley and his band.
So up and down the wooded tongue of land
That thins to where the rivers wed, awoke
The sound of many axes, stroke on stroke;
And lustily the hewers sang at whiles—
The better to forget the homeward miles
In this, the homing time. And when the geese
With cacophonic councils broke the peace
Of frosty nights before they took to wing;
When cranes went over daily, southering,
And blackbirds chattered in the painted wood,
A mile above the river junction stood
The fort, adjoining the Missouri's tide.
Foursquare and thirty paces on a side,
A wall of sharpened pickets bristled round
A group of sod-roofed cabins. Bastions frowned
From two opposing corners, set to brave
A foe on either flank; and stout gates gave
Upon the stream, where now already came
The Indian craft, lured thither by the fame
Of traders building by the mating floods.

The Song of Hugh Glass

The Song of Hugh Glass, *like* Three Friends, *is concerned with the early trappers and explorers who ascended the Missouri and Yellowstone rivers before the westward migration began. Hugh Glass was a skilled hunter; as part of the Ashley-Henry party, he rode ahead of the boatmen, found game for their evening meal, and chose a safe place for their campsite.*

One evening the party found Hugh severely mauled by a grizzly bear. Thinking he would soon die and unwilling to delay their progress, the band proceeded after leaving behind two men—one of them Hugh's young friend, Jamie. They were to care for Hugh and, if need be, to bury him. But, staring death in the face, as it were, Jamie and his more guileful companion deserted. The chapter included here, "Graybeard and Goldhair," tells the story up to this point. After awakening, Hugh Glass crawled, dragging a broken leg, one hundred miles through empty country to find his faithless friend. Anger and desire for revenge provided the needed strength for this prodigious effort, which led to a surprising outcome.

"Graybeard and Goldhair" is from *The Song of Hugh Glass* (New York: Macmillan, 1912); reprinted in *A Cycle of the West* (1949; reprinted Lincoln: University of Nebraska Press, 1963, 1991) and in *The Mountain Men* (Lincoln: University of Nebraska Press, 1971).

Graybeard and Goldhair

The year was eighteen hundred twenty three.
'Twas when the guns that blustered at the Ree
Had ceased to brag, and ten score martial clowns
Retreated from the unwhipped river towns,
Amid the scornful laughter of the Sioux.
A withering blast the arid South still blew,
And creeks ran thin beneath the glaring sky;
For 'twas a month ere honking geese would fly
Southward before the Great White Hunter's face:
And many generations of their race,
As bow-flung arrows, now have fallen spent.

It happened then that Major Henry went
With eighty trappers up the dwindling Grand,
Bound through the weird, unfriending barren-land
For where the Big Horn meets the Yellowstone;
And old Hugh Glass went with them.

                                    Large of bone,
Deep-chested, that his great heart might have play,
Gray-bearded, gray of eye and crowned with gray
Was Glass. It seemed he never had been young;
And, for the grudging habit of his tongue,
None knew the place or season of his birth.
Slowly he 'woke to anger or to mirth;
Yet none laughed louder when the rare mood fell,
And hate in him was like a still, white hell,
A thing of doom not lightly reconciled.

What memory he kept of wife or child
Was never told; for when his comrades sat
About the evening fire with pipe and chat,
Exchanging talk of home and gentler days,
Old Hugh stared long upon the pictured blaze,
And what he saw went upward in the smoke.

But once, as with an inner lightning stroke,
The veil was rent, and briefly men discerned
What pent-up fires of selfless passion burned
Beneath the still gray smoldering of him.
There was a rakehell lad, called Little Jim,
Jamie or Petit Jacques; for scarce began
The downy beard to mark him for a man.
Blue-eyed was he and femininely fair.
A maiden might have coveted his hair
That trapped the sunlight in its tangled skein:
So, tardily, outflowered the wild blond strain
That gutted Rome grown overfat in sloth.
A Ganymedes haunted by a Goth
Was Jamie. When the restive ghost was laid,
He seemed some fancy-ridden child who played
At manliness 'mid all those bearded men.
The sternest heart was drawn to Jamie then.
But his one mood ne'er linked two hours together.
To schedule Jamie's way, as prairie weather,
Was to get fact by wedding doubt and whim;
For very slightly slept that ghost in him.
No cloudy brooding went before his wrath
That, like a thunder-squall, recked not its path,

But raged upon what happened in its way.
Some called him brave who saw him on that day
When Ashley stormed a bluff town of the Ree,
And all save beardless Jamie turned to flee
For shelter from that steep, lead-harrowed slope.
Yet, hardly courage, but blind rage agrope
Inspired the foolish deed.

                'Twas then old Hugh
Tore off the gray mask, and the heart shone through.
For, halting in a dry, flood-guttered draw,
The trappers rallied, looked aloft and saw
That travesty of war against the sky.
Out of a breathless hush, the old man's cry
Leaped shivering, an anguished cry and wild
As of some mother fearing for her child,
And up the steep he went with mighty bounds.
Long afterward the story went the rounds,
How old Glass fought that day. With gun for club,
Grim as a grizzly fighting for a cub,
He laid about him, cleared the way, and so,
Supported by the firing from below,
Brought Jamie back. And when the deed was done,
Taking the lad upon his knee: "My Son,
Brave men are not ashamed to fear," said Hugh,
"And I've a mind to make a man of you;
So here's your first acquaintance with the law!"
Whereat he spanked the lad with vigorous paw
And, having done so, limped away to bed;
For, wounded in the hip, the old man bled.

It was a month before he hobbled out,
And Jamie, like a fond son, hung about
The old man's tent and waited upon him.
And often would the deep gray eyes grow dim
With gazing on the boy; and there would go—
As though Spring-fire should waken out of snow—
A wistful light across that mask of gray.
And once Hugh smiled his enigmatic way,
While poring long on Jamie's face, and said:
"So with their sons are women brought to bed,
Sore wounded!"

        Thus united were the two:
And some would dub the old man 'Mother Hugh';
While those in whom all living waters sank
To some dull inner pool that teemed and stank
With formless evil, into that morass
Gazed, and saw darkly there, as in a glass,
The foul shape of some weakly envied sin.
For each man builds a world and dwells therein.
Nor could these know what mocking ghost of Spring
Stirred Hugh's gray world with dreams of blossoming
That wooed no seed to swell or bird to sing.
So might a dawn-struck digit of the moon
Dream back the rain of some old lunar June
And ache through all its craters to be green.
Little they know what life's one love can mean,
Who shrine it in a bower of peace and bliss:
Pang dwelling in a puckered cicatrice
More truly figures this belated love.
Yet very precious was the hurt thereof,

Grievous to bear, too dear to cast away.
Now Jamie went with Hugh; but who shall say
If 'twas a warm heart or a wind of whim,
Love, or the rover's teasing itch in him,
Moved Jamie? Howsoe'er, 'twas good to see
Graybeard and Goldhair riding knee to knee,
One age in young adventure. One who saw
Has likened to a February thaw
Hugh's mellow mood those days; and truly so,
For when the tempering Southwest wakes to blow
A phantom April over melting snow,
Deep in the North some new white wrath is brewed.
Out of a dim-trailed inner solitude
The old man summoned many a stirring story,
Lived grimly once, but now shot through with glory
Caught from the wondering eyes of him who heard—
Tales jaggéd with the bleak unstudied word,
Stark saga-stuff. "A fellow that I knew,"
So nameless went the hero that was Hugh—
A mere pelt merchant, as it seemed to him;
Yet trailing epic thunders through the dim,
Whist world of Jamie's awe.
                            And so they went,
One heart, it seemed, and that heart well content
With tale and snatch of song and careless laughter.
Never before, and surely never after,
The gray old man seemed nearer to his youth—
That myth that somehow had to be the truth,
Yet could not be convincing any more.

Now when the days of travel numbered four
And nearer drew the barrens with their need,
On Glass, the hunter, fell the task to feed
Those four score hungers when the game should fail.
For no young eye could trace so dim a trail,
Or line the rifle sights with speed so true.
Nor might the wistful Jamie go with Hugh;
"For," so Hugh chaffed, "my trick of getting game
Might teach young eyes to put old eyes to shame.
An old dog never risks his only bone."
'Wolves prey in packs, the lion hunts alone'
Is somewhat nearer what he should have meant.

And so with merry jest the old man went;
And so they parted at an unseen gate
That even then some gust of moody fate
Clanged to betwixt them; each a tale to spell—
One in the nightmare scrawl of dreams from hell,
One in the blistering trail of days a-crawl,
Venomous footed. Nor might it ere befall
These two should meet in after days and be
Graybeard and Goldhair riding knee to knee,
Recounting with a bluff, heroic scorn
The haps of either tale.

               'Twas early morn
When Hugh went forth, and all day Jamie rode
With Henry's men, while more and more the goad
Of eager youth sore fretted him, and made
The dusty progress of the cavalcade
The journey of a snail flock to the moon;

Until the shadow-weaving afternoon
Turned many fingers nightward—then he fled,
Pricking his horse, nor deigned to turn his head
At any dwindling voice of reprimand;
For somewhere in the breaks along the Grand
Surely Hugh awaited with a goodly kill.
Hoofbeats of ghostly steeds on every hill,
Mysterious, muffled hoofs on every bluff!
Spurred echo horses clattering up the rough
Confluent draws! These flying Jamie heard.
The lagging air droned like the drowsy word
Of one who tells weird stories late at night.
Half headlong joy and half delicious fright,
His day-dream's pace outstripped the plunging steed's.
Lean galloper in a wind of splendid deeds,
Like Hugh's, he seemed unto himself, until,
Snorting, a-haunch above a breakneck hill,
The horse stopped short—then Jamie was aware
Of lonesome flatlands fading skyward there
Beneath him, and, zigzag on either hand,
A purple haze denoted how the Grand
Forked wide 'twixt sunset and the polar star.

A-tiptoe in the stirrups, gazing far,
He saw no Hugh nor any moving thing,
Save for a welter of cawing crows, a-wing
About some banquet in the further hush.
One faint star, set above the fading blush
Of sunset, saw the coming night, and grew.
With hand for trumpet, Jamie gave halloo;

And once again. For answer, the horse neighed.
Some vague mistrust now made him half afraid—
Some formless dread that stirred beneath the will
As far as sleep from waking.

                    Down the hill,
Close-footed in the skitter of the shale,
The spurred horse floundered to the solid vale
And galloped to the northwest, whinnying.
The outstripped air moaned like a wounded thing;
But Jamie gave the lie unto his dread.
"The old man's camping out to-night," he said,
"Somewhere about the forks, as like as not;
And there'll be hunks of fresh meat steaming hot,
And fighting stories by a dying fire!"

The sunset reared a luminous phantom spire
That, crumbling, sifted ashes down the sky.

Now, pausing, Jamie sent a searching cry
Into the twilit river-skirting brush,
And in the vast denial of the hush
The champing of the snaffled horse seemed loud.

Then, startling as a voice beneath a shroud,
A muffled boom woke somewhere up the stream
And, like vague thunder hearkened in a dream,
Drawled back to silence. Now, with heart a-bound,
Keen for the quarter of the perished sound,
The lad spurred gaily; for he doubted not
His cry had brought Hugh's answering rifle shot.

The laggard air was like a voice that sang,
And Jamie half believed he sniffed the tang
Of woodsmoke and the smell of flesh a-roast;
When presently before him, like a ghost,
Upstanding, huge in twilight, arms flung wide,
A gray form loomed. The wise horse reared and shied,
Snorting his inborn terror of the bear!
And in the whirlwind of a moment there,
Betwixt the brute's hoarse challenge and the charge,
The lad beheld, upon the grassy marge
Of a small spring that bullberries stooped to scan,
A ragged heap that should have been a man,
A huddled, broken thing—and it was Hugh!

There was no need for any closer view.
As, on the instant of a lightning flash
Ere yet the split gloom closes with a crash,
A landscape stares with every circumstance
Of rock and shrub—just so the fatal chance
Of Hugh's one shot, made futile with surprise,
Was clear to Jamie. Then before his eyes
The light whirled in a giddy dance of red;
And, doubting not the crumpled thing was dead
That was a friend, with but a skinning knife
He would have striven for the hated life
That triumphed there: but with a shriek of fright
The mad horse bolted through the falling night,
And Jamie, fumbling at his rifle boot,
Heard the brush crash behind him where the brute
Came headlong, close upon the straining flanks.

But when at length low-lying river banks—
White rubble in the gloaming—glimmered near,
A swift thought swept the mind of Jamie clear
Of anger and of anguish for the dead.
Scarce seemed the raging beast a thing to dread,
But some foul-playing braggart to outwit.
Now hurling all his strength upon the bit,
He sank the spurs, and with a groan of pain
The plunging horse, obedient to the rein,
Swerved sharply streamward. Sliddering in the sand,
The bear shot past. And suddenly the Grand
Loomed up beneath and rose to meet the pair
That rode a moment upon empty air,
Then smote the water in a shower of spray.
And when again the slowly ebbing day
Came back to them, a-drip from nose to flank,
The steed was scrambling up the further bank,
And Jamie saw across the narrow stream,
Like some vague shape of fury in a dream,
The checked beast ramping at the water's rim.
Doubt struggled with a victor's thrill in him,
As, hand to buckle of the rifle-sheath,
He thought of dampened powder; but beneath
The rawhide flap the gun lay snug and dry.
Then as the horse wheeled and the mark went by—
A patch of shadow dancing upon gray—
He fired. A sluggish thunder trailed away;
The spreading smoke-rack lifted slow, and there,
Floundering in a seethe of foam, the bear
Hugged yielding water for the foe that slew!

Triumphant, Jamie wondered what old Hugh
Would think of such a "trick of getting game"!
"Young eyes" indeed!—And then that memory came,
Like a dull blade thrust back into a wound.
One moment 'twas as though the lad had swooned
Into a dream-adventure, waking there
To sicken at the ghastly land, a-stare
Like some familiar face gone strange at last.
But as the hot tears came, the moment passed.
Song snatches, broken tales—a troop forlorn,
Like merry friends of eld come back to mourn—
O'erwhelmed him there. And when the black bulk churned
The star-flecked stream no longer, Jamie turned,
Recrossed the river and rode back to Hugh.

A burning twist of valley grasses threw
Blear light about the region of the spring.
Then Jamie, torch aloft and shuddering,
Knelt there beside his friend, and moaned: "O Hugh,
If I had been with you—just been with you!
We might be laughing now—and you are dead."

With gentle hand he turned the hoary head
That he might see the good gray face again.
The torch burned out, the dark swooped back, and then
His grief was frozen with an icy plunge
In horror. 'Twas as though a bloody sponge
Had wiped the pictured features from a slate!
So, pillaged by an army drunk with hate,

Home stares upon the homing refugee.
A red gout clung where either brow should be;
The haughty nose lay crushed amid the beard,
Thick with slow ooze, whence like a devil leered
The battered mouth convulsed into a grin.

Nor did the darkness cover, for therein
Some torch, unsnuffed, with blear funereal flare,
Still painted upon black that alien stare
To make the lad more terribly alone.

Then in the gloom there rose a broken moan,
Quick stifled; and it seemed that something stirred
About the body. Doubting that he heard,
The lad felt, with a panic catch of breath,
Pale vagrants from the legendry of death
Potential in the shadows there. But when
The motion and the moaning came again,
Hope, like a shower at daybreak, cleansed the dark,
And in the lad's heart something like a lark
Sang morning. Bending low, he crooned: "Hugh, Hugh,
It's Jamie—don't you know?—I'm here with you."

As one who in a nightmare strives to tell—
Shouting across the gap of some dim hell—
What things assail him; so it seemed Hugh heard,
And flung some unintelligible word
Athwart the muffling distance of his swoon.

Now kindled by the yet unrisen moon,
The East went pale; and like a naked thing
A little wind ran vexed and shivering
Along the dusk, till Jamie shivered too
And worried lest 'twere bitter cold where Hugh
Hung clutching at the bleak, raw edge of life.
So Jamie rose, and with his hunting-knife
Split wood and built a fire. Nor did he fear
The staring face now, for he found it dear
With the warm presence of a friend returned.
The fire made cozy chatter as it burned,
And reared a tent of light in that lone place.
Then Jamie set about to bathe the face
With water from the spring, oft crooning low,
"It's Jamie here beside you—don't you know?"
Yet came no answer save the labored breath
Of one who wrestled mightily with Death
Where watched no referee to call the foul.

The moon now cleared the world's end, and the owl
Gave voice unto the wizardry of light;
While in some dim-lit chancel of the night,
Snouts to the goddess, wolfish corybants
Intoned their wild antiphonary chants—
The oldest, saddest worship in the world.

And Jamie watched until the firelight swirled
Softly about him. Sound and glimmer merged
To make an eerie void, through which he urged

With frantic spur some whirlwind of a steed
That made the way as glass beneath his speed,
Yet scarce kept pace with something dear that fled
On, ever on—just half a dream ahead:
Until it seemed, by some vague shape dismayed,
He cried aloud for Hugh, and the steed neighed—
A neigh that was a burst of light, no sound.
And Jamie, sprawling on the dewy ground,
Knew that his horse was sniffing at his hair,
While, mumbling through the early morning air,
There came a roll of many hoofs—and then
He saw the swinging troop of Henry's men
A-canter up the valley with the sun.

Of all Hugh's comrades crowding round, not one
But would have given heavy odds on Death;
For, though the graybeard fought with sobbing breath,
No man, it seemed, might break upon the hip
So stern a wrestler with the strangling grip
That made the neck veins like a purple thong
Tangled with knots. Nor might Hugh tarry long
There where the trail forked outward far and dim;
Or so it seemed. And when they lifted him,
His moan went treble like a song of pain,
He was so tortured. Surely it were vain
To hope he might endure the toilsome ride
Across the barrens. Better let him bide
There on the grassy couch beside the spring.
And, furthermore, it seemed a foolish thing
That eighty men should wait the issue there;

For dying is a game of solitaire
And all men play the losing hand alone.

But when at noon he had not ceased to moan,
And fought still like the strong man he had been,
There grew a vague mistrust that he might win,
And all this be a tale for wondering ears.
So Major Henry called for volunteers,
Two men among the eighty who would stay
To wait on Glass and keep the wolves away
Until he did whatever he should do.
All quite agreed 'twas bitter bread for Hugh,
Yet none, save Jamie, felt in duty bound
To run the risk—until the hat went round,
And pity wakened, at the silver's clink,
In Jules Le Bon.

    'He would not have them think
That mercenary motives prompted him.
But somehow just the grief of Little Jim
Was quite sufficient—not to mention Hugh.
He weighed the risk. As everybody knew,
The Rickarees were scattered to the West:
The late campaign had stirred a hornet's nest
To fill the land with stingers (which was so),
And yet—'
    Three days a southwest wind may blow
False April with no drop of dew at heart.
So Jules ran on, while, ready for the start,
The pawing horses nickered and the men,

Impatient in their saddles, yawned. And then,
With brief advice, a round of bluff good-byes
And some few reassuring backward cries,
The troop rode up the valley with the day.

Intent upon his friend, with naught to say,
Sat Jamie; while Le Bon discussed at length
The reasonable limits of man's strength—
A self-conducted dialectic strife
That made absurd all argument for life
And granted but a fresh-dug hole for Hugh.
'Twas half like murder. Yet it seemed Jules knew
Unnumbered tales accordant with the case,
Each circumstantial as to time and place
And furnished with a death's head colophon.

Vivaciously despondent, Jules ran on.
'Did he not share his judgment with the rest?
You see, 'twas some contusion of the chest
That did the trick—heart, lungs and all that, mixed
In such a way they never could be fixed.
A bear's hug—ugh!'

                        And often Jamie winced
At some knife-thrust of reason that convinced
Yet left him sick with unrelinquished hope.
As one who in a darkened room might grope
For some belovéd face, with shuddering
Anticipation of a clammy thing;
So in the lad's heart sorrow fumbled round

For some old joy to lean upon, and found
The stark, cold something Jamie knew was there.
Yet, womanlike, he stroked the hoary hair
Or bathed the face; while Jules found tales to tell—
Lugubriously garrulous.

Night fell.

At sundown, day-long winds are like to veer;
So, summoning a mood of relished fear,
Le Bon remembered dire alarms by night—
The swoop of savage hordes, the desperate fight
Of men outnumbered: and, like him of old,
In all that made Jules shudder as he told,
His the great part—a man by field and flood
Fate-tossed. Upon the gloom he limned in blood
Their situation's possibilities:
Two men against the fury of the Rees—
A game in which two hundred men had failed!
He pointed out how little it availed
To run the risk for one as good as dead;
Yet, Jules Le Bon meant every word he said,
And had a scalp to lose, if need should be.

That night through Jamie's dreaming swarmed the Ree.
Gray-souled, he wakened to a dawn of gray,
And felt that something strong had gone away,
Nor knew what thing. Some whisper of the will
Bade him rejoice that Hugh was living still;
But Hugh, the real, seemed somehow otherwhere.
Jules, snug and snoring in his blanket there,

Was half a life the nearer. Just so, pain
Is nearer than the peace we seek in vain,
And by its very sting compells belief.
Jules woke, and with a fine restraint of grief
Saw early dissolution. 'One more night,
And then the poor old man would lose the fight—
Ah, such a man!'

           A day and night crept by,
And yet the stubborn fighter would not die,
But grappled with the angel. All the while,
With some conviction, but with more of guile,
Jules colonized the vacancy with Rees;
Till Jamie felt that looseness of the knees
That comes of oozing courage. Many men
May tower for a white-hot moment, when
The wild blood surges at a sudden shock;
But when, insistent as a ticking clock,
Blind peril haunts and whispers, fewer dare.
Dread hovered in the hushed and moony air
The long night through; nor might a fire be lit,
Lest some far-seeing foe take note of it.
And day-long Jamie scanned the blank sky rim
For hoof-flung dust clouds; till there woke in him
A childish anger—dumb for ruth and shame—
That Hugh so dallied.

              But the fourth dawn came
And with it lulled the fight, as on a field
Where broken armies sleep but will not yield.
Or had one conquered? Was it Hugh or Death?

The old man breathed with faintly fluttering breath,
Nor did his body shudder as before.
Jules triumphed sadly. 'It would soon be o'er;
So men grew quiet when they lost their grip
And did not care. At sundown he would slip
Into the deeper silence.'
                              Jamie wept,
Unwitting how a furtive gladness crept
Into his heart that gained a stronger beat.
So cities, long beleaguered, take defeat—
Unto themselves half traitors.
                                      Jules began
To dig a hole that might conceal a man;
And, as his sheath knife broke the stubborn sod,
He spoke in kindly vein of Life and God
And Mutability and Rectitude.
The immemorial funerary mood
Brought tears, mute tribute to the mother-dust;
And Jamie, seeing, felt each cutting thrust
Less like a stab into the flesh of Hugh.
The sun crept up and down the arc of blue
And through the air a chill of evening ran;
But, though the grave yawned, waiting for the man,
The man seemed scarce yet ready for the grave.

Now prompted by a coward or a knave
That lurked in him, Le Bon began to hear
Faint sounds that to the lad's less cunning ear
Were silence; more like tremors of the ground

They were, Jules said, than any proper sound—
Thus one detected horsemen miles away.
For many moments big with fate, he lay,
Ear pressed to earth; then rose and shook his head
As one perplexed. "There's something wrong," he said.
And—as at daybreak whiten winter skies,
Agape and staring with a wild surmise—
The lad's face whitened at the other's word.
Jules could not quite interpret what he heard;
A hundred horse might noise their whereabouts
In just that fashion; yet he had his doubts.
It could be bison moving, quite as well.
But if 'twere Rees—there'd be a tale to tell
That two men he might name should never hear.
He reckoned scalps that Fall were selling dear,
In keeping with the limited supply.
Men, fit to live, were not afraid to die!

Then, in that caution suits not courage ill,
Jules saddled up and cantered to the hill,
A white dam set against the twilight stream;
And as a horseman riding in a dream
The lad beheld him; watched him clamber up
To where the dusk, as from a brimming cup,
Ran over; saw him pause against the gloom,
Portentous, huge—a brooder upon doom.
What did he look upon?
                      Some moments passed;
Then suddenly it seemed as though a blast

Of wind, keen-cutting with the whips of sleet,
Smote horse and rider. Haunched on huddled feet,
The steed shrank from the ridge, then, rearing, wheeled
And took the rubbly incline fury-heeled.

Those days and nights, like seasons creeping slow,
Had told on Jamie. Better blow on blow
Of evil hap, with doom seen clear ahead,
Than that monotonous, abrasive dread,
Blind gnawer at the soul-thews of the blind.
Thin-worn, the last heart-string that held him kind;
Strung taut, the final tie that kept him true
Now snapped in Jamie, as he saw the two
So goaded by some terrifying sight.
Death riding with the vanguard of the Night,
Life dwindling yonder with the rear of Day!
What choice for one whom panic swept away
From moorings in the sanity of will?

Jules came and summed the vision of the hill
In one hoarse cry that left no word to say:
"Rees! Saddle up! We've got to get away!"

Small wit had Jamie left to ferret guile,
But fumblingly obeyed Le Bon; the while
Jules knelt beside the man who could not flee:
For big hearts lack not time for charity
However thick the blows of fate may fall.
Yet, in that Jules Le Bon was practical,

He could not quite ignore a hunting knife,
A flint, a gun, a blanket—gear of life
Scarce suited to the customs of the dead!

And Hugh slept soundly in his ample bed,
Star-canopied and blanketed with night,
Unwitting how Venality and Fright
Made hot the westward trail of Henry's men.

The Song of Jed Smith

In The Splendid Wayfaring *(1920), my father sums up the historical importance of Jedediah Smith: "His had been the first overland party to reach California, he had been the first white man to travel the central route from Salt Lake to the Pacific, and the first to traverse the full length of California and Oregon by land. . . . During three years [in the 1820s] of wandering west of the Rockies, he had covered fourteen degrees of latitude and eleven degrees of longitude. . . . The road from the Missouri River to San Francisco Bay was now open, awaiting the wagons of the settlers—and the official explorers!"*

Jedediah Smith was a mountain man who always carried his Bible with him, and throughout the Song *the reader is aware of how much it contributed to his courage, strength, and perseverance. In his thirty-third year, on May 27, 1831, he was killed by Comanche Indians at the Cimarron River in Texas.*

The sections I have chosen from The Song of Jed Smith *begin with the rendezvous meeting of three of his former comrades—Arthur Black, Robert Evans, and the Squire. Through seemingly incidental conversations of these three very different men around the campfire, Neihardt unfolds the story of hardships and triumphs experienced by the parties that Smith led.* The Song of Jed Smith *is an adventure story, but it rises to spiritual heights, and the central character is unforgettable.*

"The Rendezvous" is from *The Song of Jed Smith* (New York: Macmillan, 1941); reprinted in *A Cycle of the West* (1949; Lincoln: University of Nebraska Press, 1963, 1991) and in *The Mountain Men* (Lincoln: University of Nebraska Press, 1971).

The Rendezvous

The valley was beginning to forget
The dead June day, but southward clearly yet
The peaks remembered.

             Trappers by their gear,
With four trail-weary horses grazing near,
Two men were sitting, leaning on their packs.
Still as the shadows purpling at their backs,
They gazed upon the smoke that rose between,
Thin-fingered. From the canyon of the Green,
Low-toned but mighty in the solitude,
A never-never moaning voiced the mood
Some reminiscent waking dream had cast
Upon them. Henry's Fork that hurried past
Ran full of distant voices, muffled mirths.
A meadowlark, in gratitude for Earth's
Lush shielding, with a mounting bar that broke,
Enriched the quiet.

         And the elder spoke,
Stirring the embers into sudden fire:
"Well, that's a queer one! Was I nodding, Squire?
I swear I saw it!"

        Lifted in surprise,
With thick, black beard belying boyish eyes,

A flame-bright face regarded him. "What's queer?
I wasn't looking, Art; just sitting here
And seeing things myself."

                    The failing flare,
Across the elder's grizzling beard and hair,
Revealed the mien of one whom many snows
Would leave green-hearted. "No, I didn't doze,"
He said; "and I was thinking nothing more
Than what to do about that saddle sore
The old mare's got; and it was only now,
All still and empty. Suddenly, somehow,
I tell you, it was eighteen twenty-five!
This valley came alive with fires, alive
With men and horses! Rings on glowing rings
Of old-time faces sang as liquor sings
After a drouth; and laughter shook the night
Where someone, full of meat and getting tight,
Spun lies the way Black Harris used to do.
Then it was now again, and only you
Were sitting yonder."

                    "Art, you make me dry,"
The other said, "you make me want to cry
Into my whiskers. Thirteen years away!
That's better than a million miles, I'd say,
Without a horse, and all the country strange!"
Now while they mused there came an eerie change
Upon the world. From where the day lay dead
The ghost thereof in streamered glory fled

Across the sky, transfiguring the scene.
Amazed amidst the other-worldly green
That glowed along the flat, as though a shout
Had startled them, they stood and stared about,
Searching the muted landscape of a dream.

There *was* a cry. The bluffs along the stream
Awoke to mock it. On a low rise there
To westward, vivid in the radiant air,
They saw a horseman coming at a jog,
A pack-mule plodding after, and a dog
That rushed ahead now, halted, muzzle high,
And howled.

       The light-blown bubble of the sky,
As with a final strain of splendor, broke.
The peaks forgot; and like a purple smoke
Night settled in the valley.

          Looming dim,
The rider neared the shadows greeting him
Beside the embers, while the outer gloom
Neighed welcome. "Hitch and make yourself at home,"
One bantered: "Hang your hat upon a star,
The house is yours. Whatever else you are,
It's not a horsethief by the nag you've got!"

The stranger laughed. "If supper's in the pot,
The nag has served me well enough," he said,

Dismounting. To the growling dog, "Down, Jed,
Old-timer! They've invited us to eat."

Now hand found hand. "Except for beaver meat,
And jerked at that, you'll find the cupboard bare,"
One said; "and, short of Taos, we'll have to share
Our drinking yonder with the bird and beast."

"I never make this valley but to feast,
And water won't keep ghosts away," replied
The stranger, fumbling at the horse's side
And stripping off the saddle. "Anyhow,
The hump and haunches of a yearling cow
Have fagged the old mule here. If that won't do
To make a good old-fashioned rendezvous,
I've come from Taos—the jug's full!"

                                        Bluffs to heights
Hurrahed with glee, and in the outer night's
Star-bearing silence troubled for a space
The somber summits.
                    "Come and show your face!"
The elder cried. "I'll swear, if I don't know
That voice—though he went wolfing years ago—
My name's not Black!" He seized the other's hand
And drew him to the embers. Stirred and fanned,
They reddened till the fed twigs took the spark,
And, cut upon the onyx of the dark,
A shaven face shone—sensitive and lean,

With eyes that narrowed less upon the seen
Than with some inward gazing. Leather-skinned,
It was, hard-bitten by the worldly wind;
But more the weather of a mind that seeks
In solitude had etched upon the cheeks
A cryptic story.

        "Holy smoke!" cried Black;
"Look, Squire! Unless it be a spook come back
To haunt us, old Bob Evans hasn't fed
The kiotes yet!"

        A joyful warwhoop fled
Along the valley. Eager voices, blent
In greeting, quickened into merriment.
The dog barked gaily and the horses neighed.
Impatiently the laden pack-mule brayed
Sardonic comment.

II

      Now the jug went round
The glowing circle, while the fat hump browned
And sputtered, dripping. Night, immense and still,
With stars keen-whetted by the mountain chill,
Dreamed deep around the trio, snugly housed
In living light. From where the horses browsed,
The blowing loudened in a lapse of speech.
A wolf howled, and the farthest empty reach
Of vastness mourned, as though God dreamed in vain

141

And 'wakened, filling with a wail of pain
The nightmare void of uncreated good.

The dog whined, bristling.

                Cozy in the wood,
The tongue flame purred content. Again the bright,
Brief moment vanquished the appalling night
Of timelessness.

             The youngest laughed, and said:
"Is this a wake? If one of us is dead,
Just count me in among the other two
And cut a chunk of meat!"

                "A rendezvous,"
Mused Evans, with a far, unfocussed gaze
Upon the other. "Ghosts of better days,
With laughters never to be laughed again,
And singing from the lips of lusty men
Gone dust forever! Listen! Can you hear?
I ought to know. I've heard them year by year
With every June!"

              "Well, let them drink with us!"
The youngest chuckled. "Bob, you loony cuss,
I like you; but you always lived too far
Above the belly where the doin's are
That make men happy. This child ought to know!"
With jug presented, "Spooks of long ago,"

He mocked, "here's looking at you! Bye and bye
We'll be as dead as you! But now, we're dry,
And men at that! Tough luck to be a ghost!
Old-timers, skoal! Here's how!"

IV
                    "You're getting sober, Squire,"
Black said, and, sighing, stirred the dreamy fire
Until the dozing logs awoke in flame;
"Or else—which seems to figure out the same—
It's only getting human makes you sad.
You wish he'd taken you, and if he had
You'd know, with inside knowledge of the thing,
How buzzards soar, what makes the kiotes sing
Such mournful ditties, what the crows regret
With all their cawing. Maybe so—and yet,
Who ever saw a wolf with bowels of brass
Or bird with iron gizzard? Let it pass,—
Or, rather, let the jug!"

                        He rose and scanned
The stars awhile, eyes shaded with a hand
Against the groundling dazzle. "Night is new,"
He yawned; "and there's another nip or two
Left in the Dipper yonder, tipped to pour
Whatever angels drink. There's even more
Left in the jug. So here's regards to those
Bone-scattered where the Colorado flows
Among the damned Mojaves, and beside
The Umpqua where it bitters with the tide

Among the marshes—Jedediah's men!
And may they rise and follow him again
The other side of Jordan! Drink the toast,
Bob Evans!"

        "—Even to the cosmic coast,"
The other said, and drank, "where all stars cease,
And seas of silence answer with their peace
The petulant impertinence of life!"

"And here's to when I keep that cow and wife,"
The youngest bantered, "—just as like to be!"

"But when," said Black, "we started for the sea
That summer, Bob, not one of seventeen,
I'll warrant, cared to know what life might mean.
To ask that question is a kind of dying.
What matters to a bird a-wing is flying;
What matters to a proper thirst is drinking.
A tree would wither if it got to thinking
Of what the summers and the winters meant!
There was a place to go to, and we went,
High-hearted with a hunger for the new.
The fifty mules and horses felt so too
For all their heavy packs. The brutes were wise
Beyond us, Bob. They can't philosophize
And get the world all tangled in their skulls.
At Utah Lake the mourning of the gulls
Had seemed the last of what was known and dear;
And when we struck the bend of the Sevier

To follow eastward where it cuts the range,
The canyon seemed the doorway to a strange
New world. The ridden critters and the led,
Strung out along the river after Jed,
Pricked ears and listened. Nothing but the whine
Of saddle leather down the toiling line,
Until some cayuse at the canyon's mouth
Neighed; and the empty valley, rising south,
Was full of horses answering the din
Of horses where no horse had ever been
Forever. And the mules brayed, walking faster.
What need of any pasture, greener, vaster,
To pay them for the eager joy of striving?
If living is a matter of arriving,
Why not just start to rotting at the first,
And save the trouble? Thirty died of thirst
And hunger yonder in the desert hells.
Ask God why, when you see Him. If He tells,
You'll hardly be the wiser. Furthermore,
I'll gamble that He won't.

      The valley bore
Southeastward, and there wasn't any game.
Our packs got lighter fast. So when we came
To where a small creek entered from the west,
We followed up along it to a crest,
And saw what fed our hunger for the new
But couldn't satisfy it; for it grew
Beyond the feeding. Where a high plateau
Stretched southwardly, a million years or so

Of rain had hewed a great unearthly town
With colored walls and towers that looked down
On winding streets not meant for men to tread.
You half believed an angel race, long dead,
Had built with airy, everlasting stuff
They quarried from the sunrise in the rough
And spent their lives in fashioning, and died
Before the world got old.

              The other side
Of ranges west and south, a dim world ran
Uphill to where eternity began
And time died of monotony at last.
And when that rim of nothing had been passed,
Why surely 'twould be California then;
But would we all be long-gray-whiskered men
Before we got there? No one seemed to mind.
God only knew what wonders we might find,
And how He must be weary with His knowing!
No curiosity at all for going
And nothing new to look for anywhere!

Into the clutter of the foothills there
Below, we wound a weary way, and crossed
The valley of a stream we called the Lost—
And lost it was, if ever it had run!
The bare slopes focussed the September sun
Upon the blistering rubble. Round the few
And shallow holes that kept a brackish brew
The fifty critters pawed and fought and screamed,

Blaming each other; and the echoes seemed
To ape the clatter of the hoofs like laughter.

It wasn't any better soon thereafter
Among the tumbled hills gone bald with age
Millenniums ago. The scrubby sage
Was making out to live on memory yet,
But even it had started to forget
What rain was like. Our grub was getting low.
For days we hadn't even seen a crow
To shoot at; but we didn't seem to care,
For we were learning our first lesson there
In what thirst means; and we were walking now.
My roan was pulling like a stubborn cow
Not halter-broke, when, with a shivering slump,
He just sat down awhile upon his rump,
And then keeled over with a tired sigh.
So there was meat we couldn't stop to dry,
For need of water. Little we could eat!
It takes a proper tongue to relish meat,
And not some dead cow's crammed into your mouth!
The balance of the day we hurried south—
A creeping hurry; anyway, as fast
As we could snake the nags along. At last
'Twas night again, and not a blade of grass
Or drop of water. Seemed 'twould never pass.
You dozed, dog-weary, and the dreams you had
Of creeks and springs were just about as bad
As even waking was. A horse would dream—
Of wading, maybe, in a mountain stream—

And neigh himself and all the herd awake;
And there'd be panic neighing, and a break
That ended, in a flounder, with the ropes.
It surely didn't much revive our hopes,
When morning came, to find three others dead.

I thought 'twas kind of funny about Jed
That day. You see, I didn't know him then.
And there was peevish talk among the men
Of how he didn't seem to realize.
There'd be a freshness in his face and eyes
When he came striding from a spell of straying
Off trail somewhere. I know now he'd been praying.
You'd swear he knew a spring along the way,
And kept it for himself! He'd smile and say
We shouldn't doubt, but we should trust and know
There'd soon be water.
               And, by God, 'twas so—
'Twas so that afternoon!

                 We struck a draw—
The toughest going mortal ever saw—
A dazzling oven, crooked as a snake
And full of boulders. But it seemed to make
Downhill and southward, so we shuffled in.
To think that such a flood had ever been
As rolled those boulders, almost drove you crazy!
I mind that everything was dizzy-hazy
When someone said that Louis Pombert's mare

148

Was down. What of it? No one seemed to care
Enough to save the saddle.

                    Bye and bye—
Hours later or the batting of an eye
Was all the same, for time just sort of stood
And wobbled like a drunk—a mule sawed wood
Down yonder. Then they all began to saw,
And horses whinnied up along the draw,
If they could manage better than a nicker.
The weakest of them whimpered, stepping quicker,
And when they stumbled, staggered up again
With bloody noses. Presently the men
Were hollering down yonder like a flock
Of addled crows. Another jut of rock,
And there it was—a world of running water!"
"Aw, Arthur, make it just a little hotter!"
The younger pleaded; "just a little drier,
So I can raise a thirst!"

                    "You grieve me, Squire,"
The elder said; "I thought you'd had enough
To be half human! Water's holy stuff,
Direct from heaven! When the grass gets green,
That's worship! Bob here gathers what I mean,
Eh Bob? You mind that day; you had the most
Tough water-scrapes with Jed!"

                         "The Holy Ghost,
The dove descending," Evans mused aloud.

The youngest laughed. "This go-to-meeting crowd
Should rise and let the kiotes lead a hymn!"

"We might be singing with the seraphim,"
Said Evans.

      "Well, there was a church that night,"
Continued Black. "We circled in the light
Of one big fire; and when we had our fill
Of horse meat, which we didn't have to kill,
Because too much is deadly as the lack,
He got his Bible with the leather back
(That looked a worn-out boot-top, like as not,)
And fuzzy pages bulging with a lot
Of heavy reading. For a little while
He thumbed it, silent. No one cracked a smile
Or said a word, and there were godless cusses,
Whose on'ry fracases and rakehell musses
Had sent them where they were, among the others.
Like pious little boys who mind their mothers,
They sat there waiting, mannerly and prim.
And if they hadn't, there was that in him
To whale the devil out of any man.
I've seen him do it.

      Well, when he began
To read out loud, 'twas not as parsons do.
He said it just like anything that's true—
'The sun is shining,' maybe, or 'the birds
Are singing.' Something got into the words

That made them seem they couldn't be the same
That you remembered. For the Lord became
A gentle shepherd, real as Mr. Jones,
And he had made us rest our weary bones
In that green pasture by the waters there!
Laugh, Squire, and show your raising—I don't care;
I like to see you happy, bless your heart!"

"I didn't mean to spoil your story, Art,"
Explained the other. "Who am I to doubt it?
But what would those dead horses say about it,
Back yonder in the swelter?"

                "Well, you see,"
Black countered; "that was lack of piety.
I guess they hadn't gone to Sunday schools!"

"You reckon all of your Missouri mules
Were Holy Rollers? Not a one was dead!"
The younger chuckled.

                "Just the same," Black said,
"It wasn't funny and nobody snickered.
It scared me when a happy cayuse nickered,
The place had got so still when he was through.
And then he didn't preach, as parsons do;
He just sat silent, for the Book had said it.
What else was there to do when he had read it,
But let it soak like rain? And if he prayed,
You couldn't hear him do it.

                            There we stayed
A couple days to let the critters eat,
And jerk the leavings of the pony meat
Against the chance there'd not be game enough.
For we were down to traps and trading stuff—
Red bolted goods and blankets, fufaraws,
Like beads and looking glasses, for the squaws,
And knives and arrow metal for the men,
So be it we should ever see again
A human face but ours.
                        And then we took
Down river—just a wider sort of brook,
But 'Diah named it for the President,
The Adams River. No fine compliment,
We came to think; but not so bad at first.
'Twas still a blessing to be shut of thirst
So long as you remembered how it felt;
But when you saw the packs of jerked horse melt
To nothing, and the red-walled canyon wound,
Until you only rambled round and round
From nowhere, nowhere—not a thing to eat,
But now and then a bite of rabbit meat—
You wondered was there treason in the name!

About to kill a pony when we came
At last to where a little creek broke through
And made a valley. There a garden grew
With tasseled corn and punkin vines between!
You stood and stared, misdoubting you had seen,

But there it flickered, sure as you were born—
The yellow-bellied crawlers and the corn
Late earing in the green!

                    We yelled hurrah
For good old garden sass. And then we saw
A little Indian woman running there,
All wibble-wobble and a mess of hair,
Hell-bent for cover—and she needed some,
Not having any more on than your thumb,
But one important patch of rabbit fur!
And, like the devils that she thought we were,
Young hellions cheered her, laughing: 'Go it, Gert!'
And 'Hump it, Maggie!' But the words of dirt
They flung at her stopped quick enough, when Jed
Came riding, looking like a thunder-head
With lightning in it just about to break.
'Respect a woman for your mothers' sake,'
He said, 'or take a licking!'

                    Well, he took
Some knives and looking glasses, and the Book
For luck, no doubt, and vanished up the creek
Among the brush. It seemed a weary week
We held the herd till he appeared again,
About a dozen lousy-looking men
And women at his heels, with not a thing
Upon them but an apron and a string
Of rabbit hide. If that was human mud,

'Twas badly baked and furnished with the blood
Of rabbits. 'Diah treated them the same
As folks.

        And while we feasted, others came,
Like cringing cur-dogs that apologize
For being curs, to see with their own eyes
The four-legged spirit-critters and the gods
That rode them; for we made our thunder-rods
Spout cloud and lightning. Anyone would say
We celebrated Independence Day,
If there had been a barrel of lemonade!
For pretty soon nobody was afraid.
The women brought us cakes of pounded seeds
Messed up with cane, and strutted in the beads
They got from us. God-awful homely lasses
And scrawny grandmas peeped at looking glasses
And giggled. Men went running to their wives,
Like tickled boys, to show their shiny knives;
And wee, pot-bellied rascals dared to sneak
Just near enough to give our shirts a tweak
And show their little sisters who was scared!

It kind of looked as if the Lord prepared
A table for us!

        Well, the thought of it
Still fed us—anyway a little bit—
Down river. Anything might happen next,

The way it had, to fit the Bible text
He read that night. And, soon enough, it did!

The canyon narrowed, towering, and hid
The friendly day. A scary twilight fell.
As from the dusky bottom of a well,
We saw the blood-red rim-rock swimming high
Along the jaggéd knife-scar of a sky,
And dim stars mocked the middle afternoon!
We thought at first the place would broaden soon.
The few stars only brightened in the cut,
And, like a heavy snow of kettle-smut,
Night smothered down.

                  'Twas long before we slept.
Serenely in the diary he kept,
Jed scribbled by the fire without a word.
Unless a horse complained, you almost heard
Your thinker thinking. All the while the stream
Was like a sick man moaning in a dream
Of dying.

          We were plodding on our way
When first the rim-rock reddened with the day,
But up until the noon 'twas early morning.
It seemed that any minute, without warning,
The worst might happen. Maybe one more bend,
And there we'd come upon the canyon's end,
Some cave without a bottom, yawning black.

There was no hope of 'Diah turning back;
He wouldn't listen to the gloomy talk
Among the men. 'Yea, even though I walk
The valley of the shadow,' said the Book.
His face and eyes would have that freshened look,
When he'd been riding out of sight a spell,
As though he knew some good he wouldn't tell,
Just wanting to surprise us pretty soon.
The whole late evening that was afternoon
We plodded till the few trapped stars were bright.

The weakest of the horses went that night
To fill the pots. It didn't really matter
Which one we ate—unless the leather's fatter
In either of your boot-soles than the other.
The driftwood made a sickly sort of smother;
And while we watched the kettles in despair,
Jed asked old Rogers would he offer prayer;
And Harry would—but offer's not the word.
He took no chances that Jehovah heard,
Or interrupted with an old man's 'Eh?'—
The off ear cupped the hard-of-hearing way—
'Wha's that?' He bellered. 'Twas a fine oration!

Well, when we'd feasted on our transportation
And felt a little better, 'Diah read
Some verses from the Scripture where it said
The whole earth was the Lord's. A sneaking doubt
If that was anything to brag about
Grew big enough to dare you to deny it.

Then all at once the canyon got so quiet
The water didn't moan, the soggy wood
Quit wheezing. And the whole round earth was good,
The fulness of it—and it made you glad!
No, Squire, 'twas not the bellyful we had
Of leather soup. 'Twas far above the belt.
'Twas like old summers and the way you felt
A barefoot shaver—white clouds going over,
And apple trees and bumblebees and clover,
And warm dust feeling pleasant to your toes,
And wheat fields flowing and the corn in rows,
And stars to twinkle when the day was done,
While people rested, certain of the sun,
All safe and cozy!

               Words are mighty queer!
They try to tell you something, and you hear
Some old familiar rattle in your head
That isn't any nearer what they said
Than mules and mothers; but you think you know!
Then maybe, all at once, *they're simply so—*
And always were! They sprout like seeds and thrive!
If all the words men gargle came alive,
I wonder what would happen! 'Diah's sprouted.

And then he talked. Seemed foolish that we doubted,
So near the Spanish settlements might be.
And soon we ought to make the Siskadee
Old Ashley tried that spring to navigate,
But, getting nearer to St. Peter's gate

Than to the ocean, had to give it up.
And California! That was where the cup
Ran over!

      Well, we stumbled down that maze
And counted horses dying.—Also days
Since we had fed in yonder Indian heaven;
And number five was slow, but six and seven
Hung on so long they almost never quit.
The earth was needing axle grease a bit
Before we finished counting nine and ten!
Do you remember, Bob, what happened then,
And what we saw?"

      "The day broke overhead.
The endless canyon ended," Evans said;
And there was desert to the setting sun!"

"I guess we'd better have another one,"
Remarked the Squire, "before we undertake it!
Unless we do, I doubt if we can make it.
We've et an awful lot of harness leather!"

"The skin-rack horses nickered all together,"
The elder mused, as though he didn't hear;
"And up the haunted canyon in the rear
It seemed the dead ones answered. Starving mules
Heehawed, as if to jeer the two-legged fools
Who brought them there. We didn't make a sound;
Just looked across that country, hellward bound,

And filled our eyes with nothing, flabbergasted.
You made up stories while the canyon lasted,
But yonder was the story God had made.
It looked like even Harry hadn't prayed
Quite loud enough!

                    Jed didn't seem to care.
Spoke quietly of California there,
And pointed to the white sun blazing down
Beyond that waste! There'd be an Indian town
Along the river we were coming to,
And there we'd rest. He spoke as if he knew,
And made hope certain as geography.
Why, come to think about it, you could see
The corn fields waving by the riverside!

Well, two more horses and a mule had died,
With others on the ragged edge of dying,
Before the Adams finally quit trying
To justify the wearing of the name.
And in the dragging afternoon we came
Upon the Colorado.

                    Greasewood throve
Along the valley, and a stunted grove,
That huddled yonder by the river, made
The only promise of a little shade
In all that bowl of glare. Two yapping dogs
Came bristling; and we saw a house of logs
Squat-roofed with 'dobe in among the trees.

A nursing woman, hobbled at the knees
With frightened young ones, peeked at us and ran
Behind the cabin. Then an oldish man,
We took to be a Piute, filled the door.
If anything surprised him any more,
You didn't guess it by the look he had.
Was he amused or just a little sad
Or maybe both? The quiet, puckered way
He looked us over didn't seem to say
A thing for sure, except he didn't scare.
And when we sign-talked at him, asking where
The village was, he waved his hand around
The whole horizon, pointed to the ground,
Then tapped his chest and chuckled pleasantly.
'Twas Crusoe with the desert for a sea,
And he had built an island with his labors
Where there were only well-behaving neighbors—
The sun and moon and stars!

                    We feasted there
On garden stuff, and Jed paid more than fair
With trading goods. The mules and horses had
Their fodder, and the little ones were glad
With bells to tinkle, while their mother chose,
With happy little noises in her nose,
The gaudiest of cloth. But all the while
Old Crusoe smiled a pleasant little smile,
Observing with that quiet squint of his,
As though he sort of knew what really is
And always was and shall be evermore,

So that he wasn't bothered looking for
What isn't, wasn't, and will never be."

"Another sort of turnip, seems to me,"
The younger said; "just dumb and half asleep."

"And maybe," Evans added, "rooted deep
In what I call the other side of things,
Where running feet are stilled and eager wings
Are folded, and all seeking is forsaken,
Because there's nothing to be overtaken
In such a peace of being."

                  "Well," said Black,
"I've often kind of hankered to go back
And see if I could gather what he knew.
It must have worked on all the others too;
Nobody joked about him. All the way
Down river, when the going, day by day,
Grew harder, with the done-out critters dying,
I thought and thought of how you go on trying
And suffering to find, until you're dead,
When maybe all the while it's in your head
The way it was in his, if you could see.

But when we came to where the Siskadee
Broke out into a valley fat with tillage,
And saw the populous Mojave village
Among the trees, he didn't seem so wise;
For hadn't we arrived at Paradise,

However we had paid in Purgatory?
You're always wanting life to be a story
With some pat end to show what it's about.
Somebody's torn a lot of pages out,
If that's the case! You never quite arrive.

Well, it was mighty good to be alive
Among those gardens yellowing with plenty,
And see our critters, dwindled now to twenty,
Contented in the meadows, making fat.

Could we have read, just one year after that,
The bloody page that would be written, when
With eighteen more, Jed came that way again
From Bear Lake, fought with devils, met as friends,
And fled with eight! I guess the story ends
When anybody turns an empty page—
An ending without end. You'd swear old age
Had found them when they reached our camp beside
The Stanislaus, and told how ten had died
Bare-handed in the treacherous attack.

'Twas lucky, Bob, you didn't try it back
With Jed and Silas Gobel, your old friend
Of desert days. But what a rousing end
Old Silas made before his page went blank!
The eight had crossed, and from the western bank
They saw it happen on the further shore—
The whole tribe swimming inward, with the roar
A cloudburst makes, upon the helpless ten—

Men drowning quickly in a flood of men,
Save where old Silas, hardened at the forge,
And looming like a boulder in a gorge
Bankfull with freshet, labored with a limb
Of mesquite for a hammer at his grim
Last smithing job. If God has set the Right
To prove its mettle in the losing fight
Forever, 'twas another score for God!
Not all the horses Silas ever shod
Outweighed the burden of the spears that bowed
Those blacksmith shoulders; and the milling crowd
Rained arrows till the club no longer whirled
About him. When a howling eddy swirled
And slowly closed at last above his head,
The watchers yonder knew that he was dead
As any coward. Then the running fight—
Few rifles, many bows. And all that night
They fled until the desert blazed with day.

But that was still a good long year away,
And we were happy, being richly fed
With more than garden stuff. For Rumor said,
And 'twas the clearer being vague, somewhere
Far off beyond the jealous desert there
The ripened days of all the wide world went
To make a lazy country of content
Where it was always Spring—a dream of Spain,
Come true forever! Not a wish was vain
In yonder climate kind to all desires!
Hard-bitten youngsters, squatting 'round the fires,

Half tight already with imagined wine,
Discussed it, till you felt the soft sun shine
On drowsy vineyards; heard beneath the stars
The castanets, the strumming of guitars,
The singing senoritas! There it lay,
And only Boston clippers knew the way—
Ten thousand miles down under 'round the Horn!
To think that we, of all our breed, were born
To see it first by land!

          Our luck was good.
You, Squire, would say Jehovah understood
We'd lack for horses, and provided some.
Well, anyway, some Indians had come
Across the desert with a stolen herd
Of Spanish Mission horses! Seemed absurd
Such scurvy rascals hailed from Paradise!
What scenes had filled their slinking, sleepy eyes
That didn't seem to care! Reubasco knew
Their Spanish lingo; and the wonder grew
The bigger for the little that they told.
'Twas late October, and the moon was old,
As we were, when we hit Mojave town.
'Twas young again, as we were, going down
The trail of sunset to the Promised Land,
Our first camp out. We scooped the seeping sand
Along a wash to make a little spring,
And didn't sleep much, for the whinnying
Of horses, waiting for the hole to fill
Again and yet again.

The blue-black chill
Wore out and whitened to a withering blaze;
And after that we didn't count the days
Or nights of endless plodding, nor the sleeps
That ran to tangled dreams of water seeps
Clawed out in vain. We only counted drinks.
Dry washes running into empty sinks,
Bankfull with starlight, mocked us when we tramped
From sunset to the white of dawn, and camped,
Holed up in sand against the blistering light,
Until the purple chill came. Mind the night
We found the lake, Bob?"

                    "I can see it yet,"
The other mused. "The moon about to set;
The ghostly yucca trees around us there,
Transfigured by some ultimate despair
That filled the stillness of the solitude;
The slimy cabbage cactus that I chewed;
The rasping, hollow sound of critters panting;
The sudden clearing, and the low moon slanting—
The low moon slanting on a lake! Dry salt!
A crazy notion 'twas the yuccas' fault
Seemed true, and yet I couldn't make it track!"

"Well, even though it wasn't wet," said Black,
"It made the going easy. Anyway,
You mind it ended with the break of day
And how that cool spring sparkled in the sun
There where the river that forgot to run

Spread wide to fill the lake that wasn't wet!
'Twas something queer you wouldn't soon forget—
The spooky yucca trees that seemed to know
The end of us and didn't care—the low
Half moon across the salt! But Oh, the night
We saw the full moon glitter on the white
Peaks yonder!"

       "I remember," Evans said.
"The journey's end! And yet, the day when Jed
Went hunting water for us seems to glow
The brighter now. With burning sand for snow,
The blizzard booming down the empty river,
And 'Diah calmly praying to the Giver
Of all good things, before he left us there
Among the huddled horses! Could a prayer
Make headway yonder where the sun at noon
Ran through the howling smother like a moon
Gone mad with thirst? It seemed a cruel joke.
Yet there was something in the way he spoke
Of finding water—something in his face—"

"As if," Black said; "it might be any place
For anybody who could look that way!"

"And I believed the balance of the day,"
The other said. "But when the storm was through
At sundown, and the still cold moonlight grew
Around us, I forgot enough to doubt him.

The moon denied it knew a thing about him;
The silence said he wasn't coming back."

"It didn't know old 'Diah!" chuckled Black.
"Remember how he made us kneel to thank
The Giver of Good Things before we drank,
There where the river, hiding underground,
Came up as if to have a look around
And made a pool before it hid again?"

"The very horses kneeling with the men,
Eye-deep in joy! The moon near full and sinking,
And morning coming on while we were drinking,"
The other mused. "I like that picture better
Than yours, Art."

                    "Well, that water did seem wetter
Somehow," Black said, "than any other brew
This side of where the Squire is going to,
Unless he mends his ways. He won't, alas!
But what about the day we topped the pass
And stopped to stare—with all of that behind us,
And only missing horses to remind us
Of what it cost? The Promised Land at last!
And when we climbed the mountain, saw the vast
Land lazing there with nothing left to seek
Forevermore—the high, thin silver streak
That must have been the ocean—scattered droves
In happy meadows—greenery of groves

And vineyards! Wasn't that a better sight?
And yonder, drowsing in the golden light,
The Mission of the Padres! Journey's end!"

He thought awhile in silence. "No, my friend,"
He said, "you win. The men and horses kneeling
Around the pool, the white of morning stealing—
It's better. Queer the way a man remembers!"

He gazed awhile upon the dreaming embers,
With silent laughter mounting to his eyes.
"And so," he chuckled, "there was Paradise,
And all us lanky, ragamuffin scamps
A-faunching! What does 'Diah do? He camps
To shave his whiskers!"

The Song of the Indian Wars

As the title indicates, the fourth volume of A Cycle of the West *deals with the conflicts between the prairie tribes and the white men, beginning after the Civil War and ending with the death of Crazy Horse at Fort Robinson in the fall of 1877. The early explorers who figured in the foregoing songs had opened up the land west of the Mississippi for white settlers, and thousands pushed their way west in seemingly endless covered wagon trains. Native Americans fought against great odds, but they could not prevail against the taking of their lands and the slaughter of the buffalo.*

My father was acquainted with many officers and soldiers, as well as numerous Indians, who had participated in the wars. This Song *is based on both historical research and the first- and second-hand accounts told by the old-timers themselves. Neihardt's version of the death of Crazy Horse is one told him by Major H. R. Lemly, who was stationed at Fort Robinson when the great Sioux chief was killed, and who was so distressed by the circumstances surrounding the death that he requested and was granted a transfer out of the Indian Service.*

For this collection, I have selected the first chapter, "The Sowing of the Dragon," and the last, "The Death of Crazy Horse."

"The Sowing of the Dragon" and "The Death of Crazy Horse" are from *The Song of the Indian Wars* (New York: Macmillan, 1926); reprinted in *A Cycle of the West* (1949; Lincoln: University of Nebraska Press, 1963, 1991) and in *The Twilight of the Sioux* (Lincoln: University of Nebraska Press, 1971).

The Sowing of the Dragon

At last the four year storm of fratricide
Had ceased at Appomattox, and the tide
Of war-bit myriads, like a turning sea's,
Recoiled upon the deep realities
That yield no foam to any squall of change.

Now many a hearth of home had gotten strange
To eyes that knew sky-painting flares of war.
So much that once repaid the striving for
No longer mattered. Yonder road that ran
At hazard once beyond the ways of Man
By haunted vale and space-enchanted hill,
Had never dreamed of aught but Jones's Mill—
A dull pedestrian! The spring, where erst
The peering plowboy sensed a larger thirst,
Had shoaled from awe, so long the man had drunk
At deeper floods. How yonder field had shrunk
That billowed once mysteriously far
To where the cow-lot nursed the evening star
And neighbored with the drowsing moon and sun!
For O what winds of wrath had boomed and run
Across what vaster fields of moaning grain—
Rich seedings, nurtured by a ghastly rain
To woeful harvest!

            So the world went small.
But 'mid the wreck of things remembered tall

An epidemic rumor murmured now.
Men leaned upon the handles of the plow
To hear and dream; and through the harrow-smoke
The weird voice muttered and the vision broke
Of distant, princely acres unpossessed.

Again the bugles of the Race blew west
That once the Tigris and Euphrates heard.
In unsuspected deeps of being stirred
The ancient and compelling Aryan urge.
A homing of the homeless, surge on surge,
The valley roads ran wagons, and the hills
Through lane and by-way fed with trickling rills
The man-stream mighty with a mystic thaw.
All summer now the Mississippi saw
What long ago the Hellespont beheld.
The shrewd, prophetic eyes that peered of eld
Across the Danube, visioned naked plains
Beyond the bleak Missouri, clad with grains,
Jewelled with orchard, grove and greening garth—
Serene abundance centered in a hearth
To nurture lusty children.

                                On they swirled,
The driving breed, the takers of the world,
The makers and the bringers of the law.
Now up along the bottoms of the Kaw
The drifting reek of wheel and hoof arose.
The kiotes talked about it and the crows
Along the lone Republican; and still

The bison saw it on the Smoky Hill
And Solomon; while yonder on the Platte
Ten thousand wagons scarred the sandy flat
Between the green grass season and the brown.

A name sufficed to make the camp a town,
A whim unmade. In spaces wide as air,
And late as empty, now the virile share
Quickened the virgin meadow-lands of God;
And lo, begotten of the selfsame sod,
The house and harvest!

    So the Cadmian breed,
The wedders of the vision and the deed,
Went forth to sow the dragon-seed again.

But there were those—and they were also men—
Who saw the end of sacred things and dear
In all this wild beginning; saw with fear
Ancestral pastures gutted by the plow,
The bison harried ceaselessly, and how
They dwindled moon by moon; with pious dread
Beheld the holy places of their dead
The mock of aliens.

    Sioux, Arapahoe,
Cheyenne, Comanche, Kiowa and Crow
In many a council pondered what befell
The prairie world. Along the Musselshell,
The Tongue, the Niobrara, all they said

Upon the Platte, the Arkansaw, the Red
Was echoed word by peril-laden word.
Along Popo Agie[1] and the Horn they heard
The clank of hammers and the clang of rails
Where hordes of white men conjured iron trails
Now crawling past the Loup Fork and the Blue.
By desert-roaming Cimarron they knew,
And where La Poudre heads the tale was known,
How, snoring up beyond the Yellowstone,
The medicine-canoes breathed flame and steam
And, like weird monsters of an evil dream,
Spewed foes—a multitudinary spawn!

Were all the teeming regions of the dawn
Unpeopled now? What devastating need
Had set so many faces pale with greed
Against the sunset? Not as men who seek
Some meed of kindness, suppliant and meek,
These hungry myriads came. They did but look,
And whatsoever pleased them, that they took.
Their faded eyes were icy, lacking ruth,
And all their tongues were forked to split the truth
That word and deed might take diverging ways.
Bewildered in the dusk of ancient days
The Red Men groped; and howsoever loud
The hopeful hotheads boasted in the crowd,
The wise ones heard prophetic whisperings

[1]Pronounced Po-po-zha.

174

Through aching hushes; felt the end of things
Inexorably shaping. What should be
Already was to them. And who can flee
His shadow or his doom? Though cowards stride
The wind-wild thunder-horses, Doom shall ride
The arrows of the lightning, and prevail.
Ere long whole tribes must take the spirit trail
As once they travelled to the bison hunt.
Then let it be with many wounds—in front—
And many scalps, to show their ghostly kin
How well they fought the fight they could not win.
To perish facing what they could not kill.

So down upon the Platte and Smoky Hill
Swept war; and all their valleys were afraid.
The workers where the trails were being laid
To speed the iron horses, now must get
Their daily wage in blood as well as sweat
With gun and shovel. Often staring plains
Beheld at daybreak gutted wagon-trains
Set foursquare to the whirling night-attack,
With neither hoof nor hand to bring them back
To Omaha or Westport. Every week
The rolling coaches bound for Cherry Creek
Were scarred in running battle. Every day
Some ox-rig, creeping California way—
That paradise of every hope fulfilled—
Was plundered and the homesick driver killed,
Forlornly fighting for his little brood.

And often was the prairie solitude
Aware by night of burning ricks and roofs,
Stampeding cattle and the fleeing hoofs
Of wild marauders.

The Death of Crazy Horse

And now 'twas done.
Spring found the waiting fort at Robinson
A half-moon ere the Little Powder knew;
And, doubting still what Crazy Horse might do
When tempted by the herald geese a-wing
To join the green rebellion of the spring,
The whole frontier was troubled. April came,
And once again his undefeated name
Rode every wind. Ingeniously the West
Wrought verities from what the East had guessed
Of what the North knew. Eagerly deceived,
The waiting South progressively believed
The wilder story. April wore away;
Fleet couriers, arriving day by day
With but the farthing mintage of the fact,
Bought credit slowly in that no one lacked
The easy gold of marvelous surmise.
For, gazing northward where the secret skies
Were moody with a coming long deferred,

Whoever spoke of Crazy Horse, still heard
Ten thousand hoofs.

                  But yonder, with the crow
And kiote to applaud his pomp of woe,
The last great Sioux rode down to his defeat.
And now his people huddled in the sleet
Where Dog Creek and the Little Powder met.
With faces ever sharper for the whet
Of hunger, silent in the driving rains,
They straggled out across the blackened plains
Where Inyan Kara, mystically old,
Drew back a cloudy curtain to behold,
Serene with Time's indifference to men.
And now they tarried on the North Cheyenne
To graze their feeble ponies, for the news
Of April there had wakened in the sloughs
A glimmering of pity long denied.
Nor would their trail across the bare divide
Grow dimmer with the summer, for the bleach
Of dwindled herds—so hard it was to reach
The South Cheyenne. O sad it was to hear
How all the pent-up music of the year
Surged northward there the way it used to do!
In vain the catbird scolded at the Sioux;
The timid pewee queried them in vain;
Nor might they harken to the whooping crane
Nor heed the high geese calling them to come.
Unwelcome waifs of winter, drab and dumb,

Where ecstasy of sap and thrill of wing
Made shift to flaunt some color or to sing
The birth of joy, they toiled a weary way.
And giddy April sobered into May
Before they topped the summit looking down
Upon the valley of the soldier's town
At Robinson.
         Then eerily began
Among the lean-jowled warriors in the van
The chant of peace, a supplicating wail
That spread along the clutter of the trail
Until the last bent straggler sang alone;
And camp dogs, hunger-bitten to the bone,
Accused the heavens with a doleful sound;
But, silent still, with noses to the ground,
The laden ponies toiled to cheat the crows,
And famine, like a wag, had made of those
A grisly jest.

        So Crazy Horse came in
With twice a thousand beggars.

                And the din
Died out, though here and there a dog still howled,
For now the mighty one whom Fate had fouled,
Dismounted, faced the silent double row
Of soldiers haughty with the glint and glow
Of steel and brass. A little while he stood
As though bewildered in a haunted wood
Of men and rifles all astare with eyes.

They saw a giant shrunken to the size
Of any sergeant. Now he met the glare
Of Dull Knife and his warriors waiting there
With fingers itching at the trigger-guard.
How many comrade faces, strangely hard,
Were turned upon him! Ruefully he smiled,
The doubtful supplication of a child
Caught guilty; loosed the bonnet from his head
And cast it down. "I come for peace," he said;
"Now let my people eat." And that was all.

The summer ripened. Presages of fall
Now wanted nothing but the goose's flight.
The goldenrods had made their torches bright
Against the ghostly imminence of frost.
And one, long brooding on a birthright lost,
Remembered and remembered. O the time
When all the prairie world was white with rime
Of mornings, and the lodge smoke towered straight
To meet the sunlight, coming over late
For happy hunting! O the days, the days
When winds kept silence in the far blue haze
To hear the deep-grassed valleys running full
With fatling cows, and thunders of the bull
Across the hills! Nights given to the feast
When big round moons came smiling up the east
To listen to the drums, the dancing feet,
The voices of the women, high and sweet
Above the men's!

And Crazy Horse was sad.
There wasn't any food the white man had
Could find his gnawing hunger and assuage.
Some saw a blood-mad panther in a cage,
And some the sulking of a foolish pride,
For there were those who watched him narrow-eyed
The whole day long and listened for a word,
To shuttle in the warp of what they heard
A woof of darker meaning.

                    Then one day
A flying tale of battles far away
And deeds to make men wonder stirred the land:
How Nez Perce Joseph led his little band,
With Howard's eager squadrons in pursuit,
Across the mountains of the Bitter Root
To Big Hole Basin and the day-long fight;
And how his women, fleeing in the night,
Brought off the ponies and the children too.
O many a heart beat fast among the Sioux
To hear the way he fled and fought and fled
Past Bannack, down across the Beaverhead
To Henry's Lake, relentlessly pursued;
Now swallowed by the dreadful solitude
Where still the Mighty Spirit shapes the dream
With primal fires and prodigies of steam,
As when the fallow night was newly sown;
Now reappearing down the Yellowstone,
Undaunted yet and ever making less

That thousand miles of alien wilderness
Between a people's freedom and their need!

O there was virtue in the tale to feed
The withered heart and make it big again!
Not yet, not yet the ancient breed of men
Had vanished from the aging earth! They say
There came a change on Crazy Horse the day
The Ogalala village buzzed the news.
So much to win and only life to lose;
The bison making southward with the fall,
And Joseph fighting up the way to Gall
And Sitting Bull!

                    Who knows the dream he had?
Much talk there was of how his heart was bad
And any day some meditated deed
Might start an irresistible stampede
Among the Sioux—a human prairie-fire!
So back and forth along the talking wire
Fear chattered. Yonder, far away as morn,
The mighty heard—and heard the Little Horn
Still roaring with the wind of Custer's doom.
And there were troopers moving in the gloom
Of midnight to the chaining of the beast;
But when the white light broke along the east,
There wasn't any Ogalala town
And Crazy Horse had vanished!

                                    Up and down
The dusty autumn panic horsemen spurred
Till all the border shuddered at the word
Of how that terror threatened every trail.

They found him in the camp of Spotted Tail,
A lonely figure with a face of care.
"I am afraid of what might happen there"
He said. "So many listen what I say
And look and look. I will not run away
I want my people here. You have my guns."

But half a world away the mighty ones
Had spoken words like bullets in the dark
That wreak the rage of blindness on a mark
They can not know.

                        Then spoke the one who led
The soldiers: "Not a hair upon your head
Shall suffer any harm if you will go
To Robinson for just a day or so
And have a parley with the soldier chief."
He spoke believing and he won belief,
So Crazy Horse went riding down the west;
And neither he nor any trooper guessed
What doom now made a rutted wagon road
The highway to a happier abode
Where all the dead are splendidly alive
And summer lingers and the bison thrive
Forever.

If the better hope be true,
There was a gate of glory yawning through
The sunset when the little cavalcade
Approached the fort.

The populous parade,
The straining hush that somehow wasn't peace,
The bristling troops, the Indian police
Drawn up as for a battle! What was wrong?
What made them hustle Crazy Horse along
Among the gleaming bayonets and eyes?
There swept a look of quizzical surprise
Across his face. He struggled with the guard.
Their grips were steel; their eyes were cold and hard—
Like bayonets.

There was a door flung wide.
The soldier chief would talk with him inside
And all be well at last!

The stifling, dim
Interior poured terror over him.
He blinked about—and saw the iron bars.
O nevermore to neighbor with the stars
Or know the simple goodness of the sun!
Did some swift vision of a doom begun
Reveal the monstrous purpose of a lie—
The desert island and the alien sky,
The long and lonely ebbing of a life?

The glimmer of a whipped-out butcher knife
Dismayed the shrinking squad, and once again
Men saw a face that many better men
Had died to see! Brown arms that once were kind,
A comrade's arms, whipped round him from behind,
Went crimson with a gash and dropped aside.
"Don't touch me! I am Crazy Horse!" he cried,
And, leaping doorward, charged upon the world
To meet the end. A frightened soldier hurled
His weight behind a jabbing belly-thrust,
And Crazy Horse plunged headlong in the dust,
A writhing heap. The momentary din
Of struggle ceased. The people, closing in,
Went ominously silent for a space,
And one could hear men breathing round the place
Where lay the mighty. Now he strove to rise,
The wide blind stare of anguish in his eyes,
And someone shouted "*Kill that devil quick!*"

A throaty murmur and a running click
Of gun-locks woke among the crowding Sioux,
And many a soldier whitened. Well they knew
What pent-up hate the moment might release
To drop upon the bungled farce of peace
A bloody curtain.

　　　　　One began to talk;
His tongue was drunken and his face was chalk;
But when a halfbreed shouted what he spoke
The crowd believed, so few had seen the stroke,

Nor was there any bleeding of the wound.
It seemed the chief had fallen sick and swooned;
Perhaps a little rest would make him strong!
And silently they watched him borne along,
A sagging bundle, dear and mighty yet,
Though from the sharp face, beaded with the sweat
Of agony, already peered the ghost.

They laid him in an office of the post,
And soldiers, forming in a hollow square,
Held back the people. Silence deepened there.
A little while it seemed the man was dead,
He lay so still. The west no longer bled;
Among the crowd the dusk began to creep.
Then suddenly, as startled out of sleep
By some old dream-remembered night alarm,
He strove to shout, half rose upon an arm
And glared about him in the lamp-lit place.

The flare across the ashes of his face
Went out. He spoke; and, leaning where he lay,
Men strained to gather what he strove to say,
So hard the panting labor of his words.
"I had my village and my pony herds
On Powder where the land was all my own.
I only wanted to be let alone.
I did not want to fight. The Gray Fox sent
His soldiers. We were poorer when they went;
Our babies died, for many lodges burned
And it was cold. We hoped again and turned

Our faces westward. It was just the same
Out yonder on the Rosebud. Gray Fox came.
The dust his soldiers made was high and long.
I fought him and I whipped him. Was it wrong
To drive him back? That country was my own.
I only wanted to be let alone.
I did not want to see my people die.
They say I murdered Long Hair and they lie.
His soldiers came to kill us and they died."

He choked and shivered, staring hungry-eyed
As though to make the most of little light.
Then like a child that feels the clutching night
And cries the wilder, deeming it in vain,
He raised a voice made lyrical with pain
And terror of a thing about to be.
*"I want to see you, Father! Come to me!
I want to see you, Mother!"* O'er and o'er
His cry assailed the darkness at the door;
And from the gloom beyond the hollow square
Of soldiers, quavered voices of despair:
"We can not come! They will not let us come!"

But when at length the lyric voice was dumb
And Crazy Horse was nothing but a name,
There was a little withered woman came
Behind a bent old man. Their eyes were dim.
They sat beside the boy and fondled him,
Remembering the little names he knew
Before the great dream took him and he grew

To be so mighty. And the woman pressed
A hand that men had feared against her breast
And swayed and sang a little sleepy song.

Out yonder in the village all night long
There was a sound of mourning in the dark.
And when the morning heard the meadowlark,
The last great Sioux rode silently away.
Before the pony-drag on which he lay
An old man tottered. Bowed above the bier,
A little wrinkled woman kept the rear
With not a sound and nothing in her eyes.

Who knows the crumbling summit where he lies
Alone among the Badlands? Kiotes prowl
About it, and the voices of the owl
Assume the day-long sorrow of the crows,
These many grasses and these many snows.

The Song of the Messiah

Taking up after the death of Crazy Horse, The Song of the Messiah *is concerned with a great dream that spread in the late 1880s and in 1890 among the Great Plains Indians. They were in a pitiable condition, displaced from their ancestral lands by the conquering whites and devastated by strange diseases. A vision had come to a Paiute named Wovoka, who lived in Nevada. It brought with it the dream of a new world for the Indian people—one in which the whites would disappear, dead Indians would live again, the ravages done to the land would be healed, and the wild game would return. Under a blue, blue sky, on a green, green earth the Indian people would live happily forever. All they had to do, said Wovoka, was to paint themselves in a sacred manner, dress in the prescribed shirts, dance—and believe! It is well known that this spiritual dream had its worldly end in the blood and snow of the Wounded Knee Massacre on December 29, 1890. With the reenactment of events at Wounded Knee,* A Cycle of the West *ends.*

I have included the description of the Spirit World as told by Good Thunder after he had heard it from Wovoka, partly because this passage was a favorite of the poet, who remarked, "It feels good in my mouth when I recite it." The chapter "The Dance" is also included because it is representative of the work and provides a link with Black Elk Speaks.

"The Spirit World" and "The Dance" are from *The Song of the Messiah* (New York: Macmillan, 1941); reprinted in *A Cycle of the West* (1949; Lincoln: University of Nebraska Press, 1963, 1991) and in *The Twilight of the Sioux* (Lincoln: University of Nebraska Press, 1971).

The Spirit World

. . . eyes have never seen
The green with which that breathing land was green,
The day that made the sunlight of our days
Like moonlight when the bitten moon delays
And shadows are afraid. It did not fall
From heaven, blinding; but it glowed from all
The living things together. Every blade
Of grass was holy with the light it made,
And trees breathed day and blooms were little suns.
And through that land the Ever-Living Ones
Were marching now, a host of many hosts,
So brightly living, we it is are ghosts
Who haunt these shadows feeding on tomorrows.
Like robes of starlight, their forgotten sorrows
Clung beautiful about the newly dead;
And eyes, late darkened with the tears they shed,
Were wide with sudden morning. It was spring
Forever, and all birds began to sing
Above them, marching in a cloud that glowed
With every color. All the bison lowed
Along the holy pastures, unafraid;
And horses, never to be numbered, neighed
Like thunders laughing. Down the blooming plains,
A river-thaw of tossing tails and manes,
They pranced and reared rejoicing in their might
And swiftness. In the streams of living light
The fishes leaped and glittered, marching too;

For everything that lived looked up and knew
What Spirit yonder, even in that day,
Was blooming like a sunrise.

                       And the way
Was shortened all at once, and here was there,
And all the living ones from everywhere
Were hushed with wonder. For behold! there grew
A tree whose leafage filled the living blue
With sacred singing; and so tall it 'rose,
A thousand grasses and a thousand snows
Could never raise it; but all trees together,
When warm rains come and it is growing weather
And every root and every seed believes,
Might dream of having such a world of leaves
So high in such a happiness of air.

And now, behold! a man was standing there
Beneath the tree, his body painted red,
A single eagle feather on his head,
His arms held wide. More beautiful he seemed
Than any earthly maiden ever dreamed,
In all the soft spring nights that ever were,
Might be the one of all to look on her.
He had a father's face, but when he smiled,
To see was like the waking of a child
Who feels the mother's goodness bending low.
A wound upon his side began to glow
With many colors. Memories of earth,
They seemed to be—of dying and of birth,

Of sickness and of hunger and of cold,
Of being young awhile and growing old
In sorrow. Now he wept, and in the rain
Of his bright tears the holy flower of pain
Bloomed mightily and beautiful to see
Beyond all earthly blooming, and the tree
Was filled with moaning. All the living things,
With roots and leaves, with fins or legs or wings,
Were bowed, beholding; and a sudden change
Came over them, for all that had been strange
Between them vanished. Nothing was alone,
But each one knew the other and was known,
And saw the same; for it had come to pass
The wolf and deer, the bison and the grass,
The birds and trees, the fishes in the streams,
And horse and man had lost their little dreams
And wakened all together.

The Dance

Every day
No Water's Camp was growing near the mouth
Of White Clay Creek, lean-flowing in the drouth.
What matter if the doomed, unfriendly sky,
The loveless grudging Earth, so soon to die,

Ignored the supplication of the lean?
Rains of the spirit, wonders in the green,
Bloom of the heart and thunders of the Truth,
Waking the deathless meadow lark of youth,
Were yonder. So the village grew. And most
Who came there felt the leading of the ghost;
But if the clever in their own regard,
Amused contenders that the hills were hard
And could not flow, came mockingly to see,
They saw indeed.

           They saw the Holy Tree,
A sapling cottonwood with branches lopped,
Set in the center of a ring, and topped
With withered leaves. Around it and around,
Weaving a maze of dust and mournful sound,
The women and the children and the men
Joined hands and shuffled, ever and again
Rounding a weird monotony of song,
Winged with the wail of immemorial wrong,
And burdened with the ancient hope at prayer.
And now and then one turned a knowing stare
Upon the empty dazzle of the skies,
Muttering names, and then, as one who dies,
Slumped to the dust and shivered and was still.
And more and more were seized upon, until
The ring was small of those who could not see;
And weeping there beneath the withered tree,
They sang and prayed.

But when the sleepers woke
To stagger from the dust, the words they spoke,
As in a dream, were beautiful and strange.
And many a scoffer felt a still swift change
Come over things late darkened with the light
Of common day; as in a moony night
The rapt sleepwalker lives and is aware,
Past telling, in the landscape everywhere
About him till no alien thing can be,
And every blade of grass and weed and tree,
Seed-loving soil and unbegetting stone,
Glow with the patient secret they have known
These troubled whiles, and even men shall know.
One moment, shrewdly smiling at a show,
The clever ones could see a common pole,
The antic grandmas, little children, droll
With grownup airs, the clowning men who wept,
And dust. But suddenly, as though they slept
And dreamed till then, to wake at last and see,
Swift saps of meaning quickened to a tree
The rootless bole, the earth-forgotten thing
With starveling leafage; and the birds would sing
Forever in that shielding holiness.
A joy that only weeping can express
This side of dying, swept them like a rain
Illumining with lightning that is pain
The life-begetting darkness that is sorrow.

So there would be more dancers on the morrow
To swell the camp.

The Moon When Ponies Shed[1]
Had aged and died; and, risen from the dead,
The Moon of Fatness,[2] only in the name,
Haunted the desert heavens and became
A mockery of plenty at the full,
Remembering the thunders of the bull,
The lowing of the countless fatted cows,
Where now it saw the ghostly myriads browse
Along a thousand valleys, still and sere.
But mightily the spirit of the year,
At flood, poured out upon the needy ones
The Light that has the dazzle of the sun's
For shadow, till the very blind could see.

And then it was beneath the withered tree
Young Black Elk stood and sent a voice and wept;
And little had he danced until he slept
The sleep of vision; for a power lay
Upon him from a child, and men could say
Strange things about his seeing that were true,
And of the dying made to live anew
By virtue of the power. When he fell
The sun was high. When he awoke to tell
The silent crowd that pressed about the place
Of what he saw, with awe upon its face
The full moon rose and faltered, listening.

[1]May. [2]June.

It was, he said, like riding in a swing,
Afraid of falling; for the swing rose high;
And faster, deeper into empty sky
It mounted, till the clutching hands let go,
And, like an arrow leaping from a bow,
He clove the empty spaces, swift and prone.
Alone he seemed, and terribly alone,
For there was nothing anywhere to heed
The helpless, headlong terror of the speed,
Until a single eagle feather blew
Before him in that emptiness and grew
Into a spotted eagle, leading on
With screaming cries.

               The terror now was gone.
He seemed to float; but looking far below,
He saw strange lands and rivers come and go
In silence yonder. Far ahead appeared
A mighty mountain. Once again he feared,
For it was clothed in smoke and fanged with flame
And voiced with many thunders. On it came
And passed beneath. Then stretching everywhere
Below him, vivid in the glowing air,
A young earth blossomed with eternal spring;
And in the midst thereof a sacred ring
Of peoples throve in brotherly content;
And he could see the good Red Road that went
Across it, south to north; the hard Black Road
From east to west, where bearers of the load

Of earthly troubles wander blind and lost.
But in the center where the two roads crossed,
The roads men call the evil and the good,
The place was holy with the Tree that stood
Earth-rooted yonder. Nourished by the four
Great Powers that are one, he saw it soar
And be the blooming life of all that lives,
The Holy Spirit that the good grass gives
To animals, and animals to men,
And they give back unto the grass again;
But nothing dies.

            On every drying rack,
The meat was plenty. Hunters coming back
Sang on the hills, the laden ponies too.

Now he descended where the great Tree grew
And there a man was standing in the shade;
A man all perfect, and the light He made
Was like a rainbow 'round Him, spreading wide
Until the living things on every side,
Above Him and below, took fire and burned
One holy flame.

            "Then suddenly He turned
Full face upon me and I tried to see,"
Young Black Elk said, "what people His might be;
But there was cloud, and in the cloud appeared
So many stranger faces that I feared,
Until His face came smiling like a dawn.

And then between two blinks the man was gone;
But 'round the Tree there, standing in a ring,
Twelve women and twelve men began to sing:
'Behold! the people's future shall be such!'
I saw their garments and I wondered much
What these might mean, for they were strangely
    wrought,
And even as I thought, they heard my thought
And sang reply: 'The people clad as we
Shall fear no evil thing; for they shall see
As you have seen it. Hundreds shall be flame.'

Then I was blinded with a glow that came
Upon them, and they vanished in bright air
And wordless singing.

                Standing lonely there,
I thought about my father who is dead
And longed to find him. But a great Voice said,
'Go back and tell; for there is yet more wrong
And sorrow!'

            Then a swift wind came along
And lifted me; and once again I knew
The fearful empty speed. Face down I flew
And saw a rushing river full of foam,
And crowds of people trying to get home
Across it; but they could not; and I wept
To hear their wailing. Still the great wind kept
Beneath me. And you see that I am here."

Young Black Elk ceased; and, thinking of the dear
Good days of plenty now become a tale,
A woman, old and withered, raised a wail
Of bitter mourning: "It was even so
The way the young man saw it. Long ago
I can remember it was just the same,
The time before the bad Wasichus came,
That greedy people! All good things are dead,
And now I want to die." Her sorrow spread
Among the women like a song of pain,
As when the ponies, heavy with the slain,
Return from battle and the widows crowd
About them, and the mothers.

                When the shroud
Of moony silence fell upon their woe,
Young Black Elk spoke again: "What shall be so
Forever, I have seen. I did not sleep;
I only woke and saw it. Do not weep;
For it is only being blind that hurts.
Tomorrow you shall make these holy shirts
For us to wear the way I saw them worn.
Clothed in the Holy Spirit, none shall mourn
Or come to harm along the fearful road."

So on the morrow happy women sewed
In all the tepees, singing as they made
Of odds and ends and empty sacks of trade,
The rags and tatters of their earthly need,
Unearthly raiment, richly wrought indeed

For all the love they stitched in every hem.
And good old men of power painted them
With sacred meaning: blue upon the breast,
A moon of promise leading to the west,
The end of days; and, blue upon the back,
A morning star to glimmer on the black
And fearful road; the neck and fringes red,
The hue of life. An eagle feather sped
On either arm the homing of the soul.
And mighty with the meaning of the whole,
The work was finished.

                Death became afraid
Before the dancing people so arrayed
In vision of the deathless. Hundreds burned
With holiness.

            But when the cherries turned
From red to black, while Summer slowly died
And in her waiting hushes prophesied
The locust, and the lark forgot his song,
There fell the shadow of the coming wrong
And yet more sorrow that were left to bear.

The Agent came to see; and he was there
With all his world about him. It was sure
And solid, being builded to endure
With granite guess and rumor of the eyes,
Convincingly cemented with surmise
Against all winds of fancy and of fraud.

The height of it was high; the breadth was broad;
The length was long; and, whether bought or sold,
The worths thereof were weighable in gold,
His one concession to the mysteries.
As common as the growing of its trees,
And natural as having wakened there
Quite obviously living and aware,
His world was known.

        So clearly they were mad,
These dancing heathen, ludicrously clad
For superstitious doings in a day
Of Christian light and progress! Who could say
What devilment they hatched against the whites,
What lonely roofs would flare across the nights
To mark a path of murder!

        It must cease.

Surrounded by the Indian police,
Who sat their mounts importantly, half proud
And half abashed to wear before the crowd
Of relatives the master's coat of blue,
He spoke: "This thing is foolish that you do,
And you must stop it!" Still as though a trance
Had fallen on the interrupted dance,
The people listened while a half-breed hurled
The feeble thunder of a dying world
Among them: "It is bad and you must stop!

Go home and work! This will not raise a crop
To feed you!"

       Yet awhile the silence held,
The tension snapping with a voice that yelled
Some word of fury; and a hubbub broke.

As when across the dust and battle-smoke
The warrior hails the warrior—"Hokahey!
Have courage, brother! Let us die today!"—
The young men clamored, running for their guns.
And swarming back about the hated ones,
They faltered, waiting for the first to kill.
Then momently again the place went still,
But for the clicking locks. And someone cried:
"Your people tortured Jesus till He died!
You killed our bison and you stole our land!
Go back or we will kill you where you stand!
This dance is our religion! Go and bring
Your soldiers, if you will. Not anything
Can hurt us now. And if they want to die,
Go bring them to us!"

       Followed by the cry,
As by a stinging whip, the Agent went.

That night one mourned: "It was not what you meant!"
Alone upon a hill he prayed and wept;
"Not so you taught me when my body slept.
Great Spirit, give them eyes, for they are lost!"

Black Elk Speaks *and*
When the Tree Flowered

Five years after he completed The Song of the Indian Wars, *which ended with the death of Crazy Horse, Neihardt met the second cousin of the great Sioux chief, the holy man Black Elk. At that time he was preparing to write what would be the last volume of* A Cycle of the West, *the story of the Messiah movement, or, as it was popularly called, "the Ghost Dance craze."*

My father, hoping to meet a Sioux holy man who had participated in the ghost dancing, drove to the Pine Ridge Reservation. There he heard about "a kind of preacher" who lived in the hills near Manderson, South Dakota. With a Sioux interpreter, he went to the old man's log cabin—and found Black Elk sitting outside in a pine shade (a bower built with poles and pine boughs). Greetings over, Black Elk and his visitors sat together on the ground, smoking cigarettes brought by Neihardt. After an appropriate delay, Neihardt told Black Elk something about his years of acquaintance with the Sioux people, about what he had written, and about what he wished to learn. Although Black Elk answered his preliminary questions politely, he did so very briefly, and then lapsed into silence.

Breaking that silence, he announced—more to the empty

land in front of him that to his visitors—"I feel in this man beside me a great desire to know the things of the Other World. He has been sent to learn what I shall teach him." Astounded, Neihardt asked when he should return, to which Black Elk replied, "In the spring, when the grass is so high [indicating the breadth of his hand]."

My father did return to Pine Ridge in the spring of 1931 and conducted his now-famous interviews with Black Elk and some of his friends. The result, Black Elk Speaks, was published a year later. He kept in contact with Black Elk and again interviewed him in 1944. The material from that interview— together with the life reminiscences of another old Sioux, Eagle Elk—went into the novel When the Tree Flowered. Quite as authentic as the earlier book, When the Tree Flowered has not yet received the attention it deserves.

The importance of both books has perhaps never been better defined than by Vine Deloria, Jr., in his introduction to the 1979 reprint of Black Elk Speaks. He pointed out how much Neihardt's writing meant to a new generation of Indians "aggressively searching for roots of their own in the structure of universal reality." To them, Black Elk Speaks, in particular, had "become a North American bible of all tribes."

Although my father fully appreciated the importance of Black Elk's message and its contribution to the religions of the world, it is doubtful that he anticipated the impact it would have on the Indian people themselves.

The following selections are from *Black Elk Speaks: Being the Life Story of a Holy Man of the Oglala Sioux* (New York: William Morrow, 1932; reprinted Lincoln: University of Nebraska Press, 1961, 1979) and *When the Tree Flowered: The Fictional Autobiography of Eagle Voice, a Sioux Indian* (New York: Macmillan, 1951; reprinted Lincoln: University of Nebraska Press, 1970, 1991).

The Offering of the Pipe

BLACK ELK SPEAKS:

My friend, I am going to tell you the story of my life, as you wish; and if it were only the story of my life I think I would not tell it; for what is one man that he should make much of his winters, even when they bend him like a heavy snow? So many other men have lived and shall live that story, to be grass upon the hills.

It is the story of all life that is holy and is good to tell, and of us two-leggeds sharing in it with the four-leggeds and the wings of the air and all green things; for these are children of one mother and their father is one Spirit.

This, then, is not the tale of a great hunter or of a great warrior, or of a great traveler, although I have made much meat in my time and fought for my people both as boy and man, and have gone far and seen strange lands and men. So also have many others done, and better than I. These things I shall remember by the way, and often they may seem to be the very tale itself, as when I was living them in happiness and sorrow. But now that I can see it all as from a lonely hilltop, I know it was the story of a mighty vision given to a man too weak to use it; of a holy tree that should have flourished in a people's heart with flowers and singing birds, and now is withered; and of a people's dream that died in bloody snow.

But if the vision was true and mighty, as I know, it is true and mighty yet; for such things are of the spirit, and it is in the darkness of their eyes that men get lost.

So I know that it is a good thing I am going to do; and because no good thing can be done by any man alone, I will first make an offering and send a voice to the Spirit of the World, that it may help me to be true. See, I fill this sacred pipe with the bark of the red willow; but before we smoke it, you must see how it is made and what it means. These four ribbons hanging here on the stem are the four quarters of the universe. The black one is for the west where the thunder beings live to send us rain; the white one for the north, whence comes the great white cleansing wind; the red one for the east, whence springs the light and where the morning star lives to give men wisdom; the yellow for the south, whence come the summer and the power to grow.

But these four spirits are only one Spirit after all, and this eagle feather here is for that One, which is like a father, and also it is for the thoughts of men that should rise high as eagles do. Is not the sky a father and the earth a mother, and are not all living things with feet or wings or roots their children? And this hide upon the mouth-piece here, which should be bison hide, is for the earth, from whence we came and at whose breast we suck· as babies all our lives, along with all the animals and birds and trees and grasses. And because it means all this, and more than any man can understand, the pipe is holy.

There is a story about the way the pipe first came to us. A very long time ago, they say, two scouts were out looking for bison; and when they came to the top of a high hill and looked north, they saw something coming a long way off, and when it came closer they cried out, "It is a woman!," and it was. Then one of the scouts, being foolish, had bad thoughts and spoke them; but the other said: "That is a sacred woman; throw all bad thoughts away." When she came still closer, they saw that she wore a fine white buckskin dress, that her hair was very long and that she was young and very beautiful. And she knew their thoughts and said in a voice that was like singing: "You do not know me, but if you want to do as you think, you may come." And the foolish one went; but just as he stood before her, there was a white cloud that came and covered them. And the beautiful young woman came out of the cloud, and when it blew away the foolish man was a skeleton covered with worms.

Then the woman spoke to the one who was not foolish: "You shall go home and tell your people that I am coming and that a big tepee shall be built for me in the center of the nation." And the man, who was very much afraid, went quickly and told the people, who did at once as they were told; and there around the big tepee they waited for the sacred woman. And after a while she came, very beautiful and singing, and as she went into the tepee this is what she sang:

> "With visible breath I am walking.
> A voice I am sending as I walk.
> In a sacred manner I am walking.
> With visible tracks I am walking.
> In a sacred manner I walk."

And as she sang, there came from her mouth a white cloud that was good to smell. Then she gave something to the chief, and it was a pipe with a bison calf carved on one side to mean the earth that bears and feeds us, and with twelve eagle feathers hanging from the stem to mean the sky and the twelve moons, and these were tied with a grass that never breaks. "Behold!" she said. "With this you shall multiply and be a good nation. Nothing but good shall come from it. Only the hands of the good shall take care of it and the bad shall not even see it." Then she sang again and went out of the tepee; and as the people watched her going, suddenly it was a white bison galloping away and snorting, and soon it was gone.

This they tell, and whether it happened so or not I do not know; but if you think about it, you can see that it is true.

Now I light the pipe, and after I have offered it to the powers that are one Power, and sent forth a voice to them, we shall smoke together. Offering the mouthpiece first of all to the One above—so—I send a voice:

Hey hey! hey hey! hey hey! hey hey!

Grandfather, Great Spirit, you have been always, and before you no one has been. There is no other one to pray to but you. You yourself, everything that you see, everything has been made by you. The star nations all over the universe you have finished. The four quarters of the earth you have finished. The day, and in that day, everything you have finished. Grandfather, Great Spirit, lean close to the earth that you may hear the voice I send. You towards where the sun goes down, behold me; Thunder

Beings, behold me! You where the White Giant lives in power, behold me! You where the sun shines continually, whence come the day-break star and the day, behold me! You where the summer lives, behold me! You in the depths of the heavens, an eagle of power, behold! And you, Mother Earth, the only Mother, you who have shown mercy to your children!

Hear me, four quarters of the world—a relative I am! Give me the strength to walk the soft earth, a relative to all that is! Give me the eyes to see and the strength to understand, that I may be like you. With your power only can I face the winds.

Great Spirit, Great Spirit, my Grandfather, all over the earth the faces of living things are all alike. With tenderness have these come up out of the ground. Look upon these faces of children without number and with children in their arms, that they may face the winds and walk the good road to the day of quiet.

This is my prayer; hear me! The voice I have sent is weak, yet with earnestness I have sent it. Hear me!

It is finished. Hetchetu aloh!

Now, my friend, let us smoke together so that there may be only good between us.

The Butchering at Wounded Knee

That evening before it happened, I went in to Pine Ridge and heard these things, and while I was there, soldiers started for where the Big Foots were. These made about five hundred soldiers that were there next morning. When I saw them starting I felt that something terrible was going to happen. That night I could hardly sleep at all. I walked around most of the night.

In the morning I went out after my horses, and while I was out I heard shooting off toward the east, and I knew from the sound that it must be wagon-guns (cannon) going off. The sounds went right through my body, and I felt that something terrible would happen.

When I reached camp with the horses, a man rode up to me and said: "Hey-hey-hey! The people that are coming are fired on! I know it!"

I saddled up my buckskin and put on my sacred shirt. It was one I had made to be worn by no one but myself. It had a spotted eagle outstretched on the back of it, and the daybreak star was on the left shoulder, because when facing south that shoulder is toward the east. Across the breast, from the left shoulder to the right hip, was the flaming rainbow, and there was another rainbow around the neck, like a necklace, with a star at the bottom. At each shoulder, elbow, and wrist was an eagle feather; and over the whole shirt were red streaks of lightning. You will see that this was from my great vision, and you will know how it protected me that day.

I painted my face all red, and in my hair I put one eagle feather for the One Above.

It did not take me long to get ready, for I could still hear the shooting over there.

I started out alone on the old road that ran across the hills to Wounded Knee. I had no gun. I carried only the sacred bow of the west that I had seen in my great vision. I had gone only a little way when a band of young men came galloping after me. The first two who came up were Loves War and Iron Wasichu. I asked what they were going to do, and they said they were just going to see where the shooting was. Then others were coming up, and some older men.

We rode fast, and there were about twenty of us now. The shooting was getting louder. A horseback from over there came galloping very fast toward us, and he said: "Hey-hey-hey! They have murdered them!" Then he whipped his horse and rode away faster toward Pine Ridge.

In a little while we had come to the top of the ridge where, looking to the east, you can see for the first time the monument and the burying ground on the little hill where the church is. That is where the terrible thing started. Just south of the burying ground on the little hill a deep dry gulch runs about east and west, very crooked, and it rises westward to nearly the top of the ridge where we were. It had no name, but the Wasichus sometimes call it Battle Creek now. We stopped on the ridge not far from the head of the dry gulch. Wagon guns were still going off over there on the little hill, and they were going off again where they hit along the gulch. There was much shooting down yonder, and there were many cries, and we could see cavalrymen scattered over the hills ahead of us. Cavalrymen were riding along the gulch and shooting into it, where the women and children were running away and trying to hide in the gullies and the stunted pines.

A little way ahead of us, just below the head of the dry gulch, there were some women and children who were huddled under a clay bank, and some cavalrymen were there pointing guns at them.

We stopped back behind the ridge, and I said to the others: "Take courage. These are our relatives. We will try to get them back." Then we all sang a song which went like this:

> "A thunder being nation I am, I have said.
> A thunder being nation I am, I have said.
> You shall live.
> You shall live.
> You shall live.
> You shall live."

Then I rode over the ridge and the others after me, and we were crying: "Take courage! It is time to fight!" The soldiers who were guarding our relatives shot at us and then ran away fast, and some more cavalrymen on the other side of the gulch did too. We got our relatives and sent them across the ridge to the northwest where they would be safe.

I had no gun, and when we were charging, I just held

the sacred bow out in front of me with my right hand. The bullets did not hit us at all.

We found a little baby lying all alone near the head of the gulch. I could not pick her up just then, but I got her later and some of my people adopted her. I just wrapped her up tighter in a shawl that was around her and left her there. It was a safe place, and I had other work to do.

The soldiers had run eastward over the hills where there were some more soldiers, and they were off their horses and lying down. I told the others to stay back, and I charged upon them holding the sacred bow out toward them with my right hand. They all shot at me, and I could hear bullets all around me, but I ran my horse right close to them, and then swung around. Some soldiers across the gulch began shooting at me too, but I got back to the others and was not hurt at all.

By now many other Lakotas, who had heard the shooting, were coming up from Pine Ridge, and we all charged on the soldiers. They ran eastward toward where the trouble began. We followed down along the dry gulch, and what we saw was terrible. Dead and wounded women and children and little babies were scattered all along there where they had been trying to run away. The soldiers had followed along the gulch, as they ran, and murdered them in there. Sometimes they were in heaps because they had huddled together, and some were scattered along. Sometimes bunches of them had been killed and torn to pieces where the wagon guns hit them. I saw a little baby trying to suck its mother, but she was bloody and dead.

There were two little boys at one place in this gulch. They had guns and they had been killing soldiers all by themselves. We could see the soldiers they had killed. The boys were all alone there, and they were not hurt. These were very brave little boys.

When we drove the soldiers back, they dug themselves in, and we were not enough people to drive them out from there. In the evening they marched off up Wounded Knee Creek, and then we saw all that they had done there.

Men and women and children were heaped and scattered all over the flat at the bottom of the little hill where the soldiers had their wagon-guns, and westward up the dry gulch all the way to the high ridge, the dead women and children and babies were scattered.

When I saw this I wished that I had died too, but I was not sorry for the women and children. It was better for them to be happy in the other world, and I wanted to be there too. But before I went there I wanted to have revenge. I thought there might be a day, and we should have revenge.

After the soldiers marched away, I heard from my friend, Dog Chief, how the trouble started, and he was right there by Yellow Bird when it happened. This is the way it was:

In the morning the soldiers began to take all the guns away from the Big Foots, who were camped in the flat below the little hill where the monument and burying ground are now. The people had stacked most of their guns, and even their knives, by the tepee where Big Foot was lying sick. Soldiers were on the little hill and all around, and there were soldiers across the dry gulch to the south and over east along Wounded Knee Creek too. The people were nearly surrounded, and the wagon-guns were pointing at them.

Some had not yet given up their guns, and so the soldiers were searching all the tepees, throwing things around and poking into everything. There was a man called Yellow Bird, and he and another man were standing in front of the tepee where Big Foot was lying sick. They had white sheets around and over them, with eye-holes to look through, and they had guns under these. An officer came to search them. He took the other man's gun, and then started to take Yellow Bird's. But Yellow Bird would not let go. He wrestled with the officer, and while they were wrestling, the gun went off and killed the officer. Wasichus and some others have said he meant to do this, but Dog Chief was standing right there, and he told me it was not so. As soon as the gun went off, Dog Chief told me, an officer shot and killed Big Foot who was lying sick inside the tepee.

Then suddenly nobody knew what was happening, except that the soldiers were all shooting and the wagon-guns began going off right in among the people.

Many were shot down right there. The women and children ran into the gulch and up west, dropping all the time, for the soldiers shot them as they ran. There were only about a hundred warriors and there were nearly five hundred soldiers. The warriors rushed to where they had piled their guns and knives. They fought soldiers with only their hands until they got their guns.

Dog Chief saw Yellow Bird run into a tepee with his gun, and from there he killed soldiers until the tepee caught fire. Then he died full of bullets.

It was a good winter day when all this happened. The sun was shining. But after the soldiers marched away from their dirty work, a heavy snow began to fall. The wind came up in the night. There was a big blizzard, and it grew very cold. The snow drifted deep in the crooked gulch, and it was one long grave of butchered women and children and babies, who had never done any harm and were only trying to run away.

Why the Island Hill Was Sacred

"I did not know it then, for I was young," the old man began after a prolonged meditative silence. "All that time the sacred hoop was breaking, but I did not know. Red Cloud's people were calling us the wild Lakota, because we would not eat Wasichu food and went on living in the sacred manner. The hoop was smaller, but our country looked the same. Only what we heard was different, but the words had travelled far; and when we looked around us, the prairie and the hills were there and the round sky above them. The morning star did not forget to come. The sun measured the days and the moon the seasons. The creeks and rivers ran, the wind blew, the snow came, the rain brought forth the young grass for the bison and the elk and the deer. And Wakon Tonka heard on any hill.

"But we were living on a big island, and the Wasichus were like great waters washing all around it, nibbling off the edges, and it was getting smaller, smaller, smaller. It is very small now. The people have lost the sacred hoop, the good red road, the flowering tree. We young men heard the others talk about Wasichus killing bison along Shell River where the iron road had cut the herd in two; and beyond that, farther towards where you are always facing, the land stank with bison rotting. I heard them say Wasichus killed the bison for their tongues, so many that no man could ever count them. Our old men remembered Wooden Cup and what he saw and said before our grandfathers were born. But I was young. Sometime we would get together and kill all the Wasichus. We were young and we would do great deeds and make a story for our grandchildren, and for theirs, and theirs.

"I think I was maybe seventeen winters old when I heard about horseback soldiers with their wagons in Pa Sapa,[1] and Long Hair[2] was their chief. That was the first time I heard his name. Maybe I helped to kill him two grasses after that, for I was fighting on the hill where he died; but I never saw him. I think if our people had been living in one hoop, he and all his soldiers would have died in Pa Sapa that time. Maybe that would have been better. I do not know.

"It was our land and it was *wakon*;[3] for it was promised to us in a vision so long ago that the fire and the bow were new to our fathers then, and the sacred pipe had not yet been given to us.

"I will tell you what I heard the old men tell about Pa Sapa, and they heard it from old men, and they from others; and no one knows how long ago it was. The people were living then in land that is many, many sleeps yonder [pointing south-east]. Towards where you are always facing, there was a great water.[4] Towards where the sun comes up, there was a great water.[5] The people had become many, and I think they were not a nation yet. All were relatives, but sons did not know their fathers, nor fathers their sons, nor brothers their sisters.

[1] The Black Hills. [2] Custer. [3] Holy. [4] Gulf of Mexico. [5] The Atlantic.

These people ate small animals and birds that they could kill with rocks or maybe slingshots, and also roots and berries that they could find. Their knives were only sharp pieces of rock or shells; and all they ate was raw, because they had no fire.

"But there was a man among the people, and his name, they say, was Moves Walking, the same as with our friend who ate with us. I think he must have been the first *wichasha wakon,* for one day he had a vision of the sun, and what the vision taught him, he showed to all the people. He could bring fire down from the sun, and this he did with the soap-weed as he had seen it in the vision. The root of this plant was like hair, and when it was rotten and dry it was very soft. So he put some of this on some hard dry wood. Then he took a dry stem of this weed and made it square. The end he made pointed and round, and this he pressed down through the soft stuff against the wood. When he had made it whirl between his hands awhile, the sun gave him fire, as he had seen it in his vision. This was a wonderful thing, and after that the people could begin to be a nation.

"But they were not ready yet, for they were weaker and slower than the big animals. So another man came up among the people, and they say his name was Wakina Luta.[6] I think he must have been the second *wichasha wakon,* for one day when he was out hunting in the woods all alone, he got lost. And when he had walked

[6]Red Thunder.

and walked and could not find the way back, and was so tired he could hardly walk any more, there came a great storm of wind and thunder. So he crawled in under a rock. There was no rain. Just wind and big thunders. And there under the rock he went to sleep. All at once as he slept, there were great voices calling, and they say it was the Thunder Beings that he heard. Theirs is the power to make live and to destroy, for theirs are the bow and the cup of water; and they live in the quarter where the sun goes down. And the great voices said, 'Arise, Wakina Luta, and come with us. We are taking you to where there will be a great decision, and by it the people shall live or they shall die.' So in his dream Red Thunder arose and followed the voices flying very fast, until he came to a far place that was called the Island Hill; for it was a great hill of many hills, standing high in the centre of the hoop of the world. Therein all animals lived with the birds, and the grass was green in the valleys, and the trees on the slopes were many beyond counting, and tall. Clear, cold streams were running and leaping and sing-ing. All flowers were living there of many colours, and among them happy deer made fat and were not afraid. It was more beautiful than any land Red Thunder ever saw before; and while he looked at it from above where he was floating, the voices of the Thunder Beings came again, and they said, 'Here shall be the great decision; look about you.' And when Red Thunder looked, he saw the hoop of the world all about him, and at the centre was the Island Hill. And he saw that all the four-leggeds of the earth were gathered on one side, and on the other all the wings of the air, who are two-leggeds like us. They were all waiting for something. Then the thunder voices spoke again and said, 'These that you see shall race around the hoop of the world. If the four-leggeds win, they will eat you and the wings of the air. If the two-leggeds win, your people shall live; the children of your children's children's children shall possess this land; and the four-leggeds shall feed you.'

"Then the race began. The magpie, who knows everything, had a plan; so he flew down and sat on the ear of a bison bull and there he rode and waited. It was a long race, for the hoop of the world is great. Sometimes a big wind came, so that the wings of the air could hardly fly, and the four-leggeds were far ahead. Sometimes there would be a very hot day, and the four-leggeds could hardly run, so that the wings would be winning. A great rainstorm came roaring and many wings of the air were killed. But still the race went on, and all the while the magpie sat on the running bison's ear and waited for something. Nobody knows how long they raced, but it was long. Then one day they were getting near the end. The four-leggeds were ahead, and they began to cheer. All the kinds of four-leggeds were making the noises that they knew, howling and roaring and screaming and barking, and growling and neighing, so that the whole sky was filled with the fearful sound, and the wide earth was afraid.

"But just before the end, the magpie, who was not tired at all, rose high into the air and came swooping down upon the goal ahead of all the others. Then the voices of the four-leggeds died away, and the wide air was full of happy wings that soared and darted, swooped and floated; and the geese cried high, and the crane; the eagles screamed, and every bird that knows a song was singing.

"Then Wakina Luta heard the voice of thunder speaking once again, and it said to him, 'Your two-legged relatives, the wings of the air, have won the race for your people. Your people shall live and possess this land and the Island Hill after many snows and grasses, and the four-leggeds shall keep and feed them.' Then to the magpie the voice of thunder spoke, 'By thinking, you have won the race for all your relatives, the two-leggeds. Hereafter, you shall wear the rainbow in your tail, and it shall be a sign of victory.' And what was said is true, for you can see it yet on every magpie. Also, it was true, as the voice said, that the people should be like the birds, their relatives; for it is like birds of prey that we fought, circling and swooping, and in the beauty of the birds we dressed ourselves for battle and for death.

"For a while the world was still, until the voice of thunder filled it once again, and to Wakina Luta in his vision it was speaking: 'Your people still are weaker and slower than the big four-leggeds, so I give you this that you may be stronger than they, and their fleetness shall be slow.' And when Wakina Luta looked, it was the great bow of the Thunder Beings with a pointed arrow that was tailed for guiding as the birds are tailed for guiding to a mark. And as he looked hard to see how it was made, the bow twanged, and the arrow rose high with the whisper of wings, and swooped like a hawk or an eagle; and yonder far away a great bison bull went down with feathers sprouting from his chest.

"The thunder voice rose again, 'Behold!' And Wakina Luta in his vision saw a strange four-legged that might have been a dog, but was not, for no dog could grow so tall. It was a *shonka wakon,*[7] and as he looked and wondered, it raised its head and sent forth a high shrill voice that ran far and was like a victor singing. And the voice said, 'You shall know him after many grasses in this land, and he shall be your friend and give you fleetness.'

"Then Red Thunder awoke under his rock and the world was still. So, with the vision living in him, he found his way back to the people; and all that he had seen, he told. Also he made a bow like that he saw and a feathered arrow; and he showed the young men how to make and use them.

"After that, the old men say, another man came up among the people, and Slow Buffalo is what they called him. I think he was the third *wichasha wakon,* for what he did a vision must have taught him. One day he called all the people together, and from among them he chose the oldest and wisest to sit with him. To these he gave a name, calling them a council. And to these he told what I think a vision must have shown him, while all the people listened. He said the people had grown to be too many for that place, and now with fire and the bow they could wander and go anywhere. For the first time he gave a name to each of the quarters of the world: Where the

[7]Sacred dog, horse.

Sun Goes Down (west), Where the White Giant Lives (north), Where the Sun Comes Up (east), and Where You Are Always Facing (south). Towards the last place the people could not go, for there the great water was near, and from thence a race of strangers would come. The people should be divided into three, and each should become a nation. One would go towards Where the Sun Comes Up, one to Where the Sun Goes Down, and the last towards Where the White Giant Lives. Each as it went must name all things, and these names would be a tongue.

"Then Slow Buffalo told them about fathers and mothers, sisters and brothers, grandfathers and grandmothers. These he named for the first time. They should live together with one fire, and the fire would be holy. The old would guide the young; the young would give their strength to the old; and all together would give one strength to the nation, that it might be strong and live. The nation, he said, was itself a being with a grandfather, a grandmother, a father, and a mother. The Great Mysterious One is the grandfather, the Earth is the grandmother, the Sky is the father, and the mother is where the growing things come out of the ground and nurse with all that live. When Slow Buffalo had done this, he got together with the council and they chose leaders for the nations and called them chiefs. Each nation he divided into seven bands. Then the people started, each band with its central fire, which was holy, and its chiefs and council.

"I think the Lakotas came from those who wandered

towards the Great White Giant; and it was while they were going that a vision was sent to them. I will tell you how the old men told it. Two young men were out hunting together when they saw something coming; and when it was nearer they knew it was a young woman, very good to see, dressed in fine white buckskin, and all about her was a shining white mist. And when one of the young men saw her, he had bad thoughts of her, and this she knew. So she said to the first young hunter, 'Come, then, and do as you wish with me.' But when he came near to her, the shining mist enclosed him and became a dark cloud with lightning in it. And when the cloud was gone and the shining white mist came back, the young man's bones were scattered on the prairie. Then the young woman said to the second young hunter, 'Your thoughts are good, and to you I give this sacred thing for all the people. Behold!' It was a pipe; and while she held it out, she told the meanings that it had. The eagle feather, hanging from the bowl, meant the grandfather of all, the father of fathers, Wakon Tonka. Also it meant that the thoughts of those who smoked should rise high as the eagles do. The bison-hide upon the mouthpiece was for the grandmother of all, the mothers of mothers; and he who touched it with his lips would know that he nursed with all living things. The four thongs hanging from the stem were coloured like the quarters of the world—blue, white, red, yellow. The pipe and the morning star would stand for the power of the quarter where the sun comes up. Yonder the morning star brings light and wisdom and understanding. The pipe gives peace that comes from understanding. With the morning star and the pipe we should love each other and live together as brothers.

"I think the people forgot these things. Maybe they multiplied so fast that they got to quarrelling and split up into many new bands that grew to be strangers with different names for things, different tongues. And maybe one of these bands grew big and became our people, the Lakotas. Even then, the old men say, there was not yet any war. But once the Lakotas found one of their hunters killed and scalped by a band of these strangers. So our people were angry; and when they came upon the band that had done this thing, they cut off all the strangers' heads, so that there could be no war again. Maybe that is why the strangers used to call us cut-throats. But I think all the heads must have grown back on, for we have been fighting ever since. And after that, whatever people did not speak our tongue, we knew them for our enemies. But within the sacred hoop of our own people the ancient teaching lived and the power of the pipe was mighty.

"After these things had happened, there were many snows and grasses; I do not know how many. Then we came at last to the Island Hill that was promised long ago, and it was a sacred place. Because the pines upon it made it black a long way off, we called it Pa Sapa;[8] and all the land around it was ours.

"Farther on towards where the sun goes down, there

[8]Black heads, the Black Hills.

was a people that we called the Shyela.[9] It was they who found the *shonka wakon*[10] first. They were hunting from where they lived towards where you are always facing, and in a valley by a spring there stood this strange four-legged with long hair upon its neck and tail. It was living wild, but it was tame. At first the hunters were afraid, but after there was a council to talk about it some hunters were sent to catch it, and this they did with lariats of hide. And after some moons, this *shonka wakon* had a young one. Then one day when it was making a high shrill noise, another *shonka wakon* came, and this one was a stallion. So after that the Shyela had horses, and the Lakota traded for them, giving bows and arrows and beaded moccasins and clothing. The Arapahoes also found many horses and with them too the Lakota traded; and these peoples and the Lakota were friends after that, although their tongues were not the same. The old men said it was from the Wasichus who were towards where you are always facing[11] that the first horses ran away, and that is why they were so tame at first.

"So we had come at last to the Island Hill as the vision had foretold, and the land around it was ours and it was holy. There we lived in the sacred hoop with the sacred fire and the pipe; and the bow and the *shonka wakon* made us mighty.

"But when I was about seventeen winters old, a long dust of horseback soldiers with their wagons came down upon Pa Sapa, and I heard their chief was Long Hair.

[9]Cheyenne. [10]Sacred dog, horse. [11]Spaniards.

They came to look and went away; but they had seen the yellow metal[12] that makes Wasichus crazy; and I think the whole Wasichu nation heard about it. So when the young grass came again and died, big trouble started."

[12]Gold.

Going on Vision Quest

After putting a chunk of cottonwood in the sheet-iron stove, I sat waiting for the old man to emerge from a reverie that he seemed to be inducing with faint, dream-like tones from his eagle-bone whistle. Finally, as he had given no indication of emerging, I broke the silence: "Are you sure now that the great voice was not scolding you?"

He peered squintingly at me for a while, and said: "I am very old, and I have learned so many things that I do not know much any more. Maybe I was wiser before my ears were troubled with so many forked words.

"In the old days, it was from the seven tepees and the seven council fires that our teaching came. It was older than the oldest grandfather could remember his grandfather telling him; and more and more grandfathers before that until it was old as hills, old as stars.

"The wisdom of the teaching was from vision and the vision was from Wakon Tonka: The people could not do anything right unless the Great Mysterious One helped them; and for this they prayed and made sacred songs and dances, and had a sacred way for doing everything. When a boy was just beginning to be a man, he had to go on vision quest; for what he saw would show him the good road and give him power, so that his life might be a story good to tell. I was thinking of my vision when you bothered me."

He was silent again while he filled his pipe and lit it. Then, drawing hollow-cheeked upon the stem, he smoked awhile and brooded in the little cloud he made.

"*Dho!*" he said at length, uttering with explosive force the syllable of emphasis on something said or thought. "*Dho!*" Passing the pipe to me, he resumed aloud the tenor of his brooding. "It is so! Are the people good, and do they get along together any more? The hoop is broken and the people have forgotten. There is no voice on any hill to tell them, and they have no ears to hear.

"The hoop was breaking even then when I was happy and a boy; but then I did not know it, for the world was still as big as day, and Wakon Tonka could be found on any hill, and something wonderful could happen.

"After the Attacking of the Wagons the soldiers went away and our warriors burned their towns. And when the grass was new again there was a treaty with the Father in Washington. He said our land would be ours and no Wasichu could ever come there. You can see his tongue was forked. Red Cloud was not with us any more. The Great Father made an Agency for him on the North Platte. And that was bad; for many of our people went down there to eat Wasichu food, and take the many presents the Great Father gave them. And these they traded for the *minne sheetsha*[1] that made them crazy, so that they forgot the Mother of all and the bison and the sacred hoop.

"But our Bad Face band that had been Red Cloud's people would not go. Big Road was with us, and Little Hawk and Black Twin. Also Crazy Horse was ours; and now I see that he was greatest of them all. Sometimes some of our young men would go down there to get new guns and lead and powder, and what they told, the people talked and talked about it, and some of it I heard; but it was like a story. I think there were fifty lodges of us, and we lived the old way in the bison country of the Tongue and the Powder and the Rosebud; and with us were the Miniconjous and the Sans Arcs. I remember how they said the loafers and Wasichus at the Agency made fun of us and called us the wild Lakota; but they were the foolish ones. The hoop we lived in had grown smaller, but it was not broken yet, and the voices of the seven tepees were not still.

"I was getting stronger fast and I think it was about the time when Red Cloud made the treaty that I got my first calf. The treaty was just something people said, a little thing a long way off that maybe was not so; but the calf was very big. I gave the meat to old people, and they praised me, so that my grandmother and my grandfather and my mother were proud of me.

[1] Bad water, whiskey.

"There were more snows and grasses and I was getting tall when I heard Looks Twice telling my mother about Red Cloud's long journey to see the Great Father and of the strange things that he saw in the world of the Wasichus where the sun comes from. Looks Twice was my father then, and my grandparents did not live with us, but he took care of them, and he was good to me and taught me many things about hunting and war.

"What he told about Red Cloud was like an *ohunka* story the old folk tell only at night, and it is wonderful to stay awake and listen, but only little children must believe it. There were so many Wasichu towns yonder where the Great Father lived and the sun comes from that they could not be counted; and so big they were that a horseback could ride and ride and always stay in the town. And in those towns the Wasichus were as many as the bison when they follow the grass all together. And the tepees were made of stone, tepee on top of tepee, so that if you would see the top, you must look far up and then look again, and sometimes after that, again. And there was more and more about the great medicine power of the Wasichus. There were big iron horses breathing smoke and fire, and there was a gun so long and heavy that maybe a hundred men could not lift it, and when it shot, there was a great thunder cloud full of lightning, and the whole sky was full of thunder. And the story got bigger, the more it was told; for on the other side of a great water that was like all the prairie without grass, there were more and more Wasichus, more and more towns of stone.

"I could look around and see the world was just as it always was. Maybe Red Cloud was getting to be a Wasichu with a forked tongue like all the others. People said he had worn Wasichu clothes yonder and looked foolish. He was not ours any more and we did not like him.

"I think I was about thirteen winters old, and I was a big boy. You can see that I was tall before so many snows bent me down, and then I was almost a man. I could swim farther under water than most boys, and when we played throwing-them-off-their-horses, only an older boy could throw me off. I liked to fight, and I wanted to go to war; but Looks Twice, who was my second father, said I would be ready after another snow and that I ought to go on vision quest first. It made me feel bad when he went with a war party against the Shoshonis and told me to stay at home and look after the horses. And I felt worse when he came back with a scalp on his coup-stick and some more good horses. He always took me hunting with him, and I could kill a cow, but it was not easy for me yet, and he would come and finish killing one that was getting away from me. Sometimes he could shoot an arrow clear through a cow if the point did not strike a bone.

"Of course, I played all the games with the other boys, but we all wanted to go to war, and we would get tired playing. In the winter before the deep snow had covered the ice, we would play *chun-wachee-kyapi*.[2] We had short round pieces of wood with sharp points on them,[3] and

[2]Make-the-wood-dance. [3]Tops.

when we wrapped them with a long piece of sinew and threw them, they would spin on the ice, and we tried to break the dancing woods of the other boys by making ours dance against theirs. Or we would get tired doing that and maybe play icemark. We would fasten pieces of hard rawhide on our moccasins, then run and slide to see who could slide farthest. Or we would make little sleds with two buffalo ribs fastened together, with two feathers to guide them; and these we would throw on the ice to see whose would go farthest. We called this *huta-nachuta,* but I never knew why. Then maybe if we got tired doing that we would have a war, dividing up and fighting with blunt arrows; or maybe we would put mud balls on willow sticks and throw them at each other. Sometimes we would have very hard fights, and boys would get hurt; but they did not care.

"There was another game that showed how brave we were. It could be played with dry sunflower seeds or pieces of dry rotten wood that would keep on burning without a flame. A boy would hold out his hand and they would put the burning piece on the back of it. If his hand shook or he made a face or brushed the piece off, he lost the game and some other boy tried it. Sometimes when a boy was very brave this made a big sore, and he was very proud of it.

"When the snow was deep and it was very cold, it was good to lie back against the tepee wall with the wind outside sending forth a voice like a bull, and listen to the men telling stories about war and hunting and brave deeds. They would come over to eat and smoke, and sometimes they would stay so long I did not know when they went. If they got to arguing about something, I would just roll up and go to sleep; then it would be morning and they would not be there. I was hungry for the stories, but they made me want to go out and do something that would make a story with me in it.

"We had been camping on the Greasy Grass. The tender grasses had appeared and were a handbreadth high in the valley; and the tops of the hills were greening a little. Then my grandfather came over and talked about me with my new father; and they said it was time for me to seek a vision. So my new father caught a couple of his best horses—both of them young—and took them as a gift to an old *wichasha wakon*,[4] whose name was Blue Spotted Horse. When the old man had accepted the gift for what he was going to do, my father and grandfather took me over to his tepee. He could not see very well, and he was so old that he had something like new moons in his eyes. He looked at me a long while, and it made me feel queer, because I thought it might be a ghost behind me that he was seeing. Afterwhile he said: 'Let a sweat-lodge be prepared for this young man, and when he has been cleansed, bring him here, and I will teach him.'

"So there were two friends who made a sweat-lodge for me with willow boughs bent over like a cup upside down, and over this they fastened rawhide. At the opening of the lodge they set a stick with a piece of red cloth at the top for a sacred offering to the Spirit. Then they

[4]Holy Man.

heated rocks in a fire, and when they had put these in the centre of the little lodge, they poured water on them, and I had to go into the steam and close the flap tight. I felt like crying when I was in there again, because the other time was when my father went away and I saw him in my dream under the scaffold. Afterwhile they told me to come out. Then they rubbed me with sacred sage until I was dry and felt good all over. After that they gave me a buffalo robe to put around me and took me back to Blue Spotted Horse, and went away.

"I felt queer again and a little scared while I sat there all alone with the old man in his tepee, and maybe a ghost behind me that he was seeing. When he had looked at me that way for a long time and I wanted to get up and run away, he said: 'This is a sacred thing you are doing, and if the heart is not good something very bad will happen. But do not be afraid, for I have seen into your heart. Already you have fed old people, and you want to be a man they all praise. While you were in the sweat-lodge your father came to me, and he will help you on the hill. So do not be afraid, and I will teach you.'

"Then he filled a pipe and lit it; and after he had presented the stem to the four quarters of the world and the Great Mysterious One above and Maka, the mother earth, he held the stem to me and I touched it with my mouth. When I did that, I could feel a power running all through me and up my backbone into my hair.

"Then he taught me what I must know to go on vision quest. I did not learn it all then, but I heard it again when I was older, and this is what he told me.

"There is a great hoop; and so big it is that everything is in it, for it is the hoop of the universe, and all that live in it are relatives. When you stand on a high hill and look all around, you can see its shape and know that it is so. This hoop has four quarters, and each is sacred, for each has a mysterious power of its own, and it is by those powers that we live. Also each quarter has its sacred objects and a colour, and these stand for its power.

"First is the place where the sun goes down. Its colour is blue like the thunder clouds, and it has the power to make live and to destroy. The bow is for the lightning that destroys, and the wood cup is for the rain that makes live.

"Next is the place where the great white giant lives, and its colour is white like the snows. It has the power of healing, for thence come the cleansing winds of the winter. The white wing of the goose stands for that wind of cleansing and a sacred white herb for the healing.

"Next is the place whence comes the light, where all the days of men are born; and its colour is red like the sunrise. It has the power of wisdom and the power of peace. The morning star stands for wisdom, for it brings the light that we may see and understand; and the pipe is for the peace that understanding gives.

"Next is the place of summer, and the colour of it is yellow like the sun. Thence comes the power to grow and flourish. The sacred staff of six branches is for the power to grow, and the little hoop is for the life of the people who flourish as one.

"Then at the place whence comes the power to grow, a

road begins, the good red road of spirit that all men should know; and it runs straight across the hoop of the world to the place whence comes the power of cleansing and healing, to the place of white hairs and the cold and the cleansing of old age.

"And then there is a second road, the hard black road of difficulties that all men must travel. It begins at the place whence come the days of men, and it runs straight across the hoop of this world to the place where the sun goes down and all the days of men have gone and all their days shall go; far beyond is the other world, the world of spirit. It is a hard road to travel, a road of trouble and need. But where this black road of difficulties crosses the good red road of spirit at the centre of the hoop of the world, that place is very holy, and there springs the Tree of Life. For those who look upon the Tree, it shall fill with leaves and bloom and singing birds; and it shall shield them as a *sheo*[5] shields her chickens.

"While Blue Spotted Horse was telling me this, he drew the hoop and the roads with his finger in the ashes by the fire, and I could see it all as from a high place, like a picture.

"Then he told me how I must pray on the hill. Always before I pray I must lift both hands high with my pipe in the right, and send forth a voice four times—'*hey-a-hey, hey-a-hey, hey-a-hey, hey-a-hey!*' First I should pray at the place where the sun goes down; then at the place whence come the cleansing and healing; next where the light

[5]Prairie hen.

comes from and the days of men begin; and after that where lives the power to grow; and I should ask each power in turn to help me.

"Then I must walk the red road of spirit to the centre of the hoop of the world, and there I must present my pipe and pray for help to Wakon Tonka. And when I have done this, I must remember the ground, the mother of all, who has shown mercy to her children; I must lean low and present my pipe to Maka, the earth, the only mother, and ask her to help me; for my body is hers, and I am her son.

"When I have done all this, I have only begun; for after I have rested awhile, I must do it all over again. I must walk the black road to the sundown and pray; then back to the holiest place in the centre; then up the red road to the quarter of cleansing, and pray; then back again to the centre and over the black road to the light and the beginning of days. I must pray there, and return; and last, I must walk the red road to the place where lives the power to grow. And when I have returned to the holiest place at the centre and prayed, I can rest awhile and think hard about what I am doing.

"I cannot eat anything while I am on the hill, but I can have some water; and I must stay awake as long as I am able. Afterwhile I shall be crying, but I must keep on, for that is when the praying begins to have power.

"Then Blue Spotted Horse taught me a prayer that I must offer to Wakon Tonka at the centre of the hoop, and I said it after him six times. There is great power in that prayer, and I could feel it even then when I was a boy.

Maybe you will learn it, Grandson, Wasichu though you are, and it will help you to find the good red road and to do what you must do in this world. But when I had said it six times, all at once I was afraid; for what would happen if I could not remember it all!

"I did not say anything about this, but Blue Spotted Horse looked hard at me awhile; and then he smiled, just like my own grandfather, and he said: 'Do not be afraid, Grandson, for Wakon Tonka will remember all that you forget. There is one, there is no other, and all things are in Wakon Tonka. The powers are only the ways the one makes all things live. Take this pipe; hold fast to it and never let it go, for on this will you depend. Now you will go forth to the hill, and do as I have taught you. I will be with you there unseen; and when your prayers are heard, I will send the friends to bring you here. To me alone the vision shall be told.'

"He looked so kind when I took the pipe that I was not afraid of him at all. So I said: '*Palamo yelo, tonka schla*—thank you, Grandfather.' And as I got up and went forth into the slanting day I felt lighter on my feet than I had ever felt before."

"Hold Fast; There Is More!"

"*Dho!*" said Eagle Voice musingly, as he came slowly out of his inner solitude, "I felt queer and light when I left the *wakon's* tepee, and wherever I looked there was a strangeness like dreaming; and the sun was getting low.

"The two friends were waiting there with a sorrel horse all saddled and painted in a sacred manner for me. On his forehead was a thin new moon, because he was facing the world of spirit where the new moons lead; on his rump was the morning star to shine from behind me upon the dark road ahead; on his left flank was the sacred hoop; and on his right flank was the white wing of the goose.

"The friends did not say anything. They just took hold of me and set me in the saddle; and then we started for the hill of vision. The one who walked ahead to show the way was carrying the offerings for where the sun goes down—the bow and wooden cup—and for the place of cleansing—the white wing and the herb. The other walked behind me with a morning star made of rawhide for where the light and the days of men are born; the hoop and staff for where the growing power lives. I held the pipe; and I was holding it very tight with both hands in front of me, for on that I must depend. It was a sacred, fearful thing that I was doing, and although my legs were getting long there was still a little boy inside me. I did not look where we were going. I just looked hard at the pipe, and held it tight. There were four painted strips of skin hanging from the stem, blue, white, red, and yellow for the quarters and the powers. Also from the stem a long wing feather of an eagle hung, and that was for the Great Mysterious One. Last, upon the mouthpiece was the bison hide, and that was for the breast of Maka where all that live, with legs or wings or roots or fins, are little children nursing. I did not understand it all till I was older, but I could feel the power of the pipe.

"The sun was shining bright and level across the world, getting ready to go under, when we came to the hill standing high and alone, with shadows gathered around it like a blanket and the last of day upon its head. I felt an aching in my breast, for it was like the time we took my father to the scaffold on the hill.

"When we came to the top I could see that the friends had prepared the place for me. It was flat, and they had dug a hole there as deep as to my waist, and round about it sacred sage was scattered. Then, with the hole for centre, they had made a circle, maybe fifteen steps across, and at each quarter a stick was set, each with the proper colour on it—blue, white, red, yellow. There were strips of painted rawhide for the black road and the red; and where these crossed at the holiest place in the centre the two friends put me down. Then when they had placed the offerings at the proper quarters, they left a skin-bag full of water, and went away down the hill leading the horse. They did not say anything to me, and they did not look back. It was the way they would have done if I were dead up there and lying on a scaffold.

"With my robe about my shoulders, I stood in the hole up to my hips, holding the pipe in front of me. I watched the round red sun slip under. A thin new moon appeared low down and like a ghost. It looked lost and lonely yonder going to the spirit world. Some wolves mourned. I remembered I had heard the criers calling to the people that the village would move next day. The stars got brighter. The night was big and empty when the wolves were still. The thin new moon touched the edge of the world and sank. All at once I wanted to get out of the hole and run and run back to my people before they went away. Then I remembered my pipe. I must hold fast to it. On it must I depend. So I held it as tight as I could, and right away I could feel the power running all through me again, up my back and into my hair. I remembered the *wakon* said he would be with me, and that my father would help me on the hill. I could almost hear him saying, 'Never be afraid of anything.'

"Then all at once everything was different, and I felt like praying. So I threw back my robe and started naked for the quarter of the sunset where the bow and cup were hanging; and as I went, the world was a great shining bubble and in the midst of it the pipe and I were floating. At the blue quarter I raised both hands with the pipe in my right and cried out to the power that makes live and destroys, the power of the rain and the lightning. Four times I cried, '*hey-a-hey*'. Between the cries I waited and listened, but it was so far out yonder that no voice came back. And when I cried, 'Lean close and hear and help me,' there was nothing.

"I walked backward to the centre and waited there awhile with my face to the white quarter, where the goose's wing and the white herb hung. Then I went there, and, as before, I raised my hands and the pipe, crying out four times and asking the power of cleansing and healing to hear and help me. But the world was a big, empty bubble, and no voice came back. At the red quarter of the morning star and the sunrise, where the light is born and the days of men begin, I cried out four times and asked for help; but there was nothing. At the yellow quarter, where the sacred hoop and tree were set, I called upon the growing power for help. The voice I sent forth went far, so far it could never return, and there was stillness. When I stood in the hole at the most sacred place in the centre and raised my face and my hands and the pipe, and prayed the prayer Blue Spotted Horse had taught me, there was nothing. And there was nothing when I leaned my face and my hands and the pipe on Maka's breast and asked the mother of all to help me.

"I prayed around the hoop again and again, but still there was nothing. So I stood in the hole for a while and thought hard about what I was doing. It was not easy to find a vision, and I must try and try until I found it—like getting the first deer or the first bison calf, only harder, maybe. Pretty soon I was not thinking about the vision at all. I was in the brush by the water-hole and the deer was coming down with the fawn to drink. The cow was chasing Whirlwind and me up the hillside. I was coming into the camp with the haunch of the fawn on my shoulder. My grandmother was jumping up and down crying,

'Oh, see the vision our grandson has brought us!' Only it was not my grandmother, but the *wakon* looking that queer way at me. 'If the heart is not good something very bad will happen.'

"My head jerked, and at first I did not know where I was. Then I remembered my pipe and held it tight and began my praying all over again. I did that all night long, advancing to each of the quarters in turn and back to the centre. I did not rest long there, because I had to stay awake as long as I was able. I got so tired and sleepy that sometimes I would forget what I was saying; then I would remember the old *wakon's* eyes with the new moons upside down in them and the queer look, and then I would hold my pipe as tight as I could, and go ahead. Sometimes the coyotes would mock me when I waited and listened between cries, but that is all there was.

"The night was like always, until all at once there was the morning star out yonder and a pale streak of day beneath it. It was looking at me the way it did when I 'woke beside my father's scaffold. I remembered how I tried to hold him fast in the dream, but he melted away and the buffalo-runner too.

"When I got back to the centre that time I was crying a little, and when I put my hands and my pipe and my face on Maka's breast and asked for help, I cried harder, because I was sad for my father, and the grass on my face was soft like my own mother's breast when I was little.

"When I looked again the sun was shining. Something

was happening way off yonder. There was a big whirling cloud of dust, and things were flying around in it. Then I saw that the cloud was full of coup-sticks with scalps on them, and they were flying about in the cloud and the cloud was the whirling dust of many hoofs in a battle.

"I looked until it was not there anymore. Then there was a voice above and behind me that said, 'Hold fast to your pipe, for there is more.' When I turned to see whose voice that was, it was an eagle soaring low and looking back at me until it was not there.

"The sun was shining almost level. I had gone to sleep kneeling in the hole with my face and hands on the grass, and I thought it was still morning. But the blue stick, with the bow and cup, was where the red stick should be! The sun was shining low out of the blue quarter, and it was getting ready to go under! I had slept dead all day, and it made me feel good; but there were teeth in my belly, I was so hungry; for I had not eaten the day before.

"I filled up on the warm water in the skin and thought about what I had seen. Maybe all those coup-sticks and scalps meant I would be a great warrior. But if they meant that, what more could there be, and what did the eagle mean?

"I began to pray again as soon as the sun went under and the thin moon appeared going to the spirit land. I prayed harder than ever because of what the eagle said, and I could feel power getting stronger and stronger in me every time I came back to the centre. When I advanced to the quarters, it was like floating with the pipe in the midst of a great starry bubble. And afterwhile, whenever I began to say the prayer to Wakon Tonka at the most sacred place, the prayer the *wakon* taught me, it made me cry. And this is the prayer:

" 'Grandfather, Great Mysterious One! You have been always, and before you nothing has been. There is nothing to pray to but you. The star nations all over the heavens are yours, and yours are the grasses of the earth. You are older than all need, older than all pain and prayer. Day in, day out, you are the life of things.

" 'Grandfather, all over the world the faces of living ones are alike. In tenderness have they come up out of the ground. Look upon your children, with children in their arms, that they may face the winds and walk the good road to the day of quiet.

" 'Teach me to walk the soft earth, a relative to all that live. Give me the strength to understand and the eyes to see. Help me, for without you I am nothing.'[1]

"That is the prayer, Grandson. Maybe it will help you, Wasichu though you are, to walk the black road and to find the flowering tree.

"The lean moon was gone and the night must have been getting old when a great sudden voice roared from the quarter of the sundown where I was facing. I had not seen it coming; but all at once it was there—a heaped-up cloud coming fast towards me, with swift blue lightning on its front and giants shouting in it. And in between the shouts

---

[1] This prayer was given to me by my old friend and teacher, Black Elk, the Oglala Sioux holy man. Much of the vision also came from him.

that shook the hill I could hear the deep voices of the rain singing all together, like many warriors charging.

"I was not afraid. I felt very big and strong, and I cried back to the thunder beings as loud as I could, '*hey-a-hey, hey-a-hey*,' and they answered. Then the lightning and the voices were all about me, so that I could not hear the cries I sent forth, and the rain was a roaring between thunders. I stood there, holding my pipe high in both hands, but not a drop of rain touched me. And when the swift storm had passed and the stars were bright again, I could hear the giant voices cheering far away.

"I knew my praying had been heard and I would see. The power was mighty in me as I prayed around the hoop and back to the most sacred place at the centre.

"I was standing in the hole with my face and hands and pipe raised to the Great Mysterious One, and I was crying hard while I prayed, but I was happy and my heart sang. I was saying, 'All over the world the faces of living ones are alike.' But all at once I was not saying; I was seeing!

"I was standing on the highest hill in the centre of the world. There was no sun, but so clear was the light that what was far was near. The circle of the world was a great hoop with the two roads crossing where I stood, the black one and the red. And all around the hoop more peoples than I could count were sitting together in a sacred manner. The smokes of all the peoples' little fires stood tall and straight and still around the circle; and by the murmur of the voices of the peoples, they were happy. And while I looked and wondered, there was a tree that sprang at my feet from where the two roads crossed. It grew so fast that, while I watched, it reached the sky and spread, filling the heavens with blooms and singing leaves.

"Then I felt dizzy, and all at once I was sitting in the hole with my head on the grassy edge of it. When I looked about me, the circle of the world was empty and the sun was high above. While I sat there looking around me at the empty world, I felt homesick for what I had seen without my eyes, and there was an aching in my breast.

"Afterwhile I knew I was very hungry and thirsty. So I filled myself with water from the skin; and when I looked around me again, far off down a valley I could see the friends returning with the horse."

The old man fell into one of his prolonged silences which I finally broke with a question: "And the *wakon*? What did he say when you told him?"

"I was alone with him in his tepee," Eagle Voice replied, "and a little fire made the light. He looked hard at me for a long time when I had spoken, then he said: 'You have seen in a sacred manner and your praying has come alive. By the lightning and the thunder and the rain that fell upon you, the power to make live and to destroy will protect you to the end of the black road, and the road will be long. You shall breathe the dust of battles, counting many coups, and shall not be hurt. You shall travel far and see strange peoples; but the sacred hoop of all the peoples under the flowering tree, you shall not see by the light of the sun. It was your father talking through the eagle. Hold fast to the vision Wakon Tonka has sent you, and pray for the strength to understand it. *Hetchetu aloh!*'

"Then he waved his hand, and I went out into the low day. I was very hungry."

All Is But a Beginning *and* Patterns and Coincidences

At ninety, John Neihardt finally began to write his memoirs.
All Is But a Beginning, *covering his early years, appeared in*
1972. I include here a humorous chapter, "The Battle of Wis-
ner," and one that has caused much comment, "Four Things
Are Good."

My father had intended to record more memories, as well as
vignettes of many famous people he had known. He partially
achieved that plan in Patterns and Coincidences, *which was*
published posthumously in 1978. "The Passing of the Gods,"
one of my favorite pieces, opens with an allusion to my father's
burning of his first book of poetry, The Divine Enchantment.
Its particular value as background material prompted the inclu-
sion also of "Back Home in Bancroft." In that chapter my father
describes adventures that followed his brief stint as a reporter for
the Omaha Daily News.

The following selections are from *All Is But a Beginning: Youth Remem-*
bered, 1881–1901 (New York: Harcourt Brace Jovanovich, 1972; re-
printed Lincoln: University of Nebraska Press, 1986) and *Patterns and*
Coincidences: A sequel to "All Is But a Beginning" (Columbia: University
of Missouri Press, 1978).

The Battle of Wisner

Having procured a school to teach and completed preparations for the Grand Venture, John and I thought it proper to have a bit of recreation before leaving home.

Wisner, the center of a German community some twenty miles south of us, was about to have a rip-roaring Fourth of July celebration, according to posters scattered liberally about the country. And there we went with our borrowed horse and buggy.

It was a considerable distance from anywhere to yonder in those leisurely days when most roads were still in their rutted infancy and horsepower was still a function of horses. Also, the way would steadily lengthen with the ascension of the midsummer sun. Considering our walk-awhile, jog-awhile progress and the need for frequent pauses, with an occasional friendly drink at a roadside windmill, we'd need plenty of time for the journey. So we were up and rolling in the still, cool white of daybreak.

When we arrived, the hitching racks had begun to fill up, except along two principal business blocks of Main Street, reserved for festivities and featured events. Wagons were being parked in vacant lots and on side streets with unharnessed teams tied to the wheels and the wagon beds packed with hay.

As it seems now, there was a bodeful spell of expectancy over the town, as though it were getting set for some big effort. Our country was head over heels in the

war with Spain—our first war since Appomattox. The
Fourth fell on a Monday, and all day Sunday there had
been rumors about a great battle then thought to be in
progress between the American and Spanish fleets off
Santiago Bay. Everything was said and denied. The gath-
ering of news at the source was difficult and slow, and
there was no radio as yet. What reports leaked through
the telegraph instruments were garbled and fragmentary.
For a time it was believed that our fleet had been de-
stroyed and Admiral Cervera's invincible armada was
steaming toward our defenseless Atlantic seaboard cities.
But Santiago Bay was far away, the rumors were contra-
dictory; so the celebration would go on as planned.

The half dozen or more saloons, faithful indicators of
the social weather, were serving the casual drift of cus-
tomers. Occasionally a roistering group, making the
suds circuit of the village, might noisily breast a bar,
demanding a round of foaming tankards for all and sun-
dry. But as yet no soulful tenor had recalled "darling
Clementine," and no inspired statesman had viewed the
world situation with oratorical alarm. The veteran stein
brigades had not yet come into action; and the celebra-
tion was still an orgy of lemonade and innocence, with
wholesome fun for all the family.

To fill the time of waiting for the picnic dinner and the
great speech of the day, some of the lesser attractions, as
advertised, were being put on; the foot race of grand-
mothers, for instance. Old Grandma Copple won it in a
breeze, of course. Copples had a habit of winning their

foot races. It was in the blood. And, indeed, one of them was the fastest 220-yard man in the world. Now and then the brass band struck up encouragingly, and when it ceased with a brazen clash, the milling populace cheered raggedly. Then once again the chatter and bang of the importunate firecrackers took over in the growing swelter.

The prodigiously strong man, all bulge and brag, had offered his cool one hundred dollars ("Walk right up, folks, and count it yourselves") to any man who could stay a short three minutes in the wrestling ring with him. There were no takers, although the popular demand for the local Samson (an elephantine bartender with a falsetto voice) was clamorous and persistent.

"Take the piker, Lester!"

"Aw, come on, Lester! We're all backing you!"

"Show him up, Lester, the big slob!"

The potato race and sack derby had been run. The greased pig had finally been caught with much rough tumbling and shrill hilarity. Now the people began to drift toward the city park and trickle into the shady grove where the free picnic dinner was about to be served. Two fat steers had been barbecued over glowing logs in a pit, and there were roasted piglets for a side dish, together with all the extras and trimmings furnished by the ladies of the town.

A dripping ice wagon with a cargo of block ice and pony kegs pulled up into the shade of a spreading maple and prepared to fill tin pails at a dime apiece, pail size optional. This convivial activity was once known as "rushing the growler," and was in special favor for family groups and friendly circles.

There was a notable increase in the service after the arrival of the wagon. Meat carvers, bread slicers, sandwich makers sweated and toiled manfully, keeping the tray-bearing waiters supplied with heaped-up food for the hungry multitudes.

The hen-coop medley of tangled voices, peculiar to the feeding of any human assemblage, slowly softened into a low murmur of gastric satisfaction.

And at last it was time for the speech of the day. Firecrackers impudently loudened in the hush that fell upon the crowd as the Reverend Hiram Saunders, minister of the First Baptist Church and speaker of the day, mounted the plank platform in company with the Mayor and other local dignitaries.

No doubt the Reverend Saunders had been chosen partly for his reputation as an eloquent orator, but more for his moral and spiritual stature. Notably pious, full of good works, and a faithful servant of the Lord, his words and presence, it was thought, would tend to raise the patriotic festival to a loftier level than it had ordinarily reached in the recent past.

After a powerful invocation, which gave Providence a thorough briefing on human needs and frailties, the reverend launched forth into his oration. He began with a review of our involvement with Spain, reaching a dramatic climax in the blowing up of our battleship, the

Maine, in Havana Harbor on February fifth. Thereafter he developed his theme with mounting eloquence and dramatic power until he was dealing with nothing less than the immemorial duel between Jehovah and Satan, the endless struggle between Good and Evil (we being definitely on the side of the angels).

Finally it began to become evident that he was approaching his peroration; and indeed it was not too soon, for his voice had begun to hoarsen and crack from the outdoor straining to be heard and he was sweating profusely.

We friends and fellow Americans, he observed, were assembled there at a solemn moment in the long lists of time. A great principle was at stake. We were being weighed in the balance, and must not be found wanting. Surely it was the hour for serious soul searchings, and, verily, if we proved worthy, the God of Battles would be with us; and who then could prevail against us? Our noble boys had already flocked to the dear old flag, joining the great crusade to fight and, if need be, to die for all of high and holy.

The reverend had reached a stage of calisthenic fury. Waving his arms aloft, he shouted, "We shall triumph, for our cause, it is just. We will sweep the perfidious Spaniards out of the Western Hemisphere! We will drive the dastards into the sea!"

A sudden hush of astonishment closed over the hoarse cry.

Wh—a—t?

Did he really say it—the old fighting word we commonly spelled with a *b*? It was unthinkable but it was unmistakable!

Had one been observing the crowd from aloft, no doubt he would have noted the ripple of a shock wave spreading over the audience with the progressive realization.

Some wag, no doubt delighted to know the reverend was a regular fellow like himself, let off a roaring guffaw, leaped to his feet, and cheered wildly. Whereat the whole audience arose with laughter and cheers that went on and on. At length the brass band got into the act with the "Stars and Stripes Forever" played in a frantic tempo.

During the pandemonium the good man stood perplexed and lonely in the speaker's place, evidently wondering *what in the world—and was he really as good as all that?*

It was midafternoon now. The dust and shouting of the pony races along Main Street had subsided. The idle crowd jostled aimlessly about, having a problematical good time just being together there in the stifling slant of the sun. Now and then the *wham* of a maul came from a striking machine where the brawny exhibited their prowess to a bevy of bystanders, mostly admiring little boys.

A spell of peace and good will had descended upon the people, still pleasantly aware of a plentiful dinner with liquid refreshment. The Ferris wheel was doing a moderate business; and the merry-go-round, close-herding its galloping horses, droned its sole tune with hypnotic monotony. Even the concessionaires cried less stridently from their booths.

The spirit of *Gemütlichkeit* was abroad among the people. In the bars a stranger was no longer strange. There a snatch of familiar song made kin of those who heard; and hairy-chested men, blowing off the foam together, embraced like long-lost brothers.

Verily, we were having a right nice quiet time that afternoon, despite the drowsing heat; and we were looking forward to the big display of fireworks that would begin in the cooling of the dusk.

Then it began to happen!

The hurdy-gurdy blare of the merry-go-round died out. The Ferris wheel slowed down to a full stop with several passengers still aloft. A full-toned voice crying through a megaphone silenced the hucksters. It was the Mayor of the town who was about to make an important announcement. The word traveled slowly until all faces were turned to where His Honor stood in a wagon bed, the focal center of a spreading hush.

Ladies and gentlemen, fellow Americans!

The telegrapher at the railroad station had just handed him the first pages of an Associated Press news story then still coming over the wire. He would read it to us as it was delivered to him.

Yesterday (Sunday, July third) the American fleet under Admirals Sampson and Schley had won a great victory off Santiago Bay, Cuba. The entire Spanish fleet under Admiral Cervera had been destroyed! The cruisers *Vizcaya* and *Marie Teresa* were beached and still burning!

Spanish casualties were extremely heavy, but only one American life had been lost! The war was practically over, and the American flag was flying over the Governor's palace in Santiago!

A roar of wild applause, wave on wave, swept over the crowd, overwhelming the voice of the Mayor. Only those near where he stood could hear what he was reading, but the gist of the continuing story was abroad and spreading.

Then, as someone later remarked, all hell broke loose! The band struck up *A Hot Time in the Old Town Tonight,* playing it over and over, and the whole crowd broke into a windstorm of song.

Truly there was going to be a hot time. It had already begun, for now kegs were being rolled out into the middle of Main Street, there to be set up and tapped for free drinks on the town. And round about them jostling, singing revelers danced gaily in the dust.

I was shouldering and dodging my way through the crowd down Main Street in search of John, whom I had lost somewhere in the excitement, when I found myself jammed into the doorway of a saloon by the surging, singing crowd. As there seemed to be no escaping suffocation either inwards or outwards, I managed to emerge upwards, like a cork in a flood. There were two spacious bay windows protruding into the street, and within one of these stood a billiard table which I mounted, seizing a billiard cue by the way as a sort of accident insurance; for it was plain that a momentous debate was getting under way just below me in the boiling press of men. It seemed to be concerned with the relative merits of the Mauser rifle, used by the Spaniards, and the Krag-Jörgensen, used by the Americans. According to a beefy German bartender, the Mauser was infinitely the better rifle, if not even more so. And look who invented it. The Germans, of course! As for that clumsy fence post, the Krag, you couldn't hit a flock of tame red barns with it once out of three at a hundred yards. Even the divinely condemned Irish could have invented a better blunderbuss!

Alas! That was no way at all, at all, to address Jimmy Conley, defender of Krags and all things anti-German, for Jimmy was Irish and belligerently proud of the fact. Of middle height, slender and lean, he hardly looked the hero of his storied brawls among his natural enemies, the "Dutch."

While I prefer not to repeat Jimmy's rejoinder, I may say that it seems to have been overharsh and repugnant to family pride. At any rate, the bartender complained loudly to the world at large that no man could speak that way about his dear old mother.

Jimmy was bellied up to the bar with a foot on the rail at the moment of crisis, and the full mug of freshly drawn beer struck him squarely in the face.

That was it!

A sudden lull fell upon the uproar as Jimmy stepped back, a white glare in his eyes and bloody beer foam on his grinning face. With a catlike spring he vaulted the bar, landing a fist on a chin as he came over the top. The man with the sainted mother and the unfortunate chin disappeared beneath a tangle of Jimmys and the next of three barmen on duty. The third escaped through the door at the end of the bar, and after him raged the defender of Irish honor.

When Jimmy emerged into the agitated crowd of the barroom, the air seemed to fill with flying fists. By now he was "fighting at both ends and in the middle," as they used to say of him in those heroic days; for what he did not do with fists and heels, he did with his butting in the belly of his foe.

It was good indeed that I had seized my vantage point upon the billiard table. I had a reserved front seat, one might say, and I could look down into the melee with a minimum of risk. As for the danger of maybe drowning in that whirlpool of angry men, I backed against the wall, gripped my reassuring cue, and hoped for the best.

Of course nobody noticed me. Jimmy was fighting his way toward the front door, a ring of cautious assailants moving with him in its center like a pack of rabbit dogs about a wildcat.

When Jimmy reached the front door, the outside crowd gave way a bit before that face; and Jimmy, cupping hands about a bleeding mouth, gave forth with Irish yells that brought replying yells from here and there across the milling crowd.

Word had already spread abroad that the Dutch were ganging Jimmy Conley; and the blood cry for help had reached the Layhes and the Neary boys, as usual on the prowl for trouble and perhaps a merry fight.

The sides of my bay window gave me a clear view up and down Main Street, and I could follow the gathering of the clan by the agitation of the people where sporadic fights broke out. I fancy it would be something like witnessing the invasion of a virulent skin disease enormously magnified. I could actually see the fight infection spreading from man to man, as from cell to cell. Relatively healthy areas of the social body would suddenly flare up and swell, erupting into angry fever spots of writhing bodies. Maybe someone would hit someone on the back of the head in front of him for the cogent reason that someone had hit him on the back of his head for no reason at all. Anonymous retaliation would fall upon anonymous retaliators. Maybe a fistful of knuckles would land midmost the nearest facial features in the melee of yelling faces. Whereupon, perhaps, some bewildered innocent went under with a gratuitous wallop on the jaw. And did anyone pause to question what seemed to be the trouble, and why did someone hit him, quite likely he took his answer on the nose.

"If you see a head, for the love of God, hit it!" That, they say, made a Donnybrook Fair; and that is what I was seeing in the crowd-packed block of shouting men and screaming women.

Meanwhile, battered Jimmy, backed up against a wall, had been taking on all cautious comers as they came, biding the arrival of relief. And now a cry went up over the crowd: "The Layhes are coming! The Neary boys are coming!"

And indeed they were!

They were coming in close formation from up the street, raising the Irish yell as they came. From my window I could follow their charge by the boiling wake of tumbled, scrambling men they left behind them.

The battle did not last long after that. The unorganized opposition melted away rapidly and the fighting just petered out in the general exhaustion. They hoisted Jimmy to their shoulders for a ride of triumph, and there was desultory cheering.

Then the sun went down upon the stricken field. In the cooling of the twilight, all along the grassy parkway by the street, doctors treated the bruises of inglorious heroes; and there was reminiscent laughter over details of the fracas.

Then, while the soft summer sky blossomed with fireworks, the band played "The Star Spangled Banner" and we all stood with our hats off. After that we had "Clementine," played ever so softly, and many of us sang it together with gentle laughter.

Finally they played "The Wearing of the Green" just by way of saying "No hard feelings."

Four Things Are Good

This "younger generation" in which I claim honorary membership, regardless of my years, is caught up in the greatest social revolution the world has ever known. Discord and violence are commonplace the world over. Throughout the realm of human values the raucous yawp of anarchy is loud. In wide, densely populated areas of the planet abject misery and chronic terror are ways of life; sordid systematic killing a thriving industry, its success measured by the daily bag of "enemy" dead. It is no wonder that our youngsters would reject the mad world they have inherited. Surely there is more than frivolity and fashion in their hirsute excesses, more than clowning in their irreverence for the Established and the smug.

Do the laughing gods poke cruel fun at us?

But for all the scornful nose-thumbings at the discarded past, the discredited present, and the mistrusted future, a most hopeful sign is to be noted. Among these dissident youngsters there is an upward surge of spiritual longing. Apparently they are seeking a new, direct approach to a viable religion. Even the resort to drugs must be regarded as an attempted shortcut to the desired mystical experience.

As a university lecturer I was intimately and happily associated with young people for some years. They always seemed to be more earnestly questioning than hopeful; less joyous, and older than young people should be.

"What's it all about?" and "What's good about it?" were characteristic and often-recurring questions. They still are, especially now that I have attained this snow-topped summit of my heaped-up ninety years and more. Surely, those young people must think, having come so far and climbed so high, he must have learned some of the vital answers.

But "What's it all about?" Ask God that question. He won't tell; and if He did we would not understand. Anyway, to ask that question is to die a little. No doubt even a tree would wither if it got to thinking what the summers and the winters meant.

But "What's good about it?" That is indeed an important question, and it admits an answer. It has plagued me, too, in my darker moods.

I have a formal garden, hedge-enclosed, where I often go to pray and seek for needed answers. However the faith-inspired religionist or the scientific psychologist may explain the mechanism of prayer, I have found it a rewarding practice; and I suspect that it may be vastly more powerful than we know.

There are times when I enter my garden not to worship but just to *be*—and listen. It is such a time that I now recall. I was thinking lamely of the world's multitudinous woes, including some minor ones of my own, when the shadowy form of a cynical young friend of mine floated across my consciousness. I fancied him pressing the troublesome question upon me: "What's good about this absurd predicament in which we find ourselves? We don't know whence we came; we don't know where we are; we don't know whither we are bound. It is hard to come here, hard to remain, and sometimes very hard to get away."

I listened, and the answer came out of the silence:

"Four things, at least, are good," I found myself replying.

"First: Surely love is good—love given rather than love

received. With neither, there is nothing; with either, even sorrow and suffering may become beautiful and dear. All good things come from love, and it is the only thing that is increased by giving it away.

"Second: The satisfaction of the instinct of workmanship is good; for that instinct is the noblest thing in man after love, from which indeed it springs. Just to do your best at any cost, and afterward to experience something of the Seventh Day glory when you look upon your work and see that it is good.

"Third: The exaltation of expanded awareness in moments of spiritual insight is good. This may occur in a flash, glorifying the world; or it may linger for days, when you seem to float above all worldly troubling, and all faces become familiar and dear. This state can be spontaneously generated, but it has often been achieved through fasting and prayer.

"Fourth: Deep sleep is good.

"'Not shoaling slumber, but the ocean-deep
And dreamless sort,'

as one of my characters in *The Song of Jed Smith* remarks.

"'There's something that you can touch,
And what you call it needn't matter much
If you can reach it. Call it only rest,
And there is something else you haven't guessed—
The Everlasting, maybe. You can try
To live without it, but you have to die
Back into it a little now and then.

And maybe praying is a way for men
To reach it when they cannot sleep a wink
For trouble.' "

For some time I continued to mull over the implica-
tions of the answer. Then I was struck by the realization
that both my cynical young friend and I were of neces-
sity concerned with fragmentary conceptions; that each
"good" that I had offered involved the loss of the sense of
self in some pattern larger than self; that life, as com-
monly conceived, could be only a fragment of some
vaster pattern; and that prayer itself was a striving to be
whole.

There is a slogan that I wish to leave with my young
friends to be recalled for courage, like a battle cry, in
times of great stress. It came to me from an old Sioux
friend of mine who was recounting his experience as a
youth on Vision Quest.

He had fasted three days and nights upon a lonely hill,
praying all the while that Wakon Tonka might send him
a vision. But his prayer got lost, far out into the empty
night, and it seemed that nothing heard.

Then, on the fourth day, he fell asleep, exhausted, and
dreamed a troubled dream that had no glory in it. Any
old woman could have dreamed it, nidding and nodding
in her tepee. He wakened in despair. And as he stood
forlorn upon his hilltop he was thinking: If I have no
vision to give me power and guide me, how can I ever be
a man? Maybe I shall have to go far off into a strange land
and seek an enemy to free me from this shame.

Then, just as he thought this bitter thought, a great cry came from overhead like a fearless warrior hailing his wavering comrade in heat of battle. "Hoka-hey, brother—*Hold fast, hold fast; there is more!*" Looking up, he saw an eagle soaring yonder on a spread of mighty wings—and it was the eagle's voice he heard.

"As I listened," the old man said, "a power ran through me that has never left me, old as I am. Often when it seemed the end had come, I have heard the eagle's cry—*Hold fast, hold fast; there is more. . . .*"

The Passing of the Gods

I had experienced a sort of cleansing glory in giving my precious little book to the flames. But the glory soon faded in the commonsense light of day and left me desolate in a world gone empty. There were times when I actually considered deserting poetry for some more practical worldly interest, but the thought only left me sick at heart. Then one white night when I lay awake pondering questions without answers, the heavens opened for me again. The dynamic pattern for a major poem that I had abandoned came back upon me with a new surge of power. It had haunted me day and night for some time before the Virgin Devanaguay and her Divine Son had taken me over completely. Now it returned with much of the old excitement to fill my world again.

The Passing of the Gods. Surely it was a magnificent conception. Obviously both the title and the idea were suggested by the Scandinavian *Ragnarok,* the destruction of the Norse gods, or its Germanic equivalent, the *Götterdämmerung.* But in my plan the idea was given general scope and significance not limited by geographic or seasonal considerations. I would include all the foremost deities of the world pantheon. Even now, after these many forgetful years, I can see it all vividly as when I was a youngster. Sometimes I have even indulged in a vain, momentary desire to give it being yet.

I can see it now—the flowing host of gods that lonely

man, lost in the cosmic mystery, created in his need. Of wonderment and terror he created them; of loneliness and loss; of longing and despair—the long parade of obsolete and obsolescent gods that man had made and worshiped and outgrown. Emerging from the dreadful dark they came, a luridly self-luminous procession, tunneling the night of time. Slowly they passed before me, one by one, under the brilliant glow of now, to fade away and vanish in the dusk of ages. And then—the Man of Sorrows, still bent beneath the burden of his cross, still bound for new Golgothas.

Before I fell asleep that night I had decided to write *The Passing of the Gods,* using the Spenserian stanza as my medium. Good Spenserians are almost as difficult as Petrarchan sonnets, and I could have saved myself much effort by choosing blank verse. But I was fascinated by the gemlike quality of the strict stanza form when well fashioned. Also I had noted, as the result of much practice, that the very difficulties of structure, when fairly mastered, greatly increased the economy and power of expression.

The next day I began work on the poem; and for several years thereafter it furnished me with my principal excuse for being alive.

Back Home in Bancroft

Emboldened by my success with the "Song of the Turbine Wheel," I mailed my "Lonesome in Town" to *The Youth's Companion*. I now gave myself over, heart and soul, to the completion of my prose tale, "The Tiger's Lust."

Before my Omaha adventure I had partially conceived the plot, with no less a personage than the great Mogul Shah Jahan himself as the principal character. Several evenings had been spent in research at the Omaha Public Library, which left me with ample ignorance for the free play of creative imagination.

Also I had examined several copies of the *Ledger* by way of acquainting myself with its literary flavor. It has been more than three-score years and ten since I last set eyes upon that masterpiece and I have only the vaguest memories of it, as a whole. I do recall something about bulbuls singing in a moonlit garden, and I don't know why. But I definitely remember the final sentence of the tragic tale. It read: "And she never smiled again!"

When at length winter struck in earnest, with occasional spells of sub-zero weather, my attic room was no place for bulbuls, real or imagined; and before Christmas I was at home in Bancroft, continuing to work on my story. "The Tiger's Lust" was completed in early February and sent at once to the editors of the *Ledger*.

There followed a period of anxiety, with regular visits to the post office at mail time. Although I knew I was unreasonable in expecting a reply so soon, I was always there just the same, watching like a mousing cat, as the letters fell into the boxes. Maybe the next one would be mine!

I have previously mentioned my theory of dynamic cosmic patterns.

Although I could not know it then, I was about to be caught up into the pattern of the Indian consciousness. It was a new pattern in my experience that, in large measure, was to condition my thinking and feeling about the world the remainder of my life.

As I stood there one day eagerly mousing my mailbox, a Mr. J. J. Elkin, an Indian trader whom I knew well, asked me what I was doing. I told him I was doing some free-lance writing. He wondered if I would care to help him in his office. I would, especially as he assured me there would be time on the job when I could write.

I agreed to work for Mr. Elkin for thirty dollars a month as stenographer, bookkeeper, collector, and maker of maps showing Indian allotments.

Shortly after making the agreement with Mr. Elkin I did receive an acceptance for "The Tiger's Lust" with a check for twenty-five dollars. It was just enough to pay for my mother's false teeth.

Heirship lands had recently been released by the government for sale to the highest bidder, and, accordingly, easy money was flowing through the pockets of the notably improvident Indians. A rank money smell was abroad in the land, and money-hungry white sons of civilization flocked about the reservation like buzzards about a rotting carcass.

Business was good indeed, as indicated by the following snatch of characteristic conversation between my boss and a landowner.

My boss: "Say, Tom, how much an acre do you folks want for your Grandpa's quarter section?"

The landowning heir (importantly): "Well, now, Misser Elkin, we talk a long time about this. Then we say we guess we ask you twenty dollah. You no give us twenty, then we take ten or maybe fifteen, if you give it to us."

Obviously this was a long way from what I have called *cosmic patterns*. It was, in fact, merely one of many indications of what some of the younger Indians were becoming under the benign influence of civilization.

And here I am reminded of another episode of similar general import, although it has no bearing on the price of land. It is, rather, about the price of coffins (of all things) and a certain mixed blood by the name of Fred Leman.

Fred was an amiable, soft-spoken soul, with a singular gift of persuasion. Otherwise he was distinguished by an outsize thirst for strong drink that was always on the prowl for further refreshment.

On the midsummer day I now have in mind, Fred was headed for town with his rattletrap spring wagon and crowbait team. It was cruelly hot on the dusty reservation road and Fred was thirsty. He was getting thirstier by the mile, and he was thinking hard, we may be sure,

for he was entirely without funds. I suspect he was think-
ing fondly of me and the possibility of floating yet an-
other small loan from me—say fifty cents or maybe a
"dollah." He still owed me for the last flotation and still
does; but he has long since been gathered to his fathers.
May he rest in peace!

Several miles from town Fred came abreast of a little
tumbledown shack squatting in hopeless squalor by the
side of the road. It was full of mourning voices—*wahoo-
ha-a-a*—and the bitter wailing of children.

Evidently somebody had died in there; and, being
curious, as well as wishing to be helpful perhaps, Fred
tied his team to the hitching post and entered the house of
sorrow. I wasn't there, of course, but I knew Fred and
was familiar with the tales floating about the incident, so I
may venture to reconstruct the affair.

I can see the recently deceased, still sprawled in in-
decent abandon across the bed of death, as when the final
agony seized him. I can see the sagging jaw, the stare of
unlidded eyes, the frozen look of blank astonishment.

I see Fred, all sympathy and bustling competence,
taking charge of the sad situation like a good Samaritan.
They were going to need a coffin in that house right
away, and Fred had an inspiration. He knew the family
had recently received money at the big payment. His
team was already harnessed and hitched. He himself
would fetch the coffin; and, because he felt so sorry, he
would charge only five "dollahs" for a fine one! No
doubt Fred's exceptional gift of plausibility, aided by the

shock of grief, readily completed the melancholy business; and Fred was off on his mission of mercy.

People living along the reservation road to town used to tell with gusto, and perhaps some artistic exaggeration, the tale of Fred's wild dash for the undertaking parlor that momentous day—the skin-rack horses beaten into a stumbling lope, the rolling dust cloud with Fred bouncing therein, and plying the goad!

In our town those days, undertaking was a function of the furniture trade; and when Fred entered the establishment, it must have been clear from his disconsolate mien and manner that the next customer was not in the market for furniture.

The following version of the ensuing conversation is adapted from the popular account at the time.

"Old Man Rain Walker all time dead," said Fred in response to the proprietor's anxious question. "All time dead. Two more days, put 'im in the ground."

"What!" exclaimed the proprietor, who knew and liked the Old Man. "You don't mean to say your father-in-law, Rain Walker, is dead!"

"Yeh," Fred replied. "He get awful sick in his belly and go dead. Two more days, put 'im in the ground. I come after coffin for the Old Man, a real nice one, please. His old woman she say she give you the money when she sell her land." Hereupon, some say, Fred rubbed out a hypothetical tear or two with either fist and fetched a groaning sob.

There followed another wild dash—back to the house

of sorrow with the real nice coffin. And soon thereafter still another dash for town—and a friendly bootlegger.

The oft-told tale, in its classic form, has a highly dramatic denouement. The scene is the furniture store. The time is some weeks after the Old Man's untimely and temporary demise. He now enters, hale, hearty, and in what used to be called "high dudgeon."

Old Man Rain Walker (shaking his fist in the proprietor's face and shouting): "Next time I die I come get my own coffin!"

Curtain.

I once played a scurvy trick on Fred; and with a contrite heart I now seize this belated opportunity to confess and so perhaps make amends to a kindly soul. It was like this:

The office where I held forth was a short block from the railway station. One day, just at train time, Fred bustled into my presence all out of breath with a sad story, about as follows:

"My wife, she awful sick, Missa Naha, and she need some medicine or maybe she fall over dead. My team down in Lyons, Missa Naha, and you please lend me twenty-five cents so I buy a ticket to Lyons and get my team. My poor wife awful sick and she no get the medicine maybe she just roll over dead."

Lyons was the next town down the railway, ten miles distant.

Now it just happened that I had seen Fred's unmistakable crowbaits that very afternoon within the hour. They were moping drowsily, and quite hayless, at a hitching rack several blocks up the street.

At this moment the approaching train to Lyons whistled at the edge of town. It gave me a great idea.

"Come on, Fred!" I yelled, feeling the need of excitement for my purpose. "There's your train for Lyons. Come quick! Come quick! They don't wait long. Hurry! Hurry!"

I hustled him through the office door into the street and began herding him toward the railway station, occasionally giving him an encouraging "bum's rush." My brisk, surprise attack, together with my excited shouting, seemed to render Fred practically helpless. And, anyway, hadn't he begged piteously for a trip to Lyons?

We reached the station as the locomotive clanked and panted to a stop. I hustled Fred aboard, gave him a quarter for the conductor in lieu of a ticket, and swung off the car as it set out again for Lyons.

I must confess it still gives me a twinge of remorse to recall the incredulous, hurt look of consternation on Fred's face as he leaned out the car window looking helplessly back at me.

That evening I took Fred's team to a livery stable for a square meal and a drink.

When I next saw Fred he was the same soft-spoken, gentle soul as ever. I never knew how he got back to Bancroft, and I never had the nerve to inquire.

Literary Criticism: The Essays

During much of his career, Neihardt supplemented his income by means of literary criticism that appeared in the New York Times, *the* Kansas City Journal-Post, *the* Minneapolis Journal, *and the* St. Louis Post-Dispatch. *Many of the books he reviewed inspired critical essays that are memorable.*

The three essays included here were first published in the Kansas City Journal-Post *and the* St. Louis Post-Dispatch *in 1926 and 1927. "The White Radiance" and "Literature and Environment" express ideas that are still timely. "The Decline of Swearing" is hardly less dated, but is included largely for its unique nostalgic humor. The small piece "For What Purpose Did God Create Man?" gracefully casts light on my father's beliefs.*

"The White Radiance" was originally published in the *St. Louis Post-Dispatch,* October 30, 1926, and was reprinted in the *Prairie Schooner* 2 (Winter 1928): 3–6. "Literature and Environment" and "The Decline of Swearing" were first published in the *St. Louis Post-Dispatch,* August 15, and August 21, 1927, respectively. "For What Purpose Did God Create Man?" was originally published in the *Missouri Alumnus,* May 1957, 4–5.

The White Radiance

It is a well-known fact, and one that has furnished vast comfort to many misguided literary aspirants, that contemporaneous literary criticism has often proven ridiculously inadequate. Recently there has been published a volume entitled *Famous Literary Attacks* in which are gathered together a few choice vials of critical wrath poured upon the heads of those whom we now view as masters. It is a rather portly book, yet it is only one of many such that could be compiled. Also, if the compiler's appetite for grossly mistaken literary judgments were not appeased after so great a feast of futile ire, he might prepare an equally imposing collection of ill-fated eulogies.

Many an alleged immortal has succumbed to the inclement social weather of our world; and many an apparently puny infant has survived the croups of cultural autumns and the colics of new fruitage of the green.

Such a library of misconceived opinion, as has been suggested here, would make jocose reading for those of us who share the curious and fairly prevalent delusion that we, the first moderns, stand triumphantly unbunkable upon our height of time. But there are reasons for suspecting that we are now living in a time peculiarly liable to gross errors in artistic judgment.

Literature is merely one of many social phenomena, and the literary activities of any age are to be considered first of all with reference to the prevailing social background. Growth in society proceeds, like any other growth, by alternate periods of increasing strain—which may seem almost static in their peacefulness—and periods of sudden release and unfoldment. Slow-moving pictures of a developing plant have been seen by almost everyone no doubt, and will be remembered in this connection.

The period of release and violent unfoldment which we are now experiencing may be viewed as having begun with the French revolution—which was, broadly speaking, the triumph of the individualistic idea over the monarchic idea. The extreme of concentration had been reached in the reign of Louis XIV, after which the centrifugal, democratic, movement began. In America, its influence was dominant in the realm of economics long before it began to affect what we call the higher values— those of literature, the arts, philosophy, religion, ethics. It was not until 1912 that individualism, long triumphant in industry, struck our realm of higher values like a whirlwind.

Whether or not the storm has attained or is about to attain its maximum violence, who can say? We know that many very respectable old signboards are flying all over the place, and that many a private window, once turned serenely upon a world of what seemed eternal certainties, has been broken in by the chilling winds of doubt.

To realize the change that has taken place in literary attitudes, as a result of individualism worked out to its logical conclusions, one has only to consider the rigid rules that were laid down by absolute critical authority for the writers of pre-revolutionary France. The monarchic idea, long established in the lower realms of human activity, had penetrated to the realm of art. Then tradition was everything; now it is practically nothing. Taste was then a fixed thing imposed upon the individual by unquestionable authority; but what is taste now? The past was then the standard for the present; but now, to most, there seems only the loud moment, enormously prolific of contending whims—a bewildering spectacle!

It is the latter point that brings us to the matter of importance in attempting to judge the literature of our own time. We are witnessing the anarchic effect of extreme individualism in literature as in life. It is only the social body that lives on and on. The individual's life is but a moment in the life of the race. During an age when the social body is conceived as a unit, to which individual interests must be sacrificed, the past has tremendous meaning. For a generation dominated by the individualistic attitude, it is not unnatural that the living moment should loom larger than all time.

The result is that, being cut off from the long process that has given us all our human values, we now tend to become provincials in time. Just as the provincial in the usual geographic and social sense judges all things by the prevailing conceptions of his province, scorning the larger world, so do we now tend more and more to appraise our own literary products solely in the light that is peculiar to our agitated moment. The attempt to render absolute judgments with only the data of a limited reference scheme has always been the supreme tragedy (or is it comedy?) of human thought. But in an age like ours, it is very likely to become the rule.

The long and dearly bought experience of men, in the matter of ascertaining dependable human values, is momentarily ignored in our overwhelming passion for novel experiment. We lack the synthetic sense in literature as in life. We do not now commonly conceive all literature as organic. Its past for most readers seems to lie dead somewhere on the far side of an impassable gap. The literature that really concerns us greatly as a people is largely a sporadic phenomenon growing out of the peculiar mood of the time.

Being a revolting generation, impatient of all restraints, we are certain to overestimate the essential value of those works that most violently express the antisocial mood; and yet all of our genuine values are in their very nature social.

Doubtless Shelley had no thought of literary criticism when he wrote the strangely luminous lines:

> Life, like a dome of many-colored glass,
> Stains the white radiance of eternity,

but he expressed a truth that is applicable here. The light of understanding and persuasion by which men live is constantly changing. New generations develop new social moods within which, as in a colored atmosphere, all views are colored. When the light of time is red, as we may say, most men will think the truth is of that color;

and the blues and yellows of other generations may seem absurd or pathetic or merely curious.

Yet, what is any color but a fragment of some single white radiance? And what is the white radiance, in our special application of the figure, but a vision of the larger truth about people and the human adventure in general, as opposed to the merely fragmentary view in keeping with the bias of the moment?

Eternity is a long, long stretch, and we can not follow our poet so far. Human literary history is much briefer, and here and there, throughout the whole length of it, flashes of the white radiance may be noted by those who have the eyes to see. Even in our own confused time of stormy red, the white ray breaks in many a single line or passage; and now and then a whole book may glow with it. But it is the red which wakes the loudest clamor.

To scorn the red is to have no sympathetic understanding of one's own time—and that is a pitiful disaster. To seek the larger human values in that one necessarily transient key, is to miss the larger values.

More than once has the restless consciousness of humans passed through all the shades and colors of the social spectrum, from the naive germinating violet on through the slowly maturing blues, the flowering greens, the mellowly fruiting yellows, and the tempestuously revolting reds.

But the truth about the light was never to be perceived by the split ray.

Literature and Environment

We hear a great deal about heredity and environment in these days, and there seems to be no reason to doubt that what an individual becomes is the result of his inheritance acted upon by the environment in which he develops. Formerly the greater emphasis was placed on heredity, but there is now a growing tendency to emphasize the power of environment in shaping human beings. With a certain school of psychologists, this tendency has gone so far as to make the mind of man seem no more than the result of muscular reaction to stimuli. No doubt this tendency will lead thinkers far on the other side of truth, as generally happens when there is a new persuasion to be defended; but it is not wholly a bad tendency, since it makes society responsible for the welfare of its members.

Whatever the truth may be as to the exact relative importance of heredity and environment, this much may be taken as true: that, granting the inherited potentialities of an individual, environment is everything thereafter.

But what do we mean by environment?

Environment is that which surrounds a man. From his viewpoint, he may be regarded as the center of his environment. But what is the circumference of it? How far does it extend?

It is probable that most people think of environment only in the physical sense. A child born in dire poverty is discussed as having a certain environment characteristic of want; but the literature of biography disproves this over and over. A thousand children of all sorts are born in a country where no one seriously considers anything but the price of land and agricultural commodities; but among the thousand children, two or three may show very early in their lives that they are being acted upon by some environment greater than that of which the rest of the population is conscious. One of these youngsters, for instance, may by accident acquire a cheap copy of some great book, and such may be his hereditary traits that the book may become dear to him: so dear that he will manage somehow to get more and more joy of the same sort. And since the passion to understand develops by geometrical progression, the fixed and duller passions of the community will have little power to check the development of the youngster. He will not be the product of his county. And yet it will remain true that a man develops by virtue of his potentialities acted upon by his environment.

Then what, in reality, is that boy's environment?

There is environment in space and there is environment in time, and the latter is beyond computation the more important. It is possible to spend a lifetime in traveling all over the globe, as many illiterates have done, and never get out of the smaller environment. It is possible to dwell a lifetime in one place, yet live almost wholly in the larger environment. There is no escape from the self by changing one's geographical position. The only escape is through development of self, and the larger development of the self is the result of contact with that environment which is in time and which consists of the best that men have "thought and felt and done." The enduring literature of the world is the medium through which contact with this larger environment is made possible.

And so we come to a very thrilling fact, that great numbers of people in our time are right now able to connect with the largest environment if they care to do so. It surrounds them like an atmosphere that all but a relative few have never breathed. Wealth is by no means essential, and not very much leisure is demanded. A little well-guided reading every day will accomplish wonders in a few years, as no doubt many of our readers could testify from experience; but relatively the number of these must be small.

It is an obsession with us nowadays to be what we call "practical." By that term we mean, as a rule, little more than hustling after money. This is not strange, for need drives where greed does not, and the economic pressure is very great in a civilization that is largely devoted to the artificial stimulation of consumption, that production of commodities may be profitable.

Also, the astonishing exploits of science tend to encourage us in focusing our attention on the purely physical, the immediate thing. This, too, has its justification; for, as we have learned, there is a great deal we need to know about the purely physical, the immediate thing.

But we should not forget that we are human, and not mere brutes, only because we are able to store up human experience for the use of our posterity. We now are both ancestors and posterity. And, as posterity, is it practical for us to overlook our great inheritance—the stored-up experience of those who were before us, as recorded in the literature that has survived so many changes in the moods of men?

Three thousand years is not long. It only seems so. In fact, all the great ones, whose lives and works have been saved for us, are not so much as a minute away from us right now. They are "nearer to us than breathing, closer than hands and feet." In the realm of the greatest there is only now; and most of us may be citizens of that richest realm if we only wish to be.

The Decline of Swearing

LARS PORSENA: OR THE FUTURE

OF SWEARING AND IMPROPER LANGUAGE.

BY ROBERT GRAVES. (DUTTON)

There is no gainsaying it; the golden age of swearing is past. It is true that one who listens in the right places may still hear certain sacred names taken in vain, but such phrases, automatically uttered, have, in general, merely the status of a lazy man's superlative. The fine old ingenuity of malice is lacking. The act of "cussing" has become drably mimetic; whereas in the golden age of malediction it was, for many of its distinguished practitioners, a truly creative art. Diabolical, one grants, and highly reprehensible, one insists; but an art nevertheless.

In the old heroic days of the cowboy West, so Philip Ashton Rollins records in his classic work on that era, the "cussing match" was a regular institution; and hard-boiled, leather-skinned, two-fisted men rode miles to be present at one of these lurid vocal conflicts. Even as late as the 90's, this writer, then living in the West, remembers a few lingering exponents of the then rapidly dying art. There were two plasterers of his acquaintance whose gifts were regarded by the whole community as quite astonishing. On a sweltering afternoon when the "mud" came too slow or too fast from the mixing box one might hear this locally famous team in full blast. They had a way of operating in relays, the other beginning when his partner was quite out of breath. You never heard any threadbare oaths from those highly trained practitioners. It was commonly believed that they lay awake nights inventing and polishing the ingenious mouth-filling phrases of their next outbursts.

Often in reading contemporary novels of what may be called the "Goddam School of Fiction," this writer grows sick at heart, remembering the magnificently horrendous blasphemy of those two plasterers who reached Shakespearean heights. Alas, they are now with the kings and counsellors of the earth who built desolate places for themselves, and even this writer, who remembers, dare not record a single corruscating example of their art for dumfounded posterities. Newspapers are not printed on asbestos.

Serious students of blasphemology, in either its old creative or modern mimetic forms, or both, may now be referred with confidence to two scientific works on the subject. A dozen years ago Professor G. T. W. Patrick contributed a profound study of "cussing" under the suggestive title, "The Psychology of Relaxation." His theory, which need not be given here, was both ingenious and illuminating. But his point of view was purely psychological. It has remained for no less a man than Robert Graves, the British poet, to present a comprehensive study of the subject from the viewpoints of ethnology, sociology, economics, coprology and pornography. As to his title, "Lars Porsena," its significance will be apparent to all who remember their Macaulay. Lars, it will be recalled, was the gentleman who, in "The Lays of Ancient Rome," is reputed to have sworn, not by one god, but by nine, for which cogent reason he is chosen as the great historical exemplar of "cussing." (To what heights might our two plasterers have risen thus liberally endowed with deities!)

Mr. Graves, himself, has noted the appalling decline of the ancient art during the past generation, and seems inclined to attribute its decadence to the levelling spirit of unimaginative democracy and the standardization of a mechanical age. He looks back wistfully to the days when "the army swore terribly in Flanders," and forward to a not impossible recrudescence of the art when once more there will be "swearing without a practical element, with only a musical relation between the images it employs, swearing of universal application and eternal beauty."

Mr. Graves' essay, though written in an unmistakeable tone of high seriousness, should be avoided by all excessively serious people and by prudes. Also, devotees of the obvious might just as well stay away from the book. To all others, the unobtrusive wit of the author will prove a rare joy, and he will be a keen one indeed who is not sometimes obliged to re-read a passage by way of capturing some elusive spirit of mirth.

In response to a youth's question:
For What Purpose
Did God Create Man?

Bless that boy's heart! Of course he is entitled to a reply. As for an adequate "answer," that is a different matter!

With our painfully limited understanding, we are not even in a position to ask the question: "What was God's purpose in creating Man?" First of all, God is all a wonder and a mystery, and any definite understanding of the meaning of the term is beyond us. We only know that there is "an integrating principle" in the universe, continually operating creatively wherever we look; that everything is a manifestation thereof; and through long experience we know (some know, of course) that to live in harmony with all we can know of the creative Mystery is to be religious.

Instead of the question, why did God create us, we should strive to learn how we can live more in harmony with the divine, creative process. We can learn, as numberless men and women have learned, that we must find a way to lose our petty selves in a profound sense of the Wonder and Mystery that we call God, in our language. That is the function of prayer, which is not, in its highest form, a request for something, but a way of opening one's consciousness to the flow of that mysterious power. And whenever it flows in, love grows, love of everything; and with the love there comes increased understanding, increased power to do.

The question as asked also has the fault of placing too great stress on man's importance. Surely it seems beyond doubt that all life is one, and "holy," somehow.

As for "purpose," let our dear boy look anywhere, and he will see design, design, marvelous pattern, beautiful pattern—in any bug's shape, in any leaf, or tree, or blade of grass. There is nothing but "design" in nature from planetary systems to snowflakes.

With design everywhere, surely we need not be troubled about there being sufficient "purpose."

"Nebraska

This book was designed by Dika Eckersley and set in Linotype Bembo by Keystone Typesetting, Inc. It was printed by Edwards Brothers, Inc., using 55-pound Glatfelter, an acid-free sheet.